Unstoppable Famine

The Intern Diaries Series- Book 4

D. C. Gomez

GOMEZ EXPEDITIONS

Cover design by Christine Gerardi Designs

Edited by Cassandra Fear

Proofread by Michelle Hoffman

ISBN: 978-1-7333160-2-6 for Paperback Editions

ISBN: 979-8-9857369-1-5 for Hardcover Editions

Published by Gomez Expeditions

Request to publish work from this book should be sent to: author@dcgomez-author.com

For my family,
Cheerleaders of dreamers.
Thank you for always believing.

Chapter One

"DIE!"

It figured that was the first thing we heard when we stepped out of Storm in front of a one-story house on Northwood Street in Nash, Texas.

"I should be surprised but this is becoming the norm," Bob told me, adjusting his bulletproof vest. He walked around the driver's side of Storm—his baby-blue Ram 2500 truck—and handed me a pair of handcuffs.

"Welcome to Haven." I didn't bother checking out the house, instead I concentrated on hooking the cuffs through one of the loops in my pants. "How many of these do you think we need?"

"You can never have too many." Bob ran his hand over his sandy-blond hair, staring at the residence we were about to enter.

Bob's sea-green eyes sparkled in the streetlight, making his features more pronounced. A handsome guy in his forties, Bob was my first friend when I moved to Texarkana, both of us penniless when we first met. He'd been homeless, and I barely made a living as a waitress at Abuelita's Mexican Restaurant. Not that either one of us complained about our situation; we just adapted. Fast forward almost two years and we now worked for Death under the guidance of an egotistical five-thousand-year-old talking cat. Thanks to my position as Death's Intern of North America, we were living in the new supernatural hub of North America. What happened to my boring life?

Bob waved his hand in front of my face. "Isis! Are you hearing me?"

"Sorry, Bob." I gave myself a little shake and worked on focusing on the present situation. "I just spaced out."

"You've been doing that a lot lately." Bob scanned my face, but I had no idea what he expected to find.

"It's been a long day," I replied, breathing deeply.

"It's been a long four months and you need a break." Bob leaned closer, his eyes inspecting me, even my hair. "Isis, you have bags under your eyes, and when was the last time you got your hair trimmed? Have you seen yourself lately?"

"Bob, please ... not you, too." I dropped my head down, hoping to disappear. "How am I supposed to take a vacation? I'm the new Sheriff of Haven, and that's on top of being Death's Intern. It's not like we can ask people to stop dying."

"Exactly, people die every day." With his hands on his hips, Bob nailed his impersonation of Peter Pan, even despite his six-foot frame.

"That's not a very effective argument." Crossing my arms over my chest, I stared at Bob. I could play the stubborn game as well.

Grabbing my shoulders, Bob spun me around until I faced Storm's window, pointing to my reflection without saying a word. I hated to admit it, but Bob wasn't lying. It was scary how big the dark circles under my eyes were. My normal mocha complexion had a yellowish tone, which made me look semi-jaundiced. Even my normally long black hair looked dull and straw-like.

"Fine, so I'm looking a bit rough. It comes with the territory." I wasn't sure if I was trying to convince Bob or myself.

"It's not just your look, Isis. Your temper is super short, too" Bob whispered.

"WHAT?" I whirled around to face him.

"See what I mean?" Bob pulled away, both of his hands up in mock surrender. "You knocked that poor witch out just because she moved without your permission. That's not you, Isis. Promise me you are going to take some time off."

Bob bit his lower lip and waited patiently; his arms folded over his chest. His voice had such raw concern that my heart hurt. Was I really that out of control? I took several breaths and turned back to face Storm. Leaning my cheek against the window, I let the cool glass chill my too-warm skin.

"I'm so tired," I admitted, the words no more than an exhale. "This is the twenty-third domestic dispute we got this month, and it's only the thirteenth of March. I just want people, shifters, witches, and everyone else just to get along. This is madness."

"You know you can stop all this right now." Bob rubbed my shoulder gently.

"Are you suggesting we move?" Afraid to look at Bob, I barely shifted my head.

"You being here is the only reason there is a Haven. If you decide this is too much, you know we will follow you anywhere, no questions asked." Bob propped his shoulder against Storm, forcing me to look at him.

"I know," I mumbled. "But so many families have moved here. For every nutcase we face, three families say thank you for giving them a place stay. How can I take that away from them?

"Well, if you die or have a nervous breakdown, you will be no good to anyone."

Ouch, why did Bob have to be so blunt?

"Fine," I replied. "You made your point. I'll plan a vacation. But that means you, Bartholomew, and

Constantine are in charge of this mess."

"I'm going to kill you bitch!" As if on cue, the screams from the residents escalated.

"Did he say bitch or witch?" Bob asked me.

"Does it make a difference?" I replied, tying my hair into a tight bun.

"Unfortunately, no. Are you ready?" Bob raised his eyebrows in question.

"As ready as I'm ever going to be for these things. Let's go." I pulled out my gun—which was packed with tranquilizer bullets—and marched towards the house.

Strangely, nobody in the neighborhood had come out to find out what all the commotion was. The house was down the street from the Texas Chuckwagon. Luckily for us, the restaurant was only open for breakfast and lunch, so at this time of night, the parking lot was deserted.

After several close encounters with insane witches, we learned never to walk on the direct path that led to the houses. Because of our lesson, Bob took the right and I took the left, both of us moving in the grass. I smirked, thinking my drill sergeants would have fallen over dead if they saw us walking on the grass. Army culture could be so strange.

Crash.

A loud noise came from inside the house. Bob gave me a hand signal and mimicked knocking on the door. I nodded, letting him know I was ready. We had too much practice doing this that we no longer needed words to communicate, which wasn't something I'd ever brag about. No, I'd boast about peace and not having a routine to bust the offenders of that peace.

Bob's knock split the air, the noises inside immediately ceasing. Our eyes met, knowing that was not a good sign at all.

"Reapers Inc., open up!" I shouted in a deeper-than-normal voice.

Thirty seconds was our normal time to wait before we busted down the door and barged in. I started my mental countdown, hoping someone in there had some common sense and opened the door. Twenty-three, twenty-four, twenty-five … obviously, no common sense lived in any of the people inside that house.

"Open up or we are coming in!" Bob yelled this time.

"DIEEEEE!" a female screamed.

"Really?" I mouthed at Bob, and he just shrugged.

BANG!

The front door exploded and pieces of metal, wood, and even the door handle flew through the air. I watched the debris glide as if in slow motion, mild curiosity making my mind wander for a moment before the pieces landed in the yard with a resounding thump. That was another reason never to stand in front of doors: we always had to dodge crazy attempts on our lives. A smart being would have stopped there, but not our little friends. The exploding door was followed by several energy projectiles that unfortunately, landed on Storm.

BOOM.

Storm blew up, and not a single part was left behind. I froze, not sure if I could even attempt to move because that was the second truck Bob had to stand by and watch get blown up by an assailant.

"NOOOO!" After one last pain-filled, heart-wrenching look to the space Bob's truck occupied a moment ago, he charged inside the house.

Maybe I wasn't the only one who needed a vacation.

I ran after Bob, hoping I was in time to stop him from killing whoever was in the house, but I stopped in my tracks the moment I moved inside. The house looked like a battlefield. Holes punched in the walls, the carpet was shredded in so many different places, and even sections of the ceiling were missing. Thank goodness houses in that area didn't have basements, otherwise the place would have crumpled already. With all the damage, I didn't know where to look first, and my eyes pinged from one place to the next, finally landing on Bob. He had someone pinned under his boot.

A sound to the left pulled my attention away from the giant disaster that was the living room. I gripped my gun with both hands and made my way slowly around a demolished couch. Pieces of cushion were scattered around the floor, while a bunch of rags were scattered behind it.

Did he declare war on the furniture? Maybe the furniture was haunted?

I had seen some insane things lately, so haunted furniture could be a possibility.

I was ready to dismiss the rags when they moved. Slowly, I switched the gun to my right hand, pulling my scythe out from my pocket and holding it in my left. The magical weapon had the ability to go from a six-foot-tall deadly scythe to a six-inch tube with the touch of a button. It was also the best weapon to eliminate vampires. With a smooth motion, I extended my scythe and used the bottom of the weapon to poke at the rags.

"Die!" A ragged woman lunged at me, two knives raised in her hands.

The poor thing didn't have a chance. With a quick swing of the scythe, I disarmed her, and a roundhouse to the chest had her down for the count. It wasn't often I tooted my own horn, but I would about this. My reflexes were out of this world. We had too much practice with people attacking us to be surprised by little things like that. I retracted the scythe, slid the gun into the side holster on my thigh, and ripped the cuffs from my pants. Having multiple pockets in my combat gear made this job a little easier.

The disheveled woman groaned as she tried to stand up. Thinking she was unconscious, I rushed to secure her, but she was conscious enough to spit on me, hitting me right in the chest.

"Uh, that is so disgusting." My tone sounded whiny even to me. "This is going to hurt, I promise." Grabbing her by the hair, I dragged the wailing and flailing woman to the center of the room, but after her assault on my clothing, I had very little sympathy for her. Once she was face down, I dropped my knee on her back, holding her in place as I restrained her with the cuffs.

"You might want to wipe that off. You have no idea where she's been." Bob pointed to the glob of spit on my shirt.

"Please don't remind me." Grabbing some of the rags the woman wore, I wiped the fluid away. "Is everything okay over there?"

"I think I punched him too hard because he is out cold." Bob glanced towards the corner where nothing moved.

"At least he can't hurt anyone. Done," I told him after securing the woman and standing up.

"You are all going to die. Death is coming!" the woman screamed, her whole body convulsing.

"Sorry." I shot her in the back with a tranquilizer, and Bob eyed me. "Her screams are giving me a headache."

"Me, too," Bob agreed with a grin. "Should we search the house and figure out what all the fighting was about?"

"Do we have to?" I whined.

Bang.

Bob and I both raised our guns at the sound of the noise. Bang. The noise was coming from the back of the house. Now we were definitely going to be inspecting.

"Sounds like it's coming from that door." Bob pointed with his gun to the closed door in the back. "On three. One. Two. Three."

Bob kicked the door, and I rushed through it with my gun at the ready. The room was freezing and pitch black, and for some reason, the floor was slippery, causing me to slide across it and slam into an old wraith floating straight towards me. I landed on the floor with a thump. I blame that on Death and her magical gifts. Part of being Death's Intern meant I could see the dead. It also meant I could feel them like they still had physical forms.

From the ground, I took in the wraith, an old woman with shrunken eyes and gashes all over her face. In some places, the bones even stuck out.

A scream erupted from the wraith, her voice vibrating against my skull. "Death is coming and it's coming for you!" Pointing at me with her long, bony ghost finger, she sprayed me with some type of spit.

"Back away from her!" Bob shouted.

"DEATH IS COMING!" The being screamed even louder.

"Yes, we know. We work for her. Stop screaming!" I said, crab-walking away from the wraith, who then turned to face Bob.

"Oh, wow. It's a banshee." Bob lowered his gun, inching around the being without taking his eyes from her.

"How do you know that?" I asked, trying to wipe my face with my sleeve.

"Constantine gave me a book that describes all the supernatural creatures in the world." Bob nudged his head toward the creature. "I have no idea how they captured her, or for what purpose."

"Do we care about the purpose? If she was kidnapped, that's another charge for those two out there." Peering behind me, I made sure our villains were still where we left them.

"How are they keeping you here?" Bob edged closer, and I took a moment to acknowledge he was a brave soul. No way was I getting anywhere near her again.

The banshee appeared to understand Bob and lifted the rags around her legs. Golden shackles bound her leg, and they were connected to a chair attached to the wall. Bob rushed over to release her, but there was no way to remove her binding.

"We require a key for this." Bob glanced around the room.

"I fear one of those two idiots outside has the key." I shrugged my shoulder toward them. "And I'm not touching them again."

"We have to help her." Bob searched the room.

"I didn't say we wouldn't; I just have another idea." Before Bob could protest, I pulled out my scythe and cut the chains in two.

"How did you know that was going to work?" Bob knelt next to the Banshee and admired the clean cut in the chain.

"I didn't, but I had a feeling that was a magical chain, and since I have a magical weapon, I figured it wouldn't hurt to try." Giving Bob a wink, we both watched the magical chain evaporate. "And it makes everything a lot easier."

"Death walks with you," the banshee said as she floated in my direction.

"I technically work for Death. I'm Isis, Death's Intern in North America, and you are in Haven." I wasn't sure if I should shake hands with a banshee, but I still held my hand out and waited.

"HAVEEEEN," the banshee squealed. She floated towards the ceiling before circling back around, her features softening and making her look younger, prettier even. "Can I stay?" she asked in a whisper.

"As long as you don't cause any trouble, of course, you can stay. Do you have a place to live?" Unlike Bob, I knew nothing of banshees and housing one seemed like it might be difficult.

"A cemetery would be nice." The banshee drifted up and down, making me dizzy with all her movements.

"You are in luck. If you turn left on Kings Highway the main road that connects with this street—you will reach a very nice one. Last time I checked, no gnomes had claimed that one yet, so you should be good." I smiled at the Banshee and she swirled in the air, excitement radiating from her. When she stopped and focused on me, she was glowing.

"Can I go?" she asked.

"Yes, please. We still have to finish containing this mess." I pointed towards the door, hoping she would find her way.

"Thank you Death's Interns," the banshee said as she glided out the door.

"Should we tell her that technically you are the only Intern?" Bob stood next to me, both of us watching the banshee until she disappeared.

"Do you want to call her back?" I asked, eyeing him.

"Nah, I'm good." Bob tilted his chin and pulled his phone from his pocket. "Guess we need a ride home and a team to take these two to the station."

"I want a shower." I ran a hand through my hair, pulling out some of that weird banshee slime on it. My stomach churned. "Unless you need me, I'll be outside getting some fresh air."

"I got this. Go, just make sure you lean against the house. I don't want you passing out." Bob narrowed his eyes at me, not turning away until I nodded in agreement.

The house was in even worse condition the second time around. Weaving around the mess, I couldn't help but wonder what the two had planned to do there. Whatever it might be and based on the condition of their place alone, it wasn't working for them.

A grunt from the woman caught my attention. She stirred and her eyes fluttered open, shutting again right after. I didn't worry much. Our handcuffs were custom made to cut the powers from any magic user, so they wouldn't be going anywhere any time soon.

I stepped outside into the cool March air to find the entire neighborhood meandering around the property. It figured. Our luck was bound to run out sooner or later. With pieces of the door scattered all around and a peek into the house of horrors itself, of course it was too enticing for onlookers to pass by. So much for fresh air. Time to do damage control. Too bad I didn't have one of those devices from Men in Black.

Chapter Two

A long, hot bath followed by soft covers and a long night's sleep was all I wanted. My life was completely distorted when my greatest indulgence was sleep. I wasn't even thirty and I sounded like a seventy-year-old woman. Actually, most seventy-year-old ladies I knew were a lot more active and could tackle a lot more stuff than me. I couldn't help it, though. I was tired and beat down.

On the ride back to Reapers from Union Station, I fell asleep in Shorty's truck. That was unheard of since Shorty drove like an escaped prisoner rushing to the border. Even if Shorty wasn't driving like a maniac, the trip was less than fifteen minutes. Union Station sat in downtown Texarkana on the Texas side. Reapers, on the other hand, was at the Nash Business Park.

Falling asleep for that short amount of time took skills. Union Station was our new Headquarters downtown. It was an old train station we purchased when a door to hell manifested there. I did not want to take responsibility for the hell-portal, but I didn't have much of a choice. Supposedly, if I settled in any location for six months, the place would turn into a haven complete with its own door to hell. Couldn't I at least get a door to Disney World? Oh, no! That would be too nice for someone like me.

Owning the building solved the surveillance issue with the door and gave us a huge facility that served multiple purposes. Shorty's underground network of spies and informants worked out of the station. The group consisted of mostly street people that used to be homeless. Currently, they lived, worked, and trained out of the station.

Most of the civilians in Texarkana had no clue who ran the station or the purpose it served. Lower levels were added to function as holding cells, with the upper ones being used as registration offices, hearing offices, and all sort of other stuff I never cared to remember. We were officially running a city—more accurately multiple cities. Haven expanded from Leary to Ashdown. That was a very large area to cover, and I was grateful for all the help.

Everything was aching by the time Shorty dropped us off in front of Reapers. I didn't think it was possible for my eyelashes to hurt.

"Boss-lady, you are looking rough," Shorty told me from the driver's window as I climbed down.

"Thanks, Shorty, I've been hearing that a lot lately," I replied, taking deep breaths in hopes of clearing my head.

It was hard to get angry with Shorty. He was one of the most loyal men I have ever met, right next to Bob. When I first met him, he was paranoid, possibly drunk, and most definitely lost. Something changed in him, just like it did in Bob. They both had purpose, focus, and a huge tribe to look over. Shorty was less than five-foot-four inches, a bit scrawny but super resourceful. He was not known for sugar-coating things and said exactly what he thought. He also had the immense ability to see through people's disguises to their true core, accepting them for who they were.

"You know what that means, Boss Lady?" Shorty paused, waiting for me to look at him and answer his question.

"That I need a vacation?" What else could it mean?

"You should take one of those for sure, but you could use some meat in your life." Shorty rubbed his belly and licked his lips. "A nice, juicy steak, or maybe a pulled-pork sandwich would do the trick. All those plants you eat are not enough to keep your energy up. You should also stop running as much. It truly can't be good for you."

I was speechless, so I just stared at Shorty, dumbfounded. Bob laughed as he walked around the truck.

"That is your solution to my energy problem? To eat more fat and not work out?" I shook my head, grateful Shorty never went into medicine or counseling.

"Have you ever seen me unhappy or tired?" Shorty pointed at himself with both his hands. "Nope! Why? Because I drive everywhere now, thanks to the fur man, and I eat huge meals. Of course, that one is thanks to you since you hired us."

"How do you pass Bob's physical fitness exams?" I asked, wondering how Shorty wasn't suffering from a heart condition or any other physical ailment with his lack of health routine. "Bob, we really should start conducting health screenings on all of our employees."

"Way ahead of you," Bob announced from the door of Reapers. "And in case you are wondering, Shorty passed all of his tests with flying colors. I have no idea how, but he has the best cholesterol levels I have ever seen."

"It's in the genes, baby; I'm magical." Before I could argue, Shorty took off. He peeled out of the streets like Jake—he's the devil in case you were wondering—was chasing him.

"I just want some quiet time," I told Bob.

"That might be kind of hard since it looks like we have a full house." Bob pointed to the side of the building. "Did you notice all the vehicles parked out back?"

"I wasn't even paying attention, sorry." I was off my game. Survival as an Intern meant attention to details, and

I didn't even notice we had visitors.

To be fair, it was not that easy. Reapers was a huge, three-story metal building over sixty feet in length. How Bob noticed anything was beyond me. Reapers looked like every other building in the industrial park. The only difference was the blood-red sign outside that read: Reapers Incorporated. Like Union Station, it served many purposes besides being our home. It served as our training facility, gym, shooting range, car garage, and communication center.

We had started with only three bedrooms in the place, located in the loft at the back of the building on the second floor. When Bob was hired, an apartment was added to the front of the building on the first floor, right next to the security scanning area. To Constantine's constant dismay, I seemed to keep making friends with the other horsemen's interns and they tended to spend a lot of time here. Over Christmas, he ordered a second loft to be built over Bob's apartment. We now had enough rooms to house a small platoon.

"Are you going to make it through the security door?" Bob pressed his hands on the security panel, opening the pedestrian door of Reapers.

"You do know I'm not dying, right? I'm just tired?" Rolling my eyes, I followed him inside.

The second door of the building would not open until the first closed and the security system recognized our access. Bartholomew—boy-genius extraordinaire—had added so many layers of detection to the system that I was surprised it only took thirty seconds to clear us.

We emerged on the first floor of Reapers where the parking lot, gym, and training area were located. I expected everyone to be upstairs in the loft, but when I made it there, a large, white screen took up the whole middle of the room. Bob glanced in my direction and I shrugged. Constantine's voice drifted out from the other side of the screen.

"You know this can't be good," I whispered to Bob as we walked past the other cars.

Bob eyed Storm's empty parking space and took a deep breath. Bob was a stronger person than I was. I would have cried if Ladybug was in pieces. I gave my Mini Cooper a quick look and followed Bob around the white sheet.

"I really don't want to know what you guys are doing," I announced after seeing Bartholomew, Eugene, Eric, the Triplets, and even Constantine all wearing white suits. Constantine only had a coat on, which was still very impressive for a large cat to be wearing.

"I'm right with you on that one," Bob told me.

"You are finally here. What took you so long?" Constantine's voice was filled with irritation.

"Why are you covered in slime? Is that slime?" Bartholomew asked, moving away from the weird columns he stood by to come towards us.

"I have no idea, but a really nice banshee sprayed me with it," I told him, wiping my hair slowly.

"We have a banshee in Texarkana? Wow!" Bartholomew looked like he wanted to jump up and down with excitement.

That beautiful smile and innocent demeanor made my heart bounce. Bartholomew was only thirteen, but he was five-foot-ten inches and taller than me by an inch. His curly, brown hair was still a mess, but his hazel eyes were gorgeous. Bartholomew was my little brother, not by blood or paper but by our own personal agreement. Both of our parents were dead, and Death served as his guardian with Constantine as the overseer. It had to be the strangest combination to raise a boy—not that I was any better. I knew nothing about kids, but I was determined to protect him. Even if sometimes he took better care of me than I did him.

"I tried calling you earlier but you never answered." My eyes fell to his white tie, which of course was crooked, so I reached out and adjusted it.

"Sorry, we've been busy." Bartholomew rolled his eyes.

"Bartholomew, don't get too close now. The last thing I desire is banshee gunk all over that suit," Constantine ordered.

"Do we really have a banshee in town?" Eric asked, standing next to Bartholomew.

My brain stopped working for a minute. Eric was breathtaking. He was always drop-dead-gorgeous, and in that suit, he was out of this world. His six-foot muscular frame was well-defined, his brown hair always combed to perfection. I had a hard time meeting his brown eyes, which somehow looked even bigger than normal.

"Are you wearing eyeliner?" As smooth as always, that was the first thing I blurted. Go figure.

"Don't judge, okay? This wasn't my idea." Eric glared at Constantine.

"Doesn't it make his eyes pop," Constantine bragged from the back. "Look at all of their eyes, not just his. It was hard to make them match my perfection, but I had to try."

Carefully, I eyed the boys. Constantine was right. Each had some kind of makeup on. It wasn't so much that it proved distracting, but enough to highlight and showcase their natural beauty.

My gaze fell on Eugene, who was busy adjusting the tie of one of the Triplets and barely waved. It didn't take much to make him look fabulous. He was five-nine, smart, handsome, and if he didn't work for the devilish Pestilence, he would be the ideal guy. He had that smooth Will Smith quality about him.

Constantine had outdone himself. The triplets even looked like runway models. Shorty had nicknamed all three men triplets. They were not related and didn't grow up together—hell, they didn't even have the same nationality. Besides their absolute loyalty to Shorty, they all had one thing in common: the same first name—one I could never remember. It could be John. Maybe James. Wait, Joe? Shrugging, I wondered if Shorty named them the Triplets because he couldn't remember either.

"I know I'm going to hate asking, but what is going on here?" The curiosity finally got the best of me.

"Are you sure you really want to know?" Bob whispered in my ear.

"Probably not but it's too late now," I said as Bartholomew ran back and grabbed his laptop.

"We are at war." Constantine marched over to us and jumped on a director's chair located in front of the white screen.

"What? What war? Who are we fighting? Victoria's Secret models?" Honestly, the only war the boys were going to be fighting in those suits was a runway competition.

"Worse!" Constantine wasn't blinking when he made his statement. Not that it was hard for a five-thousand-year-old cat. "Jake."

Nobody looked at me when Constantine delivered the news.

"Jake? Like Jake, the devil Jake?" I was definitely exhausted since I had to repeat things multiple times.

"Why are we at war with Jake? Isn't that Jesus's fight?" Bob asked, standing over my shoulder.

"Good point, Bob, thank you." At least Bob had some common sense here.

"He started it, but I plan to finish it." Constantine slammed his paw against the seat and the sound echoed through the room. Gazes wandered, probably trying to figure out how he pulled that one off.

"You are planning to give me more than that, right?" I was too tired to pry information from this insane cat.

"You know I'm the YouTube King?" Constantine shouted.

"I thought it was that PewDee guy." Hoping for support, my eyes found Bob, but he just shook his head.

"His name is PewDiePie, and I'm not talking about him. In the supernatural YouTube, I'm the undisputed King of the realm." Constantine jumped from his seat and started pacing, which made me wonder if he was going to destroy his suit. "Guess what that two-timing, lying sack of feathers did?"

"'Sack of feathers?'" Bob asked, and this time, I was the one who shook my head.

"Yes, he was an angel. All angels have wings and I'm sure the prince of hell still has his. But let's not get distracted here." Constantine turned to face the boys. "Bartholomew, show them exhibit A."

Bartholomew turned his laptop around for Bob and me.

"Is this PG-13? Do I really want to see this? Because I need to sleep tonight," I told Constantine. Being traumatized by a clip made by the devil was not on my list of things to do.

"Just watch the video without the side commentary," Constantine snapped, obviously not in a good mood.

"Okay," Bob and I replied in unison.

Flames, decapitations, dead bodies, tortured souls, the depths of hell—anything in that realm would have made sense. Jake singing and dancing to Meghan Trainor's No Excuses would never have made it on my list. The whole thing was insane, but Jake pulled it off. He looked amazing in his many outfits, and his blond hair was perfectly styled. I always thought he looked like a young Brad Pitt, but in that video, he was even hotter. Not to mention his backup dancers were sexy as hell, pun intended.

"Do you have anything to say?" Constantine glared at me, and I knew anything I said would get me in trouble.

"It's different," I tried to play it off and not drool on the screen.

"Different? He has one hundred million views in less than two days!" Constantine's voice reached a new level.

"True, but he only has one million likes, which is like one percent." Listing the numbers, I hoped he would calm down.

"That's one million traitors," Constantine growled.

"You really can't blame them too much. I mean, just look at it. Adam looks amazing." I pointed at the screen.

The glare Constantine gave me could have killed me on the spot. "Adam. Always. Looks. Amazing." His size increased to that of a wildcat.

"Constantine, breathe." I waved my hands quickly in front of his face. "Jake has one video, you have hundreds. If anyone can take him down, it's you. Go forth and do great things."

"Yes, I can." Constantine slowly started to shrink to his normal size.

"Of course, you can. Why do you think we agreed to dress like snowmen?" Eugene said from the back.

"Why are you all dressed in white?" My mouth worked faster than my brain, so I couldn't stop the question before it came out.

"Payback is going to be epic. We are doing J. Balvin's Blanco song." Constantine looked straight Machiavellian as he rubbed his paws together.

"That is my signal to go." Bob turned, walking towards his apartments.

"You are not staying?" Eric asked Bob with a pleading tone. He looked so cute with his pouty lips.

"Nope. I have court tomorrow with Isis. Goodnight, boss and give Jake hell!" Bob gave Constantine a fist bump as he walked away.

"We will do that," Constantine replied.

"Are you sure you didn't pick that video because he has a cat flying all over the place?" I asked Constantine, pointing at Bartholomew's laptop.

Blanco was one of those creative, eye-catching videos you couldn't stop watching. It also had a fabulous, fetching cat in most of the scenes. So, I totally believed it had just been a coincidence that Constantine selected it.

"It's a perfect song for battle." Constantine rubbed his paws together again.

"Well, now it's my turn to go." I saluted the crew.

"You are not joining us?" Eugene whined from the back.

"Like Bob said, we got court tomorrow," I repeated for the boys.

"Do you want to go bar hopping with us tomorrow night? Early Saint Patty's treat." Eugene looked like a kid at Christmas.

"There is no bar hopping in Texarkana. Our bars are too far from each other to walk," I told him.

"We know that, but Mr. Shorty is driving us," one of the Triplets told me.

"Now that's a recipe for disaster," Eric said, shaking his head. I had to agree.

"Sorry, boys, as exciting as it sounds to live on the edge, I have a date." I gave them all a small curtsy.

"Oh God!" Eugene exclaimed. "Should I get the lab ready?"

"Very funny." I glared.

"You should," Eric added. "Who is this brave fellow? I would like to know who the victim is going to be in case he ends up in the morgue."

"I really need new friends. I don't know why I even talk to you guys." I stuck out my tongue even though I really wanted to flip them off, but I knew it wasn't their fault. My last date did turn into a zombie. "Relax, everyone. I'm going with TJ to Spring Lake Park."

"You do know that park is cursed," Bartholomew told me from the side.

"Thanks, everyone, I'm off to bed." I turned my back to them before they could torture me anymore.

"Goodnight, Isis, and don't you dare like Jake's video," Constantine commanded.

"I would never dare. Give them hell, Constantine!" The last part I shouted as I climbed the stairs two at a time.

Call me a chicken, but I could only take so much abuse from the boys. That was definitely too much for one night. All I could think about was a long night's sleep, but since it was already past midnight and I had court at eight in the morning, that probably wouldn't happen. This lifestyle was killing me.

Chapter Three

A normal person would work at getting as much rest as humanly possible. I, on the other hand, was running at six am after less than five hours of sleep. Running made me happy. It was an odd thing for people who were not runners to understand. I loved the feel of my legs hitting the pavement, the way the wind played with my hair, and the sensation of pure joy I had after I stopped. It was the ultimate high without any drugs. I probably could use more sleep and a vacation. If Bob was right and I had been snapping at people, I definitely needed happy hormones today.

I didn't have enough time for a long run, so I settled for six miles. The weather was warming up, so the temperature was perfect. It took everything in my power to head back to Reapers instead of staying outside. The boys were gone by the time I left the building, so I was surprised to find the lights in the loft on when I returned. Even Constantine required a bit of sleep every once in a while.

I entered the loft very quietly, hoping whoever had turned on the lights had decided to head back to bed.

"Why are you up?" I asked when I found Bartholomew sitting at his computer station on the opposite side of the room.

The loft was divided into sections. The bedrooms were located at the back, leaving the front area as a common space for everyone. A kitchen sat closest to the door, with a dining table right next to the sink. Leather couches were on the far side facing the TV and Bartholomew's wall of monitors. That side of the room was the command center. Bartholomew had access to every surveillance camera in the city, and even some home computers. The boy could be a terrorist, which made me happy to have him on our side.

"I got thirsty and came for water, then my trackers were going off," Bartholomew explained as he clicked all sorts of buttons on his keyboard.

"Trackers for what?" I crossed the room and joined him at the command center.

I was pretty sure I smelled like roadkill, so I left some space between us. I didn't want to traumatize him so early in the morning.

"Animal attacks." Bartholomew pointed at his screen.

"What's so special about animal attacks?" His screen was covered in different newspaper articles from all over the country.

"They all took place in major cities. When was the last time a wild panther attacked someone in Central Park?" Bartholomew turned to face me.

"What?" I didn't care that I smelled anymore. I moved closer to him. "Are all these attacks taking place in cities?"

"Yes." Bartholomew faced the screen as well.

"How many are you tracking?" I asked, my mouth dropping open. Some of the reports were extremely violent.

"With the two from last night, fifty-one." He licked his lips and stared at the screen.

"Have you found any patterns?" I was praying he had.

"None." Bartholomew leaned back in his chair. "Nothing. None of these people knew each other. Nobody remembers what happened. They were out and then some wild animal was chasing them."

"Nobody has died, right? I mean if they had, Death would have sent us to investigate," I told Bartholomew.

"Why would we investigate? People die from animal attacks every day." Bartholomew was pouting. He did that every time he was frustrated and couldn't find a solution for something.

"True, but this is really suspicious. Like you said, wild animals don't normally roam major cities." I scanned a few more of the papers before turning to face him. "Have any been reported in Texarkana. Did I miss this?"

"Relax, wonder woman, you haven't missed anything." He poked my side, making me squeal. "That's the reason I started tracking it. I figured we would eventually see one of these mysterious attacks."

"Then again, would people report it?" I asked him.

"What do you mean?" Bartholomew sat straighter.

"Think about it. These made the news because the attacks happened in a city. What about an incident that happens in the woods, at a deer lease or something like that? How would we know?" We had a huge hunter community, and it would be very difficult to track if anyone got hurt while hunting.

"I never thought about it." Bartholomew started typing a hundred words a minute on his keyboard. "An attack around here would not cause a big commotion, especially if the animal was native to the area."

"Exactly. What are you doing?" His fingers were moving over the keyboard like he was casting a spell or something.

"Scanning all the medical reports for both hospitals and clinics to see if anyone came in with animal wounds." Bartholomew never slowed down as he spoke.

"I don't want to know how you are doing that." It was more of a statement than a question. I never feared he would get caught, but I often wondered if his moral compass was completely compromised.

"It's safer if I don't tell you." Bartholomew grinned at me. In translation, it meant I probably didn't want to know.

"Thank you. I guess it's time for me to get ready." I turned to head towards my room.

"You know you really don't have to do this," he told me softly.

"Do what? Shower?" I asked.

"No, you do need a shower," Bartholomew said, rubbing his nose. "I meant court."

"I wish, but it's not like we can skip having magisterial court." I leaned against the leather couch and stretched my thighs.

"You are correct, but you don't have to be the one presiding over it all the time. You can delegate that." He looked me over several times.

"Please tell me you are not suggesting having Constantine do it." I rubbed my eyes as I remembered the last time we tried that.

"You have a point. He is a little of an extremist with his punishments," Bartholomew said, holding back a smirk.

"Bart, he ordered a guillotine be built on the roof to eliminate the pixie drug dealers," I reminded him.

"You have to admit that the selling of pixie dust dropped drastically after that." He couldn't hold back the giggles anymore. "All I'm saying is think about it. I'm sure you can find a respectable alternative who doesn't believe in executing all the prisoners."

"Let me think about it." I didn't like everyone being so worried about me. "Oh, by the way, how did the shoot go last night?"

"It was awesome!" Bartholomew informed me with both hands in the air. "Did you know that Eric is an amazing dancer?"

"Eric? Our Eric? No way!" This was huge news.

"He has some moves that even Eugene copied, and we know Eugene can move." Bartholomew just made the understatement of the year. Eugene was unstoppable on the dance floor.

"Are you telling me I'm actually going to have to watch this video?" I had hoped to stay out of this strange war, but this might be too good to pass up.

"I understand why Constantine is the reigning king of their YouTube. His directing skills are through the roof and his vision is out of this world." Bartholomew started to demonstrate some of their moves, and I couldn't wait for the final product.

"Now I'm interested in this video. When is he dropping it?" Like I didn't have other stuff to worry about.

"This evening and it's going to be hot!" Bartholomew rubbed his hands together, imitating Constantine. "I just hope this feud lasts longer than Machine Gun Kelly and Eminem."

"Why?" That was a strange comparison.

"Easy, because the videos that will come out of this feud will be priceless." Excitement bubbled out of Bartholomew, and even his cheeks were turning red. "You have to admit those two tracks that MGK and Eminem dropped were classic. Battles like that must keep going."

"I seriously think I have to start monitoring your YouTube feed." Who was I kidding? Putting parental constraints on a hacker were as useful as telling the sun not to shine. "Never mind, I'm off to shower."

"Love you, Isis." The humor was gone from his voice and he looked as sweet as any young child could.

"I love you, too, Bartholomew," I told him as I kissed his forehead. "Make sure to eat something this morning."

"Do you want me to make you breakfast?" Bartholomew had a gluten intolerance, and recently we found the most amazing gluten-free oatmeal, so the boy was in heaven.

"As long as you make some for yourself," I told him.

"Deal." He bounced off his chair and followed me to the kitchen. "Two giant bowls of peanut-butter-raisin oatmeal are on their way."

Normally, I would have taken my oatmeal with me. Today, Bartholomew was in such great spirits and he worked so hard on it that I couldn't leave him to have breakfast alone. He was the only kid I knew that wanted to make oatmeal from scratch instead of using those instant packets. I was pretty sure Bob's culinary delights were rubbing off on him. Our breakfast date put me a bit behind, though, so I had less than ten minutes to make it to Union Station for court. I drove like Shorty down New Boston Road just to make it in time.

Being Death's Intern had its benefits. I was guaranteed a parking space as close to the building as possible, which saved me some valuable minutes not having to look for one. When I did park, I rushed inside the building using the back stairs. There was a line of people already in the building by the time I walked in.

"I am so sorry," I told Shorty and the boys when I ran in to the small ante-chamber.

"Why are you sorry?" Shorty asked, inspecting me up and down.

"For being late." I glanced at my watch for confirmation.

"You are five minutes late," Bob said from behind Shorty.

"Exactly," I repeated.

"Boss-lady, are you serious?" Shorty met my eyes, a stretch for him since I was so much taller than him. "This is your court, which means you can be as late as you feel like. It's not like anyone can start without you."

"Shorty is right, Isis. This is your realm," Bob agreed.

"Then why did I just run every red light in town just to get here?" I took a deep breath to calm myself.

"It's a blast. Didn't you love it?" Shorty asked, clapping his hands together.

"No!" I told him. "It was super stressful, and I was sure I was going to kill someone."

"See, that's the problem. Those negative thoughts are definitely holding you back." Shorty shook his head and handed me a black robe.

"Unbelievable," I muttered to myself.

"Let's go Boss Lady. Time to earn some money," Shorty announced, leading the way to the court area.

Bob and I followed slowly behind him.

"Your hair looks great today," Bob whispered from behind me.

"I figured if I stopped showing up like a hot mess I might earn some respect around here," I replied just as softly.

"The team loves you, Isis, but we're worried about you. That's all." He patted my shoulder and I couldn't help but smile.

We entered our newly renovated court area. The team had done an incredible job at making the place look like a real court room, from the judge's bench to the location of the accused. Either my team had a lot of experience inside real courts, or they broke into a few just to get the blueprints to the room. I did not want confirmation for either one of those theories. Due to the nature of our population, several modifications were added to the design thanks to the help of my Godmother—the High Priestess herself. She ensured that each room was protected against spells and all sorts of magical stuff, even putting a curse on the doors that eliminated the magic of charms people might be wearing. That made for an interesting court visit.

Bob served as the main announcer, a 'pseudo officer' who made sure the ones coming forward stayed calm so no harm fell on anyone. It took us several weeks to master that little feat. Bob gave the signals to the guards at the door. We had different guards for each court, that way nobody could be targeted or corrupted.

The guards opened the doors and a handsome couple stood at the threshold. The couple was tall, slender, and impeccably dressed. They sauntered into the room like they were walking into a beauty pageant. As they crossed the entrance, their bodies shimmered. I tilted my head and waited with anticipation, knowing the spells on the door had detected a charm. When the glamor dissolved, I was left with two short, old dwarves.

"Ick!" both screamed as they looked at each other and realized their disguises were gone.

"Good morning," I said loudly enough to draw their attention towards me. "Hope you don't mind, but we prefer your true forms for these proceedings. Are you two ready to start?"

Both dwarves nodded at me, but neither of them looked happy. The female held her chin high, but her husband—if that was his status—gazed at his feet. Covered in wrinkles, their skin seemed to be made of clay, their thin hair like grass. Nothing was soothing about their presence.

"According to your record, you are being charged for trying to burn down your house. Is that correct?" I asked them, angling my head as I waited for their response.

Silence was my best ally during these proceedings since most people went crazy with it. It took the dwarves three whole minutes before cracking. Honestly, I was impressed. Most people lasted a minute and a half. Maybe it was their age that gave them more patience.

"That good for nothing, lying thief was price gouging us," the female said. "That place was a shit-hole. Just because I'm a dwarf doesn't mean I plan to live in a fetches-infested establishment. I have rights."

"Yes, you do," I replied, and the poor dwarf almost passed out.

"You agree with me?" Her features softened and she leaned closer. "Is this a joke?"

"Sorry, ma'am, we don't have time to joke here," I answered her. "You are correct, and after we are done here, the guards will take you to the next room so you can file a report against the landlord. Mr. Shorty will be over there today to inspect the facilities."

The female looked around the room, searching for Shorty, no doubt. With a mischievous demeanor, he waved at her, and even her husband raised his head to glance his way.

"But that doesn't excuse your behavior," I told them both.

Both dwarves turned to me, their faces changing to a paler color, which I thought might be their version of blushing.

"We have a list of certified housing that you can use to avoid incidents like this," I continued. "In order to keep the safety and welfare of everyone, conditions like this must be reported. It's the only way for us to know what is going on. Is that clear?"

"Yes, your magistrate," both dwarves replied.

"Good. For your sentence, you will assist in the building of the new playground downtown." I read over my notes as I spoke.

"What?" the male asked.

"It says you have exceptional skills in building, is that correct?" I leaned over my desk, eyeing the dwarf closely.

"Yes, but ..." he trailed off.

"But what?" I said, trying to move it along. Since we had over thirty cases to be heard today, we didn't have time to dally.

"Aren't you going to sentence us to the dungeons, to clean dragon poop and feed the alligators?" Because he said his words to the floor, I struggled to hear him correctly.

"We have alligators in the cells? And what dragon?" I looked over at Shorty for clarification, but he was already chattering to anyone around him, more than likely asking them the same things I just asked the dwarves. "Who told you that?"

"Our landlord," the female replied for her husband. "That's why nobody comes forth ... because that's what happens to snitches."

I slapped my head with my hand. It was going to be a long day.

"Oh, I got dragons and alligators for his ass. Don't worry, Madam Boss Lady, we got this," Shorty announced to the room and the rest of the guards gave me wicked smirks.

"Thank you, Shorty," I told him. "Please pay a visit to all the establishments this week. I want to know the status of every one of them. Ensure that the residents know the law and that they can come see us to report violations anytime."

"We are on it." Shorty saluted and left the court.

I was afraid what the inspections would reveal. Shorty did not appreciate his reputation and that of this organization being tarnished, so this accusation was a straight insult.

"Any other questions on your sentencing?" I asked the pair.

"How long do we serve?" the male asked, finally meeting my eyes.

"It's only for a week, but we would appreciate if you could help us finish it. After the week is served, we will pay you for any additional work you do to complete the project." We had too many projects and not enough artisans, so I hoped they took the deal.

"Yes," the female replied before her husband could say anything.

"Thank you. The guards will escort you to the registry office." I nodded to the guards on my right and they led the dwarves away.

"Smooth," Bob whispered to me.

"We need help and they have talents, so why not?" I told him.

"You might be right," Bob said, glancing at his clipboard.

"About what?" I asked, leaning back in my seat.

"I don't know who could do this job better than you." Bob winked at me and signaled for the door guards to let the next one in.

Another pair of beautiful people stood at the threshold. The guards ushered them in, and just like the first pair, they shimmered. Their bodies glowed and they morphed. This time our supermodels transformed to ten-foot-tall trolls.

"It's going to be one of those days," I whispered to Bob.

"Yes, it is," Bob replied.

I made myself comfortable and got ready for ten hours of pure fun. Not. At least lunch was being catered from The Flying Crow and that always made my day better. I was hoping they had Peanut Butter Pie today because I was going to need a good dose of sugar after all the cases we were facing.

Chapter Four

It was official; I was getting an understudy. I looked at my reflection in the window of Ladybug after parking inside Reapers. Ten hours of listening to crazy stories, horrible scenarios, and coming home covered in even more slime had been too much for me.

Did I even have enough shampoo to get this crap out of my hair?

I looked like I got run over by a horse and flushed down a sewer pipe. I would be delegating this to someone else, at least long enough for me to take a proper nap.

The soles of my sneakers kept getting stuck on the steps due to the disgusting concoction covering me. I took them off and carried them the rest of the way up. I hadn't seen the boys and hoped they were all out bar hopping with Eugene.

"Hi, Isis." A chorus of voices welcomed me home.

"I couldn't be so lucky," I muttered to myself.

"How was—?" Constantine stopped mid-sentence. "What happened to you? I thought you were going to court. Why are you covered in slime again? Oh, my senses, why do you smell so nasty?"

"I got doused by a pot of goblin stew," I announced to the group, turning slowly in a circle to show off my fabulous new look.

"They actually eat that stuff?" Constantine gagged. "I'm going to be sick. This is too much for my sensitive nose."

"Fine, I'm going to shower." I raised my hands in surrender.

"Leave your clothes and your shoes outside your room," Constantine yelled back.

"Why? Are you planning to wash them?" I eyed the group from the door.

"Wash them? There is no saving them." Constantine fanned himself with his paw as he draped himself over the couch like he had the weight of the world on him or something. Overly dramatic much? "We are burning all that stuff. Eric, can you make some powerful fire, right?"

Eric dismissed him and conjured a fireball in his palm. "Of course, I can."

"Good, we are going to need it." Constantine turned back to me. "Don't worry, Isis. We got this."

"I really like these shoes." I glanced at my perfectly broken-in Converse and almost cried.

"I will buy you three new pairs, but those are gone." Constantine didn't seem even a little sorry for sentencing my shoes to total destruction. No, he just continued to fan himself.

Court was not my favorite place anyways, but after what it had caused, the way I felt about it was even worse today. I headed towards my room and dropped my poor shoes outside my door. Bartholomew, Constantine, and I had rooms on this side of the loft, each one with a very distinct flare. From what I was told, I had the largest bathtub in Reapers—a fact I was not ashamed of. Constantine claimed I required it since I was prone to injuries and required constant soaking. I was convinced he just enjoyed picking on me.

As soon as I turned on the light, soft jazz filled the room. The air smelled of roses and chai tea. Bartholomew had rewired my room so my sound system was now connected to the lights. He also sound-proofed the room to give me space to play my instruments. Music was a huge part of my life, and Death only enhanced my skills. I had the power to make people do whatever I wanted based on the music I played. Too bad the only things I had mastered were knocking people out, making them clear a room, and getting them to dance all night. I should focus on my repertoire more.

If Constantine was planning to burn my clothes, there was no point in carrying them to my bathroom. I undressed by the door. As I slid the clothes outside, I took a whiff of my shirt.

Holy Mother of God, that was nauseating! I should apologize to Constantine because he hadn't lied. And his sense of smell was twenty times more sensitive than mine, so I couldn't believe he hadn't passed out.

"Constantine they are outside, and I'm so sorry!" I shouted through the crack in the door.

I didn't wait for his reply. I knew he heard me even if nobody else did. The stew had made its way down my back and chest, and the stickiness was disgusting. I ran into my bathroom and jumped in the shower. While a bath would have been amazing, I needed as much running water as possible for this mission. I turned the faucet as hot as I could handle and started pouring shampoo over my head.

The shower took a lot longer than I expected, and even though I knew it would take a while, no matter how much I scrubbed I couldn't make the smell disappear. After going through three bottles of shampoo, two bottles of body soap, and washing so hard I'm surprised my skin was still intact, I gave up and hopped in the tub. My Godmother had given me jasmine oil to help with healing. The only problem was every time I used it, I smelled like jasmine for days. These were desperate times, though, so I didn't care. I soaked everything in the water, including my hair. The bath was the strangest sensation I experienced in a long time. While the water was super-hot, the oils made my skin and scalp tingle.

I texted TJ as soon as I got out of the bath, but it still took me forty-five minutes to get dressed. Dates were not my thing, and I had no idea what to wear. I only had a handful of female friends—no comparison to the amount of men I hung around. Calling them for something this silly was embarrassing. I tried ten different outfits and hated them all. Staring at my closet confirmed the fact that it was filled with all sorts of clothing. My job required me to dress as many different characters, that was for sure. I just had nothing that screamed "Date Night."

This was a horrible way to start a date.

I finally settled for a pair of boot-cut jeans that, according to Constantine, pushed my butt into a bubble shape. I had no idea how that crazy cat knew about bubble butts, but he insisted it was a good thing. TJ was over six feet tall, so I could pull off a pair of boots with a bit of a heel. We were going to be outside, so I found a baby-blue cardigan that hung off one shoulder and fell past my hips. I hated make-up, and since this wasn't a real date—we were just going to the park—I only brushed lip-gloss on and added mascara. Hopefully, it didn't scream desperate girl.

The only thing I did differently from my everyday life was my hair. Normally, I had it tied in a braid or a ponytail, but today I decided to let it down. Bob was right again; my hair was almost to my hips. I could really use a nice haircut, but I would think about that tomorrow. I was already super late.

I ran out of my room to find Eugene and Eric still in the common room. Constantine and Bartholomew were both pressing buttons at the computer station and Bob was busy in the kitchen mixing stuff in a bowl.

"Wow, look at you." Bob gave me a little whistle.

"You do know most ladies would find that very offensive?" I informed Bob with my hands on my hips.

"Should I apologize?" Bob raised an eyebrow.

"Not this time. I really don't care." I beamed. "I'm just warning you in case you decide to start courting ladies here."

"You are out of control." Bob chuckled and went back to mixing. "I thought your date was at eight."

"Yes, I'm late. But I couldn't get the smell off me." I sniffed my arm one more time to make sure it was gone. "Wait a minute, how did you get yours off?" Bob got soaked with the same stew as I did.

"Baking soda bath gets rid of any obnoxious odors in fifteen minutes," Bob told me.

"You didn't consider that would be important information to tell me?" My voice was a little higher than I intended.

"You were moving with such a purpose that I thought you knew." He turned to hide in the fridge, pretending to pull jars out.

"Next time, please check. I'm pretty sure I destroyed six layers of skin tonight." I was busy examining said skin when Eric walked over.

"Do we need to save TJ?" His voice startled me so bad that I slammed into him. "Sorry Isis, didn't mean to scare you."

"It's my fault. Sorry about stepping on your foot." I looked down to find a big footprint on his shiny, white shoes.

"Don't worry, I'm sure I can clean them," Eric said softly.

"You look great, Isis!" Eugene shouted from across the room.

"Yes, you do," Bartholomew concurred. "You should leave your hair down more often."

"Only if I want it to be used as a weapon against me," I replied as I tossed my hair over my shoulder. It was such a girly move, but my hair was everywhere. "What are you guys doing over there?

"Constantine dropped the video," Bartholomew told me, sliding off his chair.

"And?" I asked.

"And like I expected, this baby is soaring to the moon. We have ten million views in under an hour. Jake is going to eat crow." Constantine was almost purring when he spoke.

"Does Jake even know you two are fighting?" I knew it was an obvious question, but I wasn't sure if anyone had asked.

"Oh, trust me he does, but it wouldn't matter if he didn't," Constantine replied.

"It really does. He can't eat crow if he doesn't know you two are competing," I pointed out the obvious to my fearless guardian.

"Aren't you late for a date?" Constantine asked.

I looked at my watch and it was past nine. "Oh God, I'm so late. Bye, everyone."

Running out the door without waiting for a reply, I was happy not to hear any more comments about saving TJ. I already knew I was bad at dating, so I didn't want any more proof.

Chapter Five

Spring Lake Park was not one of my favorite places to hang out. Somehow, horrible things kept happening to us at this park. It sucked because it was a beautiful place in the center of Texarkana. The city planned many events there and it had such a great view. Still, it gave me the creeps. Maybe today I could start making happy memories there, though.

Why did I agree to come in separate cars?

The park wasn't huge like Central Park, but with it being dark, it would take forever for me to find him.

Ring. The ringing of my phone came through the speaker in my car. It was a blessing Bartholomew knew how to program everything because this was amazing.

"Hello," I answered before the phone announced who the caller was.

"Hey, you just drove past me," TJ told me.

"I did?" I looked around, hoping to figure out where he was.

"Yeah, I was doing cartwheels and you didn't even see me," he teased.

"Now you are just pushing it," I replied, really hoping I hadn't actually missed him doing cartwheels.

"Fine, don't believe me." TJ's voice was masculine yet gentle. "If you turn around, there is a small entrance to your right. You will see my truck in the parking lot."

"Okay, give me two minutes." I disconnected the call and tried to make a U-turn in the small road.

I didn't want to draw too much attention to myself, and thankfully, a Mini Cooper can turn anywhere. I slowed drastically to make sure I didn't miss the turn again. It didn't take me long to find it, and I was surprised that I'd missed it the first time. TJ's white truck was the only one in the lot and he was leaning against it. In fact, slanted against it the way he was, he kind of looked like he belonged in a vehicle commercial. His brown hair had that carefree look that only guys could pull off. I didn't know how but I could have sworn his hazel eyes glowed when the light hit them.

I parked Ladybug next to his truck, and the true gentleman that he was, TJ came over and opened the door for me.

"Are you ready for a night of surprises and mind-blowing experiences?"

Unsure how to answer his question, I bit my lip. "I hope so." My voice came out hesitant, the words drawn out.

"Don't look so terrified, Isis. It's going to be fine." TJ took my arm and led us down the path.

"Did we miss the movie?" I asked as we passed the big-screen TV and all the movie goers.

"It started at eight, unless you don't mind watching the end of it?" TJ stopped at the edge of the clearing where the movie was playing.

"I'm so sorry," I told him, and I had no other words in my arsenal to convey how sorry I actually was.

"Don't be. Work happens to all of us," he told me in an understanding tone.

"It happens to me a lot more than most." I took a deep breath and tried to smile.

"What's wrong?" He led us down the curving path of the park. "And don't tell me nothing because you look miserable."

"Uh," I muttered, wishing I could scream. "Everyone keeps telling me I need a vacation."

"Do you think they're right?" TJ looked at me when he asked.

"I guess so, but it's hard to take time off with everything we have going on," I said, wishing someone would understand my side of things.

"You are probably right, but there is never a good time for a break." He squeezed my hand a little. "You just take one before you burn out. I'm sure that's what everyone is hoping to avoid."

"I know you are right but it doesn't help." I stretched my shoulders a little, trying to release the tension that was accumulating between my shoulder blades. "Where are we going?"

"I want to show you something." We walked a little further off the trails and into the tree line. "I know you don't like this park, so I wanted to give you something fun to remember it by. Here, kneel with me."

We are in the middle of a bunch of weird bushes and falling limbs, and this is the place he wants to show me?

The thoughts were flashing in my mind faster than I could breathe. I worked on clearing my mind before my face betrayed me, then knelt next to TJ and waited for the amazing surprise to show up. If this was it, I had to say this would go down as the strangest date ever.

"We should stay very still," TJ whispered in my ear, and his warm breath made goosebumps dance down the back of my neck.

TJ squeezed my hand again, and I took a few deep breaths to relax before facing him. The night was beautiful, only a few clouds covering the quarter moon and the stars. Perfection.

"Look." TJ pointed to the left and I followed his hand.

Out of nowhere, hundreds of fireflies appeared. They coated the bushes and the semi-dead trees. It was like watching a living Christmas tree full of lights. The little bugs created such a magical feeling that it was easy to forget we were still in Spring Lake Park.

"They are beautiful," I whispered, afraid to scare the little bugs away.

"I found them last spring by accident," he said, his voice just above a whisper. "I'm not even sure if they are native to this area, but I couldn't stop staring at them."

It was hard not to be mesmerized by their lights. The tension in my shoulders disappeared and my heart filled with wonder.

"Thank you," I told TJ. "It is beautiful." I leaned on his shoulder and watched the little light show created just for us.

"I'm glad I could make your day better," TJ told me as he wrapped his arm around me.

Unfortunately, our show didn't last forever. The fireflies slowly dispersed back to where they came from.

"That was fun. Now what?" I asked TJ like a little kid in a candy store.

"Well, I have a picnic basket in the truck. I know you are always rushing everywhere and barely eating. How about a late dinner by the lake?" TJ stood up and pulled me to my feet.

"You thought of everything. Oh look, the moon." The quarter moon became visible as the clouds floated away.

TJ screamed.

"Oh God, what's wrong?" I asked as he pushed me away.

"Isis, RUN!" TJ growled at me.

"What? Are you nuts?" I reached for him, but he just pushed me away.

"Please, run." TJ convulsed, his whole body shaking with tremors so hard his teeth clacked together.

"I'm not leaving, we need to get you to a hospital. Now." I reached for his arm, but fur sprouted from it, sharp claws extending from his fingers.

"Isis, go. I'm turning and I can't control it. It's not safe for you." He dropped on all fours and it looked like that moment out of Thriller when Michael Jackson starts changing.

"TJ, you are a shifter?" I asked, my feet inching towards him without my permission.

"RUN!" TJ ordered as his teeth extended and pointy feline ears grew from his head.

"If this is not safe for me, it's probably not safe for anyone else," I told him, watching as his face mutated even more. "TJ, I'm so sorry."

I pulled a small revolver from my boot and aimed it at his head. Fear, anger, and hunger all showed on TJ's face.

"Isis, do it."

Hardly able to recognize his voice in his new form, I took a quick breath and pulled the trigger. He dropped on the ground. Without any warning, his hair and the fur that was starting to appear also fell off. He was completely hairless.

"What in the hell?" I looked at the gun like it should have directions written on it. "Nobody ever mentioned something like this would happen."

With the increase in werewolf gangs in Texarkana, Constantine had made me carry this new gun. According to him, the bullets were designed specifically for werewolves. I wasn't sure how we would test these kinds of weapons, but this side effect was something to keep in mind. TJ was going to kill me when he woke up and found himself hairless.

"TJ, I don't know if you can hear me but I'm so sorry." I knelt next to him and turned him around. "Why didn't you tell me you were a shifter?"

The transformation had shredded his shirt in several places and even his jeans. The boy was completely hairless, but his chest was extremely well defined. I'd always known he was in great shape, but I never imagined he would have an eight pack.

Do shifters come with incredible muscle definition? Maybe that was a possibility ... Focus! This was not the time to be checking out his body. I had to get him back to Reapers before Eugene left for the night and was too drunk to help. Wait, could Eugene even get drunk? Being Pestilence's Intern made him immune to drugs, plague, and probably alcohol.

"The real question is, TJ, can I carry you back to Ladybug?" I guessed I was going to find out.

TJ was a lot heavier than he looked, probably due to his bulging muscles. It took me almost twenty minutes to drag him back to the parking lot. I avoided the movie goers and any other pedestrians in the park. Explaining why I was carrying a half-naked man that looked half human/half animal would be impossible.

By the time I made it to Ladybug, sweat dripped from me and my muscles burned from the exertion. I was also pretty sure I was going into muscle failure. I hoped Bob was at Reapers when I got there because there was no way I could carry TJ up those stairs.

Shoving TJ in the car, I noticed the bumps and bruises marring his skin. Eugene could treat those as well, so I buckled him in and rushed to the driver's side.

"This park is cursed," I told TJ, wondering if he could hear me.

I adjusted his head one last time and took a deep breath. If that tranquilizer wears off in this car, I'm one dead girl.

"Happy thoughts, Isis." Desperate times had come when I began talking to myself.

I started Ladybug and left the park as slowly as I could. I wanted to gun the engine and head to Reapers, but I really did not want to get pulled over. Discretion was of the essence.

Chapter Six

Please God, let TJ be alive.

Driving out of Spring Lake, I prayed TJ wouldn't wake-up during the ride to Reapers. In the last thirteen minutes he hadn't stirred once—not even an eyelid. I had never used that crazy werewolf tranquilizer, though, so part of me worried I killed him. He had a pulse, but it was so faint.

God, Eric was right! I was a walking nightmare for dates.

"TJ, if you can hear me, please hold on. We are almost at Reapers." I turned off Interstate Thirty to Highway Eighty-Two,

One of the greatest things about living in a small town was traffic issues were nonexistent. I took the sharpest right turn I'd ever done to enter the business park. I didn't bother calling Reapers ahead of arriving, mainly because my ego wasn't ready to be humiliated by the boys. Pulling around the building to the vehicle entrance of Reapers, I found both Eugene's company car, the Hearse, and Eric's red Jeep still there. The vehicle entrance had as many security sensors as the pedestrians', but the latter took twice as long.

The minute scan felt like an eternity. I started counting the seconds in my head to avoid reaching for TJ again and checking his pulse. By the time the gate opened, I gunned Ladybug, screeching to a stop into my space. My heart was pounding, and I could hear my heartbeat like drums in my head. I broke free from my seatbelt and ran to TJ's side of the car.

"Constantine. Bob. Bartholomew. Help!" I struggled with TJ's seatbelt.

Doors crashed open from all directions. "ISIS!" Constantine screamed.

Bob was the first one to reach me as he sprinted from his apartment. Constantine leaped down from the second floor. I had no idea how he didn't break all his bones, but like a true cat, he landed on his feet and kept on running. Bartholomew, Eugene, and Eric were not far behind.

"What's going on?" Bob held me steady by the shoulders.

"TJ." I pointed at his body with my chin.

Bob crept past me towards the open door of Ladybug. Constantine walked on the hood of the Deathmobile— Death's Mustang—to get a better look.

"What happened?" Constantine asked me as he watched Bob examine TJ.

"I have no idea. We were talking and then he told me to run. He started turning but he couldn't control it." I covered my face with my hands, not ready to look at the boys.

"Isis," Eric's voice was a soft whisper.

"Eric. Please." I raised my hand to push him away.

"Are you okay?" he asked, and until his hand went under my chin and lifted my face to look at him, I hadn't noticed he'd moved so close. "Did he hurt you?"

"No," I barely mumbled. "I shot him before he finished turning."

Was Eric actually concerned about me? He searched my arms and legs to make sure I wasn't hurt. This was definitely the strangest night of my life.

"Turning? What do you mean by turning?" Bartholomew made his way to the side of Ladybug.

"That thing that people do to become werewolves." Pulling away from Eric, I faced Bartholomew.

"He is no werewolf," Constantine announced, hopping off the Deathmobile and joining Bob. "I knew I liked this one for a reason. Our dear TJ is a Lynx Rufus."

"Thanks, Constantine, but that didn't really help," I told my guardian as I struggled to see anything from my angle.

"TJ is a Bobcat," Bartholomew clarified, smirking from ear to ear. "Which makes total sense since Bobcats are native to this area. This is so cool! Can we keep him?"

"Bartholomew, focus! He is not a pet," Constantine chastised.

"It might just be me, but I don't get why he was shifting during your date?" Eugene said, his statement more a question as he scribbled notes into a small notebook.

Often, I forget Eugene was actually a brilliant scientist and he lived for these types of riddles.

"He saw the moon. Isn't that what triggers it?" I was oblivious to these things. As the sheriff of the only Supernatural community in North America, I should take lessons on all my citizens.

"The moon shouldn't have any effect on him at his age." Constantine strolled over to me. "TJ is not a kitten, so he should have full control of his abilities. Something else forced the shift."

"Oh, wow. He is much heavier than he looks." Bob struggled to get TJ out.

"Let me help you." Eric made his way over and grabbed TJ's lower half.

"How did you get him in the car?" Bob asked me, peering over his shoulder.

"That was a struggle," I admitted. "What I want to know is why he lost all his hair? Have you guys ever tested that stuff?"

All the boys went dead silent. None of them looked in my direction and all pretended to be busy with their own tasks: Eugene with his notebook, Bob and Eric moving TJ, Constantine inspecting his claws, and even Bartholomew was staring at the ground.

"Never mind." I raised my hands in defeat. "Next time, somebody please warn me that the poor people are going to end up looking like raw chicken meat after I shoot them."

"That was a good call, Isis," Constantine told me as he jumped on the Deathmobile again. "Out of control shifters can be deadly."

"Shifters! That's it!" Bartholomew screamed and ran up the stairs.

"Where are you going?" Constantine shouted back.

"The animal attacks ... they are not random," Bartholomew replied from the top of the stairs.

"What is that boy talking about?" Constantine turned to face the rest of us.

"Bart has been tracking an increase in animal attacks across the country in major cities." My stomach turned, and I thought I was going to puke. "Oh, God. If he is right, it means shifters have been attacking and eating humans."

Bob and Eric almost dropped TJ. Eugene paled and Constantine froze on the hood.

"Why haven't we heard about this before?" I could tell Constantine was trying not to growl at me, but he needed to try a lot harder because he failed.

"There was no pattern." I couldn't take my eyes off TJ's comatose body. "All the animals were different. The victims were in different areas, different settings. Nobody had reported anything unusual. All we had were random animal attacks."

"Were any of the animals found?" Constantine asked in a softer voice.

"No, they weren't." I hadn't paid attention to that part before. "Bartholomew has been tracking over fifty cases and none of the animals were ever located."

"That wasn't a big enough pattern?" This time, Constantine definitely growled.

"Hey, I just found out today so calm down," I ordered.

"Could we continue this conversation a little later? TJ is pretty heavy here." Bob adjusted TJ one more time.

"Let's take him to the lab. I think I have something I can give him to keep him knocked out," Eugene told Bob as he headed towards the back of Reapers.

"Are you turning my shooting range into a lab again?" I followed Eugene towards the enclosed range right next to the vehicle's entrance. "It took me over a week to get all the simulators and targets back in order."

"We have done some renovations lately," Eugene informed me, not bothering to turn around. "It appears the demand for a lab is going to be a permanent requirement in your world, so we adjusted."

"'We?' Who is 'we?'" There were too many people making decisions around here when I was not at home.

"Who else?" Constantine answered for Eugene.

"I should have guessed." If anyone would make major changes to my world, it would be Constantine.

Eugene opened the door to the range—one of my favorite spaces at Reapers. Gun racks lined the wall adjacent to the door, with targets spread on the opposite side. Simulators were dispersed in the middle of the room, making the space look like an arcade center. We had the latest technology to test everything from hand and eye reflexes to expert-level marksmanship. The one thing missing from the range was Eugene's lab equipment.

"Do we have to get your supplies from your shop?" Glancing at Eugene, I hoped he had a plan.

Pestilence's lab was located in Hope, Arkansas, underneath a chicken plant. While Hope was only a thirty-five-minute drive from Reapers, we didn't have an hour to spare to search for medicine in another state.

"We have taken care of everything." Eugene winked at me and flipped a switched by one of the gun racks.

The floor started to move and my simulators dropped to the ground. Gun racks disappeared along with everything in the room that resembled a firing range. Instead, lab tables, cabinets, and even medical beds replaced my favorite place, like a giant transformer had mutated the room into something it shouldn't be. As I watched, the lights were even switched out for brighter ones, so I stood by the door with my mouth wide open, completely speechless.

"Bob, Eric, please put TJ on the bed," Eugene ordered. "I'm not sure how conscious he is going to be when he wakes up, so let's restrain him. I don't need a wild Bobcat attacking me."

"Wow," I finally said, speaking of the transformation because it was pretty amazing.

"Thank you," said Constantine.

"Can you cure him?" I asked Eugene once my mind had accepted the new state of the room. TJ's skin had paled even more, and since he was hairless ... it just didn't look good. "And is he going to stay like that for long?"

"One question at a time," Eugene replied, pulling a huge needle from one of his cabinets. "The curing part I have no idea. I would want to know what caused this thing in order to reverse it or cure it. Two: the hair loss, well ... he should grow his hair back normally, but if you want me to, I can give him something to speed up the process."

"No!" we all screamed at the same time.

"What?" Eugene asked, his eyes moving to each of us.

"Eugene, you are brilliant and absolutely my favorite mad-scientist, but you don't do anything in moderation," Constantine explained.

"What does that mean?" Eugene raised his eyebrows.

"What Constantine is trying to say is we don't want TJ going from a plucked chicken to a full-grown ape in a matter of minutes." I pointed to poor TJ on the bed for extra emphasis.

"That is such a horrible mental picture," Eric told me. "I'm never going to be able to look at TJ the same way. I'm going to be thinking raw chicken meat every time. Thanks, Isis."

"How do you think I felt when all of his hair fell off in front of me?" That image would forever be burned into my mind.

"Can we focus on the shifter with no control and leave the hair discussion for another day?" Constantine made his way to the table, sniffing TJ's head.

"Yes, that would be great," I agreed with Constantine. "What do you need, Eugene?"

"Ideally? To find out what caused this—whatever this is?" Eugene examined TJ's eyelids while checking for his pulse.

"Is he in pain?" TJ was stuck in the middle of his shift, his face, legs, and arms a mix of his animal form and his human one.

"He shouldn't be," Eugene told me. "The formula is powerful enough to knock them totally unconscious and stop the process. Unfortunately, it doesn't reverse it. We have to wait for TJ to wake up in order for that to happen."

"Is that safe?" Bob finally spoke, having been so quiet I almost forgot he was there.

"It would be if we wait until sunrise," Constantine told us as he moved TJ's face from one side to the other.

"I thought you said the moon had nothing to do with this?" I crossed my arms and glared at Constantine.

"I said the moon was not the cause of his shift, but once he is in this form, that damn thing provides an extra layer of instability to our situation." Constantine moved down the table to study TJ's claws. "I'm impressed. This boy is an incredible specimen. Absolutely my favorite."

"What can we do, Eugene?" Bob asked, leaning against the wall.

"We have to find out what TJ has been doing, taking, eating ... you name it. Anything that would tell us how his habits have changed." Eugene turned to look at me and the other three did the same.

"How am I supposed to know that?" I backed away from the group.

"We should check his apartment. Maybe his roommate knows," Bob suggested.

"I don't know where he lives." Admitting that meant I was a horrible friend, but I couldn't lie. I'd never gotten around to asking.

"I do." Bob winked at me.

"How do you know that?" Eric saved me from asking.

"Easy. I know the addresses of all the people that we interact with on a daily basis." Bob pulled a small notebook from his backpack that I had never seen before.

"Wow, that is impressive," I admitted to him.

"Or paranoid, depending which one you prefer," Bob corrected me playfully.

"I prefer impressive." It was my turn to grin at him.

"Perfect," Constantine announced from the bed. "Bob and Isis, go search TJ's place. Eric, check your police records for any animal attacks in the area."

"Bartholomew already checked," I blurted out, instantly regretting the words.

"I don't want to know if that boy has hacked the police department again." Eric covered his face with his hands.

It must be hard being a witch, friends with Death's team, and a civilian cop. Eric must enjoy his world being complicated. At the same time, it was very handy having a friend on the inside of the police station.

"Some things are safer not knowing, Eric," Constantine told him, shrugging.

"Tell me about it." Eric didn't meet any of our gazes. "Someone please call me if anything changes with TJ. I'll head in right now."

"We will," Bob answered.

"For the record, Isis, I'm glad you are okay, even if you have the worst dating record in the history of dating ever." With a wicked grin, Eric left the room.

I was growing on him.

I couldn't help but giggle. Normally, Eric never showed this much emotion. Especially towards me. In fact, I drove the poor guy nuts since he served as my martial-arts instructor.

"Bob, let me change into some work clothes before we go." My work clothes were not that much different from what I was already wearing, but I required more pockets so I could add more weapons. A lot more.

"That's a good idea," Bob concurred. "Boss, do you mind if we take the Camaro?"

"It's ready to go." Constantine's eyes never left TJ. "Just don't let Isis blow it up. I really like the Camaro formerly known as Bumblebee."

"We could take Ladybug," I suggested, mainly because I could never get Bob to ride with me.

"Nope," he said, the one-word answer all he gave me.

"You can't possibly think a yellow Camaro is more discreet than a Mini Cooper?" Normally, Bob's argument for not riding with me was that my car drew too much attention.

"Maybe, but I can hide a lot more firepower in the Camaro than in Ladybug. We are taking the Camaro." Bob raised one eyebrow as he waited for my reply.

I could accept when I was defeated, and that was one of those times. "Okay, I can't argue with that. I'll be back."

I left the converted-into-a-lab range and ran up the stairs. I knew it wasn't my fault that TJ had started to shift, but it was my fault he was stuck in the in-between state. The sooner we figured out what was going on, the faster my life could go back to normal. But what was normal anymore?

Chapter Seven

If Friday the thirteenth was an odd day for me, this Saturday was not going any better. It took us less than ten minutes to leave Reapers. TJ lived at the Westridge Apartments in Texarkana. It was an easy ride, but I kept fiddling with my pockets. I couldn't stay still, and my adrenaline level had me ready to run a few miles.

"Isis, are you hearing me?" Bob almost shouted from the driver's side.

"How long did I tune you out this time?" I scrunched my face, hoping to convey my embarrassment.

"At least five minutes," Bob answered, focusing on the road. "Are you sure you are okay?"

"Yes, I guess." I leaned my head against the headrest and took several deep breaths. "Do you think I'm cursed?"

"Cursed?" Bob snickered softly, and I narrowed my eyes at him. "Oh, you are serious."

I nodded.

"Isis, you are not cursed." Bob shifted, angling his head in my direction. "You have been on two dates in the last two years."

"Yes, and they both have ended horribly." If this was baseball, I would have the best record in the league.

"True but neither one of those was your fault." Bob made a right turn and drove to the back of the complex.

"Since when have you been this sensitive about dating?"

"Ana is getting married, and she asked me to be her maid of honor." Ana was the coolest human friend I had. She'd had a transition from out-of-luck girl to an incredible lady.

"Oh, that explains a lot," Bob said, pulling into a visitor's parking space.

"I don't want to be that girl who is always a bridesmaid ..." I couldn't finish the rest of that sentence.

"Considering you have very few female friends, I'm sure that is not going to be a problem." Bob pulled another gun from the center console in the Camaro. "Besides, can we just work on sending you on a vacation? That part is difficult enough without trying to add dating into the mix."

"You do have a point," I agreed, checking my weapons one last time.

"Which part do you agree with?" Bob fixed his hard stare on me.

"All of them are very valid points. This will be the first and last wedding I'll be invited to." Translation: I needed more friends.

"How come when you say it that way it sounds so bad?" Bob asked. Since he was the ultimate optimist, I had to be driving him nuts today.

We exited the Camaro and faced a row of identical apartments. I hoped Bob would find the apartment quickly because this place was creepy at night. The trees created extra shadows around the corners. The lights from the dealership next door added a weird glow making it look like a scene out of a Sci-Fi movie.

"Bob, where are we going?" I wanted to get back to Reapers as soon as possible.

"Corner apartment on the second floor," Bob told me, leading the way.

"Do you think his roommate is home?" Arriving at TJ's door, the lights in the room were off, although a strange sound came from inside. "Do we want to know what that sound is?

"We are going to find out whether we want to or not." Bob got in position to one side of the door and knocked loudly.

Nothing happened. We waited patiently for a few minutes and then Bob knocked again. The weird sounds increased, and I was ready to tell Bob to kick the door down.

"Who's there?" a young man asked as he cracked the door open.

"We are friends with TJ," Bob explained. "He sent us to pick up a few of his things but forgot to give us the key."

"Oh, okay. Come in." He opened the door for us.

"Oh God!" I screamed when I saw the young man who was totally naked.

"No, name is Roger not God, but nice try." Roger tilted his head and grinned with a disoriented stare.

"Of course, Roger. Which way to TJ's room?" I asked, keeping my eyes focused above his neck.

"The one to the right," Roger told us, but he pointed to the left.

Bob and I looked at each other and decided to follow his hand signal instead of his verbal directions.

"Thank you, Roger," Bob told him, rushing down the hall.

Hurrying behind him when Roger started some weird, interpretive dance in the middle of the living room, I had no words for what I'd just witnessed. "That was so weird," I told Bob. "Do you think he is a witch and is casting some incantation on the house?"

"Nope. I'm sure he is high and has no clue what is going on." Bob glanced over my shoulders as Roger jumped over the couch and landed flat on his face.

"Ouch." I headed inside the room before I witnessed any more of Roger.

"Poor TJ really should get a new roommate." That was the understatement of the year coming from Bob.

"Why is he naked?" Somebody should address the elephant in the room.

"He is not naked." Bob glanced one more time towards the living room. "He has knee-high socks on."

I rolled my eyes at Bob. "How did I miss that?"

"The boy is making a fashion statement," Bob told me, frowning deeply as he stared at the disaster in the living room.

"Do I want to know what he is doing?" I really didn't, but because the scene was so bizarre, I couldn't help but ask.

"He just ran into the glass door leading to the porch area and face-planted on the floor. He is going to be in pain tomorrow." Bob faced TJ's room, probably not wanting to witness anymore of the madness happening in the other room. "This room is ..."

"Even more immaculate than yours," I pointed inside, doing my best version of Vanna White.

Bob's apartment was the ultimate perfection of interior decorating. It could be used for the cover of any housing magazine. TJ's room was on the same level. Everything was meticulous, organized, and super clean. His bed was perfectly made in the same manner soldiers made theirs in the Army, with all the corners properly tucked in and the sheets as tight as possible. There wasn't a speck of dust anywhere in the room. Even the sketches on his walls were organized to create a lovely display.

"I didn't know TJ could draw," Bob told me as he examined the drawing on the walls.

"I had no idea either, but these are gorgeous." TJ was a talented artist.

I was starting to feel bad going through his stuff without him being here. I wouldn't enjoy it if people did that to me.

"How are we going to find out what we need?" I looked around the perfectly organized room and had no idea where to start.

"I hate to say this, but we should start with the roommate." Bob pointed towards the door one more time.

"Do we have to?" I was not ready to see the "streaker wannabe" again.

"I don't think we are going to find any answers here, not when we don't have a clue what we are searching for." Bob just had to be the voice of reason here.

"Fine, but if he starts wiggling around me, I'm shooting him," I warned Bob, holding up my gun.

"That is fair," Bob told me, then he stepped out of the room and I followed him like an obedient soldier.

"Hey, Roger," Bob said to the naked boy in the same tone he used to soothe terrified kittens or wild animals.

"Yes?" Roger answered from behind the couch.

"What are you doing there?" The words were out of my mouth before I could stop myself.

"They are coming and I'm building an escape pod." Roger popped his head up, scanning the room for I guessed whoever was coming.

"Who is coming?" Bob asked.

"We don't want to know," I told Bob, slapping his arm.

"We need him to talk to us, so I'm building a bond." Bob took a few steps towards Roger.

"The little people are coming," Roger replied, ducking behind the couch and peeking out with only his eyes.

"When you say 'little people,' are you referring to small children, midgets, or something else entirely?" If I had to play along with this madness, I was determined to at least get more details.

"Not those little people." His eyes dashed to the left and to the right, and I followed his gaze.

"I don't think they are here," I told him as I gazed at the living room.

"They are coming ... they are miniature men and they have wings. They can fly." Roger was on the ground doing a very similar imitation of the high crawl.

Two years ago, I would have recommended locking this boy up and throwing away the key. Today, I worried if it was my fault the poor thing had a horrible encounter, and probably with a pixie.

"If you keep the patio doors closed and pull the blinds tight, they won't get in." Bob walked over to the patio door and locked it for Roger, pulling the shades shut.

"Do you think I'm safe now?" Roger asked, hiding behind Bob.

"As long as you don't go outside to buy any dust, you should be good," Bob confirmed.

"You know about the dust?" Roger sat on the floor and crossed his legs, rocking back and forth.

"We are wasting our time. He is high on pixie dust and won't remember anything," I told Bob, leaning against the doorway.

"This might take a minute," Bob said, taking a seat on the couch. "Hey, Roger, have you noticed anything different about TJ?"

"Different? Different how?" Roger stopped rocking and popped his head up to see Bob.

"You know, like has he been hanging out with strangers, eating new foods, going to different places—things like that." Counting each item he listed on his fingers, I couldn't help but wonder how that line of questioning would help.

"No, no, no," Roger mumbled. "TJ is super boring. No new people, trips, same boring job, so nothing new."

"Basically, everything is as normal as it has always been?" Bob pushed a little harder.

"Yeah, besides this health kick he is on. He's all about being healthy now when he never used to be." Roger flipped to his hands and knees, high crawling again.

"What kind of health kick?" Bob asked, folding over the couch to look at Roger on the floor.

"He ordered these super-powerful supplements for your abs that burn fat in no time, see!" Roger bounced to his feet and pointed to his abs.

I had avoided peering at Roger's body, but after a quick glance, he had some very well-defined abs.

"Are you telling me you actually took pills to get those abs? That's impossible." Because if it wasn't, I desired those pills in my life.

"Absolutely. Mine came faster but TJ is catching up." Roger flexed, showing off his biceps and triceps along with his abs.

"Isis, check the cabinets," Bob told me.

The apartment had one of those tiny kitchens that looked more like a hallway with appliances than an actual place where one could cook food. I didn't miss those types of spaces at all. While the living room table had been covered with takeout containers and papers, the inside of the cabinets was meticulous. Each shelf was organized by item and then size. All the cups were arranged in descending order by length. TJ's handiwork could be seen all over this side of the apartment.

I opened all the doors and found the plates, the cups, and finally in the last cabinet I opened, I found the seasoning and medicine area.

"Bob, we have like six here. Which one should we take?" These boys had absolutely too many pills here.

"I have no clue. Just grab them all." Bob was not taking any chances.

I seized every bottle I could find and stuffed them in my pockets, then closed the cabinets and joined Bob in the living room. Roger was walking on the couches watching for flying people on the ceiling. It was a horrible picture, so I turned to face the wall.

"Hey, Roger," Bob said a little louder than necessary.

"Oh hi. Are you here to help me find Mrs. Glitter pants?" Roger asked.

"We are going to go and find TJ, so why don't you sit down on the couch until we get back?" Bob asked Roger in a gentle voice.

"I can't ... must find them," Roger mumbled.

"If you just sit here for just one minute, I will help you look for them," Bob offered.

"Okay, but only for a minute," Roger replied, and I glanced over my shoulder as Roger sat on the couch.

"Good night, Roger." Bob pulled his tranquilizer gun out and shot Roger in the chest. Poor guy dropped like a sack of potatoes on the couch.

"Isis, grab me a blanket for him." Bob pointed towards a stack of blankets on top of a loveseat. "Was that necessary?" I asked Bob as I handed him a blanket.

"It's safer than having him drive all over town high as hell." Bob covered Roger.

"You do have a point." I opened the front door and headed out of the apartment. "Poor TJ."

"At least you know he is never bored with that one," Bob told me as he pulled the door closed behind him.

"I think I'd rather have a boring life than a naked roommate." If those were my only options, boring would always win.

"Don't forget high and drunk," Bob added with a chuckle.

"Yes, let's not forget that," I replied.

Saturday had definitely been a lot stranger than Friday. It was hard to believe I now measured the type of day I had based on how strange and outlandish it ended. I would never complain about Constantine singing in the middle of the night again. At least he was covered in fur and could carry a tune.

Chapter Eight

Bob took a few short cuts I'd never known about on our way back to Reapers. Speeding, I worried he had been spending too much time with Shorty, and when we passed a state trooper who only waved at him, my worry doubled.

"You have that kind of relationship with every cop?" I got stopped all the time—granted it was mostly by Eric—so this didn't seem fair at all.

"I make friends with everyone. It keeps things simple." Bob didn't bother glancing at me. "Besides, we are driving Constantine's vehicle, which comes with extra privileges."

"Do civilians know this baby belongs to Constantine?" That thought had never occurred to me.

"I'm pretty sure everyone knows this car belongs to Constantine, or at least to someone they should seriously avoid." Bob accelerated, his eyes on the road.

I was glad when we pulled into Reapers. My mind was filled with horrible theories of TJ dying in our lab. Even worse, I was afraid TJ would get stuck in that in-between state. I rubbed my eyes and tried to cover a yawn with my hand.

"It's been a very long day," Bob told me in a soft voice as he parked the Camaro.

"Every day is a long one around here," I replied.

As soon as Bob turned the engine off, I headed back to the lab—hopefully, with answers. Constantine was sitting on one of the tables across from TJ's bed, one leg straight in the air. How could that cat be so flexible?

"Well, it took you long enough," said Constantine, his leg still in the same position.

"Stretching?" I couldn't help myself.

"Learning how to levitate," Constantine replied.

"Really?" That took me by surprise.

"Of course not, girl!" Constantine flipped on his back, arching as his legs extended. "This is a stretch, and that was grooming. You know better than that."

"Just needed to confirm since it's been such a weird night." I sat on the table next to Constantine, my gaze spanning the room. "Where is Eugene?"

"Upstairs getting food." Constantine wiped his eyes with his paws. "His stomach was growling like a runaway tiger and he refused to acknowledge it. I finally had enough and sent him to eat. Now I'm doing kitty watch."

"You are doing a great job." I patted his stomach.

"Not the fur." Constantine swatted my hand away. "I just spent the last twenty minutes cleaning that spot. I don't know where your hands have been." He made a face. "I got Isis cooties all over me."

"Hey, I shower all the time." I looked at my hands to confirm they were clean. "Unfortunately, we just met TJ's roommate and who knows what crazy stuff he was doing before we got there. My bad!"

"Gross! I'm never going to be clean." Constantine licked his stomach furiously while giving me passing glares. For a cat, he had issues with germs.

The door to the lab opened and Bob entered the room followed by Eugene. When he handed me a tomato and cheese sandwich, I could have hugged the man.

"Thank you, Bob." I held my hands together in front of my chest and gave Bob a low bow in salutation. He was my hero.

"This might help cheer you up." Bob placed a bowl of ice cream in front of Constantine. The man was a genius.

"See how it's done, you come in a room bearing gifts." Constantine pointed at his bowl before demolishing the dessert.

Eugene swallowed the last piece of his sandwich before he spoke. Whatever was in his sandwich was probably delicious because he almost licked his finger. I couldn't blame him. If Bob had created it, the food had to be out of this world. Eugene had changed to a white lab coat while we were gone, which he adjusted carefully.

"Okay, family. I'm ready. Hit me with what you found," Eugene announced while rubbing his hands together.

I pulled the bottles from my cargo pockets while balancing my sandwich in my mouth. I'm sure the process would have been a lot smoother if I'd just put the sandwich down, but around these boys, that would be considered dangerous. Food had a way of disappearing from my plate very quickly. I placed all the bottles of supplements and vitamins on the counter.

"Holy Jesus Christ!" Eugene exclaimed as he backed away from the bottles.

"Damn, not that." Constantine froze mid lick and stared at the bottles.

"What's going on?" I asked, and both Eugene and Constantine stood as still as statues. "Eugene, please tell me this is not your merchandise and somehow it got compromised?"

"That is definitely not ours," Eugene told me, making a cross with his index fingers.

"Constantine, what is going on?" I dared to place my sandwich back on the plate and glanced at Bob for support.

Bob shrugged and inspected the bottles one by one. "Boss, what are we missing?" he asked, reading the labels.

"This is bad; this is really bad." Constantine's fur stood on end. "We must call Death.

"This is not bad, it's horrible if we need to call Death." I pushed away from the bottles because I was afraid they might explode now. "You never want to call Death, so what is going on?"

"It seems you might finally get to meet the fourth horseman," Constantine whispered the last words and my heart stopped.

If Constantine was that upset about our last family member, it couldn't be a good sign. He despised Pestilence, but he never got this upset when he had to deal with her. War didn't count since Constantine was probably his number one fan. The only one left was Famine, and I was not making the connection between the bottles and that particular horseman.

"I should go." Eugene tried to run but slammed into TJ's bed instead.

"Eugene, slow down." Bob moved towards Eugene, his arms up in a calming gesture.

"You don't understand. We are forbidden to see, talk, or even be in the same proximity of Famine." Eugene turned in quick circles like he was searching for a way out.

"Eugene, breathe. Famine is not here," I reminded my desperate friend.

"Right, right. Breathe. Breathe." Eugene said as if he was talking to himself. Truthfully, he probably was.

"Why does the queen of evil hate her brother so much?" I asked, hoping someone would answer.

"Don't call Famine that," Constantine hissed.

"Don't call him brother?" Was Famine a female?

"Or sister while you are it." Constantine crawled in my direction. "Famine is unique."

Several minutes passed while Constantine's gaze scanned the room. Scared that was all he would tell me, I decided I had to ask very specific questions to ensure I got some real answers.

"While Death becomes whatever people believe Death to be, Famine refuses to claim any existence at all." Constantine sighed. "Famine is neither male nor female and barely recognizes the fact of having a human body. Famine is just Famine."

"Does Famine have a human shape?" I was not ready to meet with a three-headed alien that served as the fourth horseman.

"There's the rub. Famine embodies a gorgeous androgynous human," Constantine explained.

"What do we call Famine?" Bob saved me from asking the obvious question.

"Famine, Boss, or they and them if necessary." Constantine returned to his ice cream, running his claws over the melting cream. "Why couldn't it be Pestilence?"

"We are doomed if you would prefer to work with Pestilence on this." I dropped on the table, letting my head hang over the edge. "Are you calling Death?"

"He already has," Death announced from the door.

Looking at Death from my position, she was stunning. Today, Death wore a three-piece black Versace suit. I made it my hobby to learn designer clothes just to be able to identify Death's wardrobe. Thanks to my ridiculous salary and amazing fringe benefits, I could afford to buy a few pieces. I enjoyed admiring Death's instead, though, since she pulled it off so well. With her dark, silky hair and her gorgeous dark eyes, Death was the envy of any supermodel, if the supermodel had the same vision of Death as I did.

"Sorry for the late house call," I said softly.

"To have Constantine call me in the middle of the night to the lab I figured it had to be urgent." Death crossed the room and stood over TJ. "What happened to him?"

"That's one of the things we are trying to find out," Constantine informed his boss.

"Eugene, you haven't been able to figure it out?" Death inspected Eugene from across the room.

"Death, I can't touch those. The mistress would kill me." 'Mistress' was the name Pestilence made all her interns call her. I still cringed when Eugene said it.

Death let out a loud sigh. "Please tell me it's not what I'm thinking."

Constantine pushed the bottles to Death, and she examined each one without saying a word.

"Can someone explain the connection between those supplements and Famine?" I asked the group, who only stared at the bottles.

"You haven't told her?" Death asked Constantine.

"Not yet. Wanted to get you here as soon as possible," Constantine replied.

Constantine and Death had a weird connection. They could communicate mentally regardless of how far they were from each other. Constantine didn't talk much about it, but the ability came in handy since I wasn't allowed to call Death unless I was dying. We had weird intern rules that made no sense to anyone. One of the rules was I couldn't tell anyone I worked for Death, even though everyone already knew. It was like having a secret that was published on Facebook. Go figure that.

"Well, I'm here. Please make the explanation brief," Death told Constantine as she adjusted her suit.

"Famine runs the diet industry," Constantine told me.

"Well, that was definitely brief." That was all I could think to say. Constantine took his orders seriously today for sure.

"You are not planning to elaborate on that?" Death gave Constantine a murderous glare with one of her perfectly arched eyebrows raised in the same fashion as the Rock.

"You said brief," Constantine countered, taking on his favorite sphinx pose.

It was a match-off. Death only glared, and Constantine ignored her. Neither one spoke, and the rest of us held our breaths to see who would crack first.

"Oh God, I can't take this!" Eugene cracked first and he wasn't even playing. "You know how each horseman has a business, or form of a business, right?"

I nodded. I wasn't sure what our official business was, but according to our mission statements, we were in the transportation business. How exactly we made money transporting souls I didn't want to know.

"Famine's business is the most extensive and brilliant out of all of them." Eugene took a deep breath like it hurt to admit that out loud. "Famine figured out how to get humans to starve themselves and make a killing at it."

"No pun intended on that." Throwing a wink at Eugene, his shoulders dropped, showing he'd finally relaxed a little.

"Famine found a way to exploit our vanity, selling us millions of diet pills, supplements and all sort of toxins to makes us thinner and more beautiful." Eugene pushed the bottles close to me with one of his pens.

"Which company do they own?" There were dozens of diet companies, and manufacturers all over the world.

"All of them," Constantine answered.

"You are kidding me." My mouth fell open.

"Just like War has infiltrated every military in the world, Famine has majority stocks in all the industries, companies, and diet explosions that come out each year." Death walked around TJ, examining him closely without touching him. "Are you sure Famine is involved?"

"No," Constantine told her. "But the only thing out of the ordinary that TJ has been taking are one of those supplements."

"This could be an isolated case, though. Maybe TJ has a bad reaction to the pills," Death told him.

"It's not." Bartholomew walked in the room carrying a stack of papers. "I knew it wasn't normal."

"What are you talking about?" Death stopped and looked at Bartholomew.

"Fifty-one, well fifty-two if we count Isis and TJ, have been attacked, and that's just in the last month." Bartholomew spread the papers between Constantine and me, immediately pointing at landmarks. "Once I knew we were dealing with shifters, the pattern emerged. I ran all sorts of combinations of what each area had in common, from foods to products. The one thing that kept coming up was a new product just released within the last month to reduce fat and expedite muscle development."

"I've been trying to reach Famine for over three weeks and nothing," Death admitted.

"Is that normal?" I knew nothing about this mysterious horseman, and I didn't want to jump to conclusions.

"Yes and no. Famine can be reclusive at times, but we have a different relationship," Death said softly.

"Translation: Famine is Death's favorite and Famine can do no wrong!" Constantine spat the last part.

"Don't be so dramatic, Constantine." Death turned to face the wall. "We need to find Famine and get some answers."

"Great, let me get the jet ready." Constantine stood, ready to leap off the table.

"No time for that," Death announced, and I did not like how that sounded. "Eugene, please stay here and watch over TJ. The rest of you are coming with me."

"Where are we going?"

I never got an answer to my question. Instead, Death closed her eyes and snapped her finger. My vision went dark, and I felt like my body was being run through a blender. I hated traveling like this.

Chapter Nine

My entire body was shaking by the time my feet hit solid ground. According to my watch, it took less than a minute, but every cell in me screamed like it had actually taken an eternity. My vision was blurred, so I leaned on the closest wall I could find and closed my eyes.

"Wow. Where are we?" Bartholomew asked. "This place is magnificent."

It took me a minute to open my eyes again. I had no idea why Bartholomew recovered so quickly or if he was even affected the same way. My world was no longer spinning, and Bartholomew was right. We were standing in the biggest room I had ever seen in my life. The ceilings were probably thirty feet high, with intricate columns in each corner for support. A glass wall separated the main room from a huge outdoor terrace that ended with an infinity pool.

"Whose mansion did we just break into?" I asked. This was the type of place you saw on MTV Cribs.

White-leather couches were artistically arranged in the main area, with a black-leather recliner near a fireplace at the back. Everything in the room was white or black, and it screamed wealth.

"This is Famine's place," Death told us.

"Why is it so humid here?" Bob asked, waving his hands over his face.

"Because we are in Miami and overlooking the ocean," Constantine said, wiping down his face.

"Billionaire Famine owns a mansion in Miami and this doesn't draw attention?" How good was Famine at hiding their identity?

"Famine is Famine," that was all Constantine told us.

"We are going to search this whole place. Isis and Bob, start upstairs and check every room, closet, and anything you can think of. The rest of us have this floor." Nobody questioned or challenged Death's orders.

We quickly marched to our assigned areas, hoping to find Famine fast. It was close to three o'clock in the morning and I was dead tired. I wasn't sure how much longer I would be able to stay on my feet. I focused on one room at a time, but the mansion was enormous. We searched over twenty rooms just on the second floor. Famine had guest rooms, study rooms, a library, gym, entertainment center, and even a massage room. Why would anyone get all this? Even with Bob and me moving from room to room, it took us over half an hour to search the whole floor.

"Let me guess, nothing?" Death asked as we marched downstairs.

"This place is enormous," I answered.

"Do we have to search the rest of the property?" Constantine asked, staring out the glass windows.

"No. Famine is here; I can feel it," Death said.

"Does this place have a basement?" Bartholomew asked, regarding his surroundings.

"Bartholomew, you are a genius." Death pinched Bartholomew's cheek as she walked towards the back of the house.

"I know that." Bartholomew's smile spread from ear to ear. "I'm taking that as a yes."

"Famine mentioned once that they created a bomb shelter as a basement." Death marched down several rooms and hallways.

"Why does a horseman need a bomb shelter?" I couldn't help asking the question because the place was out of control.

"Same reason Famine needs the mansion," Death answered.

"Because Famine wants it, and that's the only reason," Constantine added, strolling down the hall.

I wondered if Constantine was holding back the urge to scratch the furniture. He kept extending his claws a little too often to be normal.

We arrived at the kitchen and I was in love. I wasn't the only one. Bob walked around in circles, opening every cabinet and running his hands down the appliances.

"Next time we build, we are getting a kitchen like this," Bartholomew said. "You two are way too happy about it."

Bob and I nodded at each other and continued to stare at the granite countertops, mahogany cabinets, and the top of the line in appliances. Famine even had a crystal chandelier in the kitchen.

"I agree, this kitchen is impressive, but unless you brought us here to get a snack, shouldn't we be checking for the basement?" Constantine followed closely behind Death.

"The entrance to the basement is here." Death pressed each of the doorknobs as she made her way around the room.

"Famine is also paranoid, huh? Lovely." I shook my head. This was getting better and better.

"Here!" Death clapped her hands together as she pulled the fridge from the wall, revealing a long stairwell leading down.

"This bomb shelter is not for the weak," I told Bob, who just snickered at me.

Death flipped the light switch at the entrance of the stairwell. I was glad because going down creepy stairs in empty mansions was not my idea of fun. At the same time, I was descending with Death and a five-thousand-year-old talking cat, so how could I be worried? Famine was meticulous, even in the building of their shelter. The stairwell was carpeted, which muffled our footsteps. The basement itself was one large room with soft-tan paneling and recessed lights all around. Expecting an empty room, I startled when my eyes landed on a figure sitting in the middle.

"Famine." Death rushed toward the horseman and the rest of us followed.

Constantine had not been lying; Famine was painfully gorgeous but completely androgynous. Aqua eyes with shimmering black hair made the contrast breathtaking. Famine was duct taped to a chair and their pinstriped suit was now wrinkled. I didn't know what to make of the situation.

"Is that a sippy cup?" Bartholomew was the first one to speak.

"I don't want to know." Constantine turned around and headed towards the staircase. "Death, zap me back to Texas. This is already madness."

"Constantine, get over here," Death ordered the whiny cat.

"Should we take the tape out of their mouth?" The pronoun situation was going to take me a minute to get used to.

"Allow me." Death volunteered and the rest of us waited.

Rip.

The sound of the tape being pulled off Famine's face was awful. I waited for the scream, or even profanity to come, but instead Famine gave Death the tenders expression I had ever seen.

"Hi, Death." Famine was so chipper it was a bit overwhelming.

"Famine, what are you doing here?" Death pointed at the empty basement.

"I'm kidnapped," Famine said, sitting straight in the chair.

"Is that possible?" I asked softly to Constantine.

"No! It is not possible!" Constantine shouted. "Why are you in that chair?"

"I told you, I was kidnapped," Famine sounded like a demented five-year-old on sugar.

"You were kidnapped in your own house?" Death leaned down, eyeing her sibling with raised eyebrows.

"Nobody knows this place exists," Famine explained.

"Except you and the kidnappers, obviously." Constantine marched circles around Famine.

"Do you know who kidnapped you?" I asked, walking closer to Famine.

"Who is this?" Famine whispered to Death.

"Famine, meet Isis, my North American Intern," Death said. "Over there is Bob, and the young man over here is Bartholomew."

"Do they know I'm a you-know-what?" Famine was still whispering.

"Yes, they know you are a horseman, you lunatic!" Constantine shouted. "Everyone who meets you knows you're a horseman, except you, of course."

"My kidnappers have no clue," Famine bragged.

"How do you know that?" Bartholomew asked, trying not to stare at Famine.

"Because they work for me." After Famine dropped that bomb, nobody said a word. We all just stood there with dumbfounded expressions.

"I'm sorry, but did you say your employees kidnapped you?" Bob was a brave man to ask that question.

"Yes." Famine grinned as if nothing at all was the matter.

"That's it. Death, let me strangle them. It would take me three seconds. I promise I'll make it quick." Death grabbed Constantine, restraining him so he didn't choke Famine to death.

"Famine get up from that chair," said Death.

"But they tried so hard," Famine whined. "They even gave me a sippy cup with dinosaurs."

"I knew Famine had a sippy cup," Bartholomew repeated.

"FAMINE. GET. UP!" Death shouted, making Bob, Bartholomew, and I jump at least three feet off the ground.

"Fine." Famine pouted, but with a snap of their finger, the duct tape and chair disappeared. "Better?"

"Much," answered Death.

"How long have you been sitting down here?" I asked, my eyes roaming over the empty space.

"Two, maybe three, weeks. I lost track of time." Famine adjusted the suit that was not cooperating.

One more snap and Famine was wearing a white suit in the same design as Death. Constantine started gagging and Death just shook her head. This family lacked some serious counseling. The dynamics of the horsemen would give Dr. Phil hours of material to analyze.

"What is the emergency that made you come all the way over to Miami to see me?" Famine turned to look at Death. "Oh wait, this place is so gloomy."

Snap.

We were now sitting in the outside patio of the mansion overlooking the city and the ocean. I was a little dizzy, but at least Famine had the courtesy of depositing me on a chair. Bob was stretched out on a hammock, Constantine was lying on a tall throne, while Bartholomew floated on an inflated bed in the pool. Death just stood next to the pool scowling.

"I'm slacking at my duties. Food?" Famine didn't wait for anyone to answer. Trays of food appeared around each person in an instant.

A large cup of Columbian coffee was in the center of my tray. The horseman was absolutely weird, but right now, I was in heaven. I took the coffee in both of my hands and inhaled the rich aroma. The smell alone brought me back to life, but the taste was mind blowing. Where in God's name did Famine get this coffee from?

"Colombia," Famine told me.

"Can you read my mind?" I asked, holding my cup with both hands.

"Don't be silly dear, but that is the most asked question. Do you like it?" Famine hovered over me as they waited for my response.

"It is amazing," I confessed.

"That's what I love to hear." Famine beamed with joy and even skipped in the direction of Death. "What can I get for you dear?"

"Your undivided attention would be nice." Death narrowed her eyes at her sibling. I wouldn't want to be in Famine's shoes right now.

"Fine, what is going on?" Famine grabbed a glass from the tray near Death and sat down.

"We have a significant number of animal attacks that we think are being triggered by one of your supplements!" Bartholomew shouted from his position in the pool.

"Why would anyone be giving supplements to animals? That is absurd?" Famine asked.

Constantine slapped his face and took a huge bite of some pastry in front of him. Based on Bartholomew's statement, Famine's answer made perfect sense.

"Unfortunately, these are not regular animals but shifters doing the attacking," Death clarified.

"Oh." Famine moved from sitting in the chair to pacing so fast I couldn't follow them. "Not good."

"You know about this?" Death asked very slowly.

"Yes, but the supplement shouldn't be on the market." Famine waved both hands in front of them. "It needs additional testing and major modifications."

"What does it do?" Constantine asked without glancing Famine's way.

"The finished product is supposed to accelerate muscle development, give the users incredible tone definition, increased appetite, and make people lose drastic weight," Famine told us, shrugging.

"You created a magic pill," I said, my tone more of a question than a statement. Every human would want to get their hands on that pill if word got out. "How will you make money?"

"You have to keep taking the pill to maintain the effects, except you will have to increase the doses every few months," Famine explained. "Which will eventually lead to kidney failure and then death."

"Oh, okay. I keep forgetting the job of every horseman is to kill humanity." My mouth was dry, and the coffee felt cold in my hands. "Remind me never to take supplements."

"Trust me, I would never let you!" Constantine shouted from his throne.

"Thank you," I replied.

"You said it wasn't supposed to be on the market yet, why?" Death brought us back on track.

"The process was too fast." Famine stood, pacing in front of their chair. "Humans were going into organ failure within a few weeks and some shifters developed an unstoppable hunger that couldn't be contained."

"Unless they ate human flesh," I finished for them.

"Exactly," Famine concurred.

"Why were you kidnapped again?" I realized Famine never explained that.

"My CEOs decided they didn't like the way I was handling some companies," Famine told us, showing very little emotion. "The kidnapping was part of a coup to take over my business."

"Are these the same CEOs that released the supplements?" I was hoping this mess could have a simple solution.

"Maybe." Famine stopped, tilting their head from side to side. "That would make sense and it's definitely possible."

"Great. Then all we have to do is march to your office, stop your CEOs, and send out a cure for the supplements." Sounded easy enough, but I had a feeling it wouldn't be.

"Not really," Famine whispered.

"Why not?" Constantine asked this time.

"I need my notes for those supplements, and the notes are in my special lab, and I can't show up because I'm kidnapped, and nobody knows I'm a horseman, and—"

"Stop!" Death shouted, cutting of Famine's rambling. "One thing at a time. Can you create a cure?"

"Well,..." Famine started, stretching the word out.

"It's a yes or no question," Death told Famine.

"Yes, as long as I have my notes and the formula for the supplements," Famine explained.

"Fine. In which lab to do you have them?" Death's tone was ice-cold against the warm Florida weather.

"In my lab in Mount Pleasant," Famine said the last part very slowly, and I had to lean in to listen.

"Mount Pleasant where?" Constantine and I asked at the same time.

"Texas," Famine said, not facing us.

"Why?" Constantine drooped on his throne.

"Please tell me it's not underneath a chicken plant," I said, afraid to hear the answer.

"How did you know?" Famine asked with wide eyes.

"Where else would it be?" was all I said because I had no other words at that moment.

"Exactly," Famine answered, jumping up and down.

"They keep following us," Constantine whined, and I couldn't blame him anymore.

Each of the other horsemen had a secret location extremely close to us. No wonder Constantine was so paranoid about them. Their obsession for using chicken plants for hideouts was nuts. I wondered which one started the trend first. Was that the reason Pestilence hated Famine?

"Let's start by creating a cure for these little supplements of yours, then we can move to figuring out what to do with your CEOs," Death told Famine. "I'm not excited to find a bunch of mutilated bodies that would draw serious attention to us. Is that clear?"

The last part was directed at us, so I sat up straighter in my chair. "Yes, Death," I answered as the official Intern in the group.

"In that case, let's get back to Reapers. It sounds like everyone has work to do," Death said, but it was more of an order than a statement.

"When you said, 'let's get back,' who's included in that statement?" Famine asked, their eyes down as they fidgeted with the buttons on their suit.

"You are coming with us, and you will follow Constantine's directions exactly. Otherwise, I'll let him strangle you." Death turned to face Constantine. "You have my full permission to hurt Famine."

"Yes!" Constantine did backflips on his throne. "Let's go home because I've got some whipping to do."

"Constantine, only if Famine steps out of line, am I clear?" Death glared between Famine and Constantine.

"Absolutely." Constantine smirked.

"I recommend you put the coffee down, Isis. We are leaving now," Death told me in a much sweeter voice than the one she'd used with Famine.

"Absolutely." I placed the cup on the tray and stood up.

It was probably a mental thing, but I found it easier to handle Death's little trips standing. After a quick inventory of the team, Death snapped her fingers. I was ready to be home, but I would prefer a nice, calm jet.

Everything went dark again.

Chapter Ten

The common room in Reapers never looked as good as it did when we transported back. Even after the fabulous coffee Famine had given me, my eyes were drooping. I glanced at my watch and it was almost six in the morning. No wonder I was exhausted...I had been up for twenty-four hours. This day did not want to end. I leaned down on the kitchen counter checking for a way disappear to my room.

"Famine, I swear you better listen to Constantine," Death said, leaving what would happen if they didn't open ended as she walked away from Famine, who was at the computer desk.

"Fine." Famine pouted like a two-year-old requiring a diaper change.

"Constantine, try to behave while I'm working," Death warned Constantine, who headed over to Famine.

"Do you really think Famine will listen to Constantine?" I whispered to Death.

"Famine might try to play it off, but there is not a being on this planet more feared than Constantine," Death answered, monitoring Constantine stalking circles around her sibling.

"Even the horsemen fear him?" Not that it was hard to believe or anything because Constantine was a menace.

Death arched an eyebrow at me. "Look at him. The cat is fearless, he enjoys slapping people around, and he doesn't mind blowing stuff up to get his point across. Pestilence might detest him, but even she would not declare war on that one. Famine will behave or Constantine will send them to the fifth door of hell."

"Just what I always wanted to hear: more confirmation that Constantine is psycho." Maybe Constantine made such an effective Guardian because he was not impressed by titles or positions.

"You should rest." Death placed her hand on my shoulder and gave it a light squeeze.

"I am tired," I confessed to Death.

"The spring equinox is around the corner, so you have to prepare for it." Death headed toward the door.

"Prepare for what?" Not another supernatural holiday to create more chaos and panic in this city.

"You have a visitor out here," Death told me from the loft's balcony area.

I followed Death out the door, trying to see our mysterious visitor. Death headed down the stairs, revealing Eugene sitting on the stairwell.

"What are you doing out here?" I asked him as I joined him on the steps.

"Is Famine here?" Eugene asked, and I nodded. "I can't be anywhere near Famine or Mistress will kill me. It's better if I just stay at the lab."

"Pestilence has some strange rules, but okay." I patted Eugene's arm. "How is TJ doing?"

"He is going to be fine in a few hours," Eugene said softly. "His body is shifting back, but unfortunately all of his clothes are ruined. We can't have him walking around like he was attacked by a wild cat."

"Darn. I never even thought about clothes when we were at his apartment." My mind couldn't pay attention to all the details because there were just too many of them.

"I can go get some if you give me the address," Eugene volunteered.

"We locked the door and knocked the roommate out, so getting in might be a bit tricky." I rubbed my face with my hands, thinking of an alternative.

"I can take Eugene," Bob told me as he stepped out to the balcony.

"Are you sure?" I asked, even knowing Bob didn't mind volunteering for anything.

"Constantine is busy giving instructions to Famine and I'd rather skip that entire process." Bob shook his head and took a deep breath.

"I will go watch TJ while you guys are gone," I offered, mainly because I didn't want anything to happen to him.

"Go to bed. How about I stay with TJ?" said Bartholomew as he sneaked out of the loft on his tiptoes.

"Are you avoiding the Constantine lecture?" I asked Bartholomew, who kept glancing over his shoulder.

"Definitely." Bartholomew moved closer to the balcony. "Famine is doing lots of eye rolling and Constantine has a list longer than the Bible. If I stay there, I might get volunteered to do something too traumatizing to describe."

"All three of you have lost your minds, but I won't argue. Thank you, Bart." I fluffed his hair.

"Don't worry. We will take care of TJ, but you really should head to bed," Bartholomew told me. "You look like you are going to fall over any minute."

"I'm too tired to argue but if something happens, you better call me immediately," I ordered.

All three of them gave me a crooked salute. I shook my head and headed inside before I said something I might regret in a few hours. Constantine was still lecturing Famine when I walked into the loft.

"Do you have any questions?" Constantine's loud shout echoed in the cavernous room.

"Yes, I need a shower," Famine started. "Where could I take care of that?"

"You technically do not need a shower and I know you know that," Constantine growled.

"No, but I want one. Is that better?" Famine pouted.

"Better," Constantine answered with a nod. "Let me check to see if I have anything inappropriate in my room before letting you in."

"What kind of inappropriate stuff do you have in your room?" I asked him when he walked in front of me.

"Nobody is asking your opinion, Missy. Why are you not in bed yet?" Constantine didn't look in my direction when he spoke.

"Heading that way now, but I'll just wait until you get back." I hopped on the kitchen counter and made myself comfortable.

If I sat on the couch, it would be all over. That stupid couch was a sleep trap. It didn't matter if you were tired or not, that piece of furniture would take you out in under three minutes. I was exhausted, but I was too close to my bed to fall out here.

"Good idea. Don't let them touch anything," Constantine commanded.

Famine's pronoun was killing me, but it was better than calling Famine he/she. Constantine headed towards the bedrooms to inspect who knew what in his room.

"How does Death do it?" Famine whispered less than two inches from my ear.

I screamed and almost fell off the counter. I never saw Famine move and the fact that they were so close to me was terrifying.

"I'm sorry," I told Famine as I held my hand over my chest, hoping to prevent my heart from exploding. "What were you asking?"

"How does Death do it?" Famine repeated, examining my face.

"Do what?" Why couldn't Famine just ask a full question like a normal person?

"You know, get attached to you guys." Famine reached for my hair, but I pulled away.

"I don't know." That wasn't a lie, either. I had no idea why or how Death did anything.

"Humans are so fragile. Why get attached when you guys are just going to die?" Famine turned around and headed to the couch.

"Aren't you lonely?" I asked Famine.

"Maybe, but I'm a horseman. Nobody understands what that means," Famine answered.

"Pestilence and War are horsemen and they also have interns." I slid off the counter as slowly as possible just in case Famine made any more lightning moves.

"Why would anyone want to be an intern for a horseman?" Famine focused their stare on me and my cheeks warmed.

"The benefits are to die for," I mumbled, moving towards the backdoor.

Famine mocked me. I was three seconds away from sprinting to my room and leaving Famine alone in the common area when Constantine stepped back in.

"Okay, Isis. Head to bed. I got this." Constantine strolled towards Famine like a runway model.

"Thank you so much." I dashed out of the common area without waiting for an answer.

Constantine could play fifty questions with Famine. I was too tired to process information and provide educated answers to their philosophical issues. I locked myself in my room and debated between taking a quick shower or dropping to sleep. My bed was so soft that the temptation to climb in fully clothed was too much. At least I could take off my shoes before calling it a day. I sat at the edge of the bed and started to take off my combat boots when my phone went off.

"Hello," I said, not having the energy for a more elaborate greeting.

"Hi, sweetie, did I catch you before your run?" The melodious voice of my godmother filled the speaker.

"Hi, Godmother." I grinned at my phone. "No run today."

"Oh wow, are you okay? You are not getting sick, I hope. Should I send you some stuff?" My Godmother had raised me after the death of my parents, and at times, she forgot I was in my late twenties.

My Godmother had always been eccentric and free spirited. It wasn't until recently I found out that she was the high priestess of the Order of Witches in the United States. I only recently discovered it when she was mediating a treaty between the vampires and elves. I had been highly disappointed, but I also failed to tell her that I was Death's new Intern. Godmother blames Constantine for the whole thing, but I had no idea why.

"I'm not sick, Godmother, just had a late night at work." I wasn't technically lying.

"Isis, you work too many hours and that job is way too risky." Godmother had given me the same lecture at least ten times in the last four months after she found out of my new position.

"Godmother, I'm sure you didn't call me to give me a lecture, right?" I was too tired to handle this conversation with no sleep.

"I'm sorry, dear, I just worry about you." Godmother slowed down, her voice much calmer. "I'm just confirming that I will be landing on Wednesday to get everything ready for the equinox party."

"What party?" I stopped rubbing my face and gave the phone my undivided attention.

"That furball didn't tell you?" Godmother's voice dripped with sarcasm.

"Obviously not, so what are you talking about?" Why am I asking? I'm not going to like the answer.

"Your evil overlord is planning a huge equinox celebration this Thursday and wants me to officiate it. Something about bringing blessings and good wishes to haven." Godmother really didn't like Constantine.

"You agreed to it?" I was absolutely sleep deprived because I couldn't be hearing this conversation correctly.

"I hate to admit it, but it is actually a really good idea," Godmother told me in a soft voice. "A blessing by the Order to the newly-found haven would show a sign of solidarity and the blessing of the Goddess would shower the community. Besides, you need as much protection as I can send you."

"You do know I can take care of myself?" If my Godmother could lock me up in my room, she would do so from Salem.

"Sweetie, I know you are very talented, and your skills and abilities have increased drastically, but the horsemen have many enemies." Godmother let out a long breath. "I'm not interested in losing you because you become collateral damage in the middle of their madness."

"Nothing is going to happen to me," I reassured her. "Besides, if it does, you will burn half the city to the ground. I'm sure fear is instilled in the heart of every evil doer."

"Isis, this is not funny," Godmother was trying hard to sound serious. "But you are right. Texarkana would become a small dot on the map if something does happen to you. Make sure that it doesn't."

"Yes ma'am," I replied back.

"You are a mess, child." Godmother cackled. "In the meantime, tell that good-for-nothing guardian of yours that he better have everything ready for my arrival. I love you sweetie."

"I love you, too." I disconnected the call and tossed the phone on my bed.

Constantine and I must have a long talk, just not right now. I laid on my bed for a quick nap and then I'd have a long discussion with the evil overlord on proper party planning in the city. My eyelids were so heavy that before I knew it, I had visions of dancing witches and cats jumping over the moon.

Chapter Eleven

Chirp, chirp, chirp.

Where did all the birds come from? Birds? What birds?

My arms were stiff, and my eyelids were not cooperating. The chirping sound was coming from somewhere to my right and it took me a minute to realize it was my phone. I accidentally ran a hand over my mouth to find out I had drooled all over my face.

"Gross." That was enough to wake me up.

I reached for my phone that wouldn't stop ringing.

"Hello." My dry mouth was barely able to form the words.

"That was one hell of a date if you are still in bed," Katrina pronounced.

Katrina was War's Intern and single-handedly the most-deadly soldier I had ever met. She was also a drop-dead-gorgeous blonde and sweet as pie. Katrina was a walking contradiction, and it didn't help she was over seventy years old but appeared to be in her twenties. One of War's gifts to his interns was youth for one-hundred years while they served their term. That sounded more like a jail sentence instead of an enlistment contract.

"You don't even know. He almost shifted to a bobcat and ate my head off." I tossed over on my side, grabbing a pillow.

"Please tell me that is a code for some new dating game," Katrina replied.

"I wish," I mumbled. "It seems some weird supplement is forcing shifters to turn uncontrollably and making them attack humans."

"You did smack Eugene around for being super careless again?" Katrina's tone was light, but I knew she meant the smacking part.

"That would have been too easy. Pestilence is innocent this time." That was hard to believe, even for me. "It seems our missing relative has finally made an appearance."

"Oh no, Isis, not Famine!" Katrina shouted.

"Basically, I'm the last one to know about Famine?" I was always the last one to learn about everything around here.

"There is no time for jokes. Avoid Famine like you would the plague," said Katrina.

"Like I avoid Pestilence?" I stretched my legs out on the bed to help me wake-up.

"Worse than Pestilence." Katrina's tone indicated how deadly serious she was.

"Famine does not look worse than Pestilence." That was a horrible thing to say about anyone. "Famine is like a spoiled toddler."

"Famine is definitely spoiled, but with a very short temper and uncontrollable rage." Katrina forced her voice to slow down. "Whatever you do, don't make them mad. Just avoid Famine."

"That will be impossible because Famine is here at Reapers," I announced to Katrina, and after a thump, I had a feeling she dropped her phone. "Katrina, are you there?"

"Sorry about that, I will be on the next flight over," Katrina told me.

"Hey there, slow down." I really could not handle Katrina joining forces with Constantine against Famine. "Don't panic. I have plenty of back-up."

"Are you sure?" Katrina insisted.

"Yes. Besides, we just have to pick up some notes from their secret lab, Famine makes the cure and bang, all done." That sounded pretty simple.

"Isis, nothing is that easy when the horsemen are involved. You know that." Katrina was starting to sound like Constantine during one of his lectures.

"Why are you raining on my parade?" I whined.

"Because you are not taking this seriously," Katrina told me, still in her lecturing tone.

"Fine," I said to make her stop bossing me around. "I will be careful and if things get super crazy, I'll call you."

"Perfect," Taking shorter breaths, Katrina sounded fairly pleased with herself. "Also, are you planning to join me in Hawaii this weekend? It's the best surf competition in the world."

"First of all, I don't surf," I said, irritation swimming in my words because we'd had this conversation before and she wouldn't listen. "Secondly, I have court."

"You always have court," Katrina dismissed my argument. "I'll call you after the equinox to see what you decided. Now be careful with Famine."

Katrina hung up and didn't even wait for me to say goodbye. I shook my head. Constantine's habits were rubbing off on everyone. I planned on going back to sleep until I saw the time. My short nap turned into six hours.

"Oh, crap!" I screamed as I jumped off the bed.

This was not how I wanted to start my Sunday. I was surprised none of the boys stopped by to wake me up. I ran to the bathroom to shower so I'd be fully awake and ready for battle. If Famine was as dangerous as Katrina said, I needed to wear all my gear today.

Thirty minutes later, I entered the kitchen to find TJ sitting at the table and Bob pouring him coffee like nothing had happened. Famine, Bartholomew, and Constantine were leaning over the computer, pointing at things on the screen. My feet were stuck to the ground, and I had the urge to run back into my room.

"Isis." Too late. TJ noticed me.

"Hey there," I responded.

TJ shuffled from the table towards me wearing a pair of jogging pants and a very tight t-shirt. Whatever those supplements were doing had created some serious definition in his abs and chest. He stopped at arm's length, gazing shyly at his shoes.

"I'm so sorry," TJ told me.

"For what? Trying to eat my face or not telling me you were a shifter." My tone was a lot colder than I expected. I didn't realize how angry I was with him.

"Both, but in my defense, how do you bring that up in a conversation?" TJ tilted his head, making his eyes sparkle.

I would not be distracted by his cuteness.

"You could have tried," I said a little softer. "It's not like you don't know who I work for."

"You have never confirmed you work for Death before." TJ was sticking to technicality.

"Because I couldn't. Because that's part of the rules." My voice got louder with each word. Damn those stupid rules.

"Isis, it's not the easiest subject to breach. People are extremely judgmental about shifters." TJ turned around to face the glass wall.

"I work with Constantine, so how could you possibly think I would be judgmental when my guardian is a five-thousand-year-old talking cat? How do you validate that?" I was pointing at Constantine from across the room.

"She's got you there, boy," Constantine told him.

"I was planning on telling you, just didn't know when," TJ went back to the table.

"When were you going to tell me about the supplements?" I asked, trying to lower my voice.

"There was nothing to tell. I got them from a couple of guys in town," TJ explained. "They help with fat reduction and muscle development."

Bob and I met each other's eyes before glancing back at TJ.

"They were also the reason you couldn't stop the change," Bob clarified as he gave TJ more coffee.

"That is impossible. I've been taking them for two weeks and this has never happened." TJ rubbed his abs and avoided the hard stare I threw his way.

"Prolonged exposure to the pills brings on the condition," Famine explained. "The longer you take them, the less you will be able to control it. Eventually, you'll lose all sense of self and conscious thought."

"What does that mean?" TJ asked, shaking a little.

"You would most likely get stuck in your animal form," Famine said.

"You never mentioned that yesterday," I exclaimed.

"There was so much going on it was hard to keep up." Famine waved their hands in the air and turned back to the computer. "I will need the detailed formula for those supplements, as well as any of my notes for them."

"You are a horseman, right? So, why can't you remember it?" Shouldn't the horsemen be above normal issues like memories?

"Do you know how many formulas I have up here?" Famine pointed to their head. "One single element can be the difference between total immobility and kidney failure."

"I'm never taking another pill in my life," Bob told me, walking to the fridge with an empty plate.

"Oh, relax. The process is supposed to be very slow so no one can make a connection back to us," Famine bragged. "The products will give you amazing results and still fulfill their ultimate purpose. I need to know if my CEOs were able to modify the original."

"Can they modify your work?" Bartholomew spoke from his corner.

"I hire brilliant scientists," Famine said. "Once I create the first strand, I send it to them to be modified and adjusted for each variable we want. I trained them that way." They raised their chin in the air. "The rift happened when my scientists wanted faster results to increase profits quicker."

"You wanted the results to be slower?" I would like to believe Famine was concerned for the health of their clients, but that was not the case for most of the horsemen.

"Like I told you yesterday, an expedited process would kill humans before they are able to finish their first bottle." Famine flipped their hair with one hand and sucked on their other thumb.

Between Famine and Pestilence, humanity was doomed. TJ's mouth hung open as he looked at Famine, who was still sucking their thumb when Constantine coughed, bringing everyone's attention to him.

"Got it. Dead humans, bad for shifters, but what about the other supernatural beings?" Constantine asked the distracted horseman.

"We didn't have enough research to see the full effects of the pills," Famine explained. "Initial tests with high dosages showed uncontrollable hunger, rapid shifting stages, and loss of higher thinking power for the shifter. Nothing major for the other groups."

"Wait, you test your pills on live subjects?" My eyes widened. I really hoped that wasn't the case, but I had a feeling it was.

"Of course," Famine said, putting their hands on their hips. "How else am I going to find out the true results of my products?"

"What if they die?" I asked, my fists clenching at my sides because I wanted to choke Famine.

"Then it's a good indication the formula is too strong and must be adjusted." Famine's tone was matter-of-fact. No remorse whatsoever came from their voice or their expression.

"What happens after they die?" I asked, unable to let it go.

"You work for Death, don't you? Do I really have to explain what happens to people after they die to you?" Famine shifted their weight to one side, their big eyes probing me.

"That's not what I mean. What do you tell their families and everyone else that expects them to come back alive?" How do you explain to people their loved ones died during the trial experiment of illegal drugs?

"They sign a full disclosure agreement," Famine said, doing a semi-circle to face the computers again. "If anything happens to them while at one of my facilities, the families will be taken care for life. Typical transaction."

"And your people don't see anything wrong with this?" Bob jumped in since all I could do was blink. This was madness.

"They understand it's the price for doing business," Famine replied over their shoulder to Bob before training their attention on Bartholomew. "Here it is. That's my passcode to the lab. That should let you in. That bottom one will give you access to my system. You are a very smart little boy, but please don't hack my labs because I would hate to hunt you down."

Famine knew how to deliver a threat with a pleasant demeanor and still make it completely terrifying. Bartholomew swallowed and moved as far away as he could from Famine while still staying on the chair.

"If you try to hurt him, I will rip out your eyes, little one," Constantine told Famine with the same cheerful tone Famine had used.

My stomach turned and I thought I might puke. I leaned against the counter and took a few long breaths.

"Here." Bob handed me one of Eric's super shakes.

I stopped asking what was in Eric's shakes since it was a combination of natural ingredients and magical stuff. At times, I questioned if I was the only person Eric practiced his craft on. The good news was the shakes were delicious, rejuvenated me, and reduced all sorts of aches and pains.

"Thank you," I whispered.

"Not to be a downer, but we are running out of time," Famine said. "If my supplements have been on the market for the last two or three weeks, that means humans will start dying pretty soon, and shifters will be wild animals permanently. Not that I mind a bunch of shriveled dead people, but that would cost me millions."

"Why do you care about the money?" Constantine asked.

"I'm aiming to surpass Pestilence in revenue this year and I can't afford to take a hit like that. She would never let me live it down." Famine adjusted their fabulous suit and Constantine looked ready to shred it to pieces.

"Sibling rivalry at its best," I told the group as I gulped my shake. "What happens if people just stop taking the supplements? Wouldn't that end the process?"

"Unfortunately, no. The chemicals are already in their system." Famine did not look sorry as they cleaned their nails with a pen. "The humans won't die as quickly but they will still perish before their time. After examining our friend here, I have a theory. If I'm correct, every time a shifter changes, the transformation will become harder to control and they will still lose their human side."

"You were examining me while I was unconscious?" TJ wrapped his hands around his body.

"It was nothing major. A closer look at your cell development, and I just took a little of your blood to test my theory." Famine smiled at him like a demented toy doll. "I should have the results of it in a few hours."

"Okay, everyone, it sounds like we need to hurry." I put the cup in the sink and pointed to the door.

"Yes, please hurry." Famine clapped their hands together. "I'm awfully bored here."

"How could you be bored? You spent two weeks in a basement with nothing but a sippy cup." I asked Famine. Did they forget that?

"But that was different because I was binge watching all my favorite series on Netflix." Famine spun around in circles.

"Go, I will entertain looney toons here." Constantine walked over to the controls on the desk and turned on the large-screen TV.

Like magic, Netflix was on and Famine was mesmerized by the moving images. Bartholomew snuck out of his computer area with all his notes and made his way in our direction.

"Have Eugene take TJ home," Constantine told us softly so he wouldn't disturb our deranged guest.

"Eugene is still here?" I hadn't seen him at all.

"He is hiding in my apartment as far away from you-know-who as he can be," Bob told me, pointing at Famine.

"Got it. Guess we better get going," I told the boys, but before I moved, I remembered my Godmother. "I almost forgot. My Godmother called, and she says she is heading here on Wednesday. Care to explain?"

"Unfortunately, that will have to wait for your return. Now, you have to go." Constantine pushed us out of the door and refused to answer my question.

Bob, TJ, Bartholomew, and I exited the loft and walked down the stairs.

"Isis, are you mad?" TJ looked so young, fidgeting with his fingers and staring at the floor.

"I'm not mad, TJ, just disappointed," I admitted. "It feels like people don't trust me with their real story—first my Godmother and now you. I have to deal with it. But right now, we must find an antidote so you don't start eating your clients at Big Jakes." I hated when people lied to me, even if they thought it was for my sake.

"Gross," Bartholomew said.

TJ followed Bob to his apartment without saying a word.

"We are taking Killer, so make yourself comfortable," Bob told us from across the bay.

"What's Killer?" I asked Bartholomew before turning to face the line of vehicles.

"That would be Killer!" Bartholomew announced, hopping up and down.

A blood-red Land Rover Discovery was parked in Storm's old spot. The vehicle was beautiful. I preferred smaller vehicles, even if at one point in my life I did cruise around in a blue minivan I called The Whale. I had to admit that Killer deserved respect.

"What happened to Bob's obsession with trucks?" I asked Bartholomew.

"After getting the last two blown up, he is ready for a change," Bartholomew replied, trying to hide his amusement.

"You are blaming this on me, aren't you?" It was hard to look down at Bartholomew now that he was taller than me.

"You have to admit this only happens to him when you are around." Bartholomew poked me in the stomach.

"A giant coincidence." I tried to play it off, but Bartholomew was right. "But why red?"

"If you want to make a statement, you go all out," Bartholomew announced "Go big or go home. He can now install that 50Cal he has been wanting."

"Remind me to kill Katrina," I told Bartholomew as I climbed in the passenger's side of Killer.

Katrina had installed a 50Cal in all her SUVs and Bob loved the idea. Nobody needed that much fire power in Texarkana. Then again, at the rate we were going, maybe we could use a 50Cal around here.

I was still fatigued from my never-ending Saturday. Killer was not only impressive, but the seats were incredibly comfortable. I leaned my seat back and closed my eyes. Unless Bob needed me for a firefight, I was planning to sleep the whole hour-long drive.

Chapter Twelve

The stench of the chicken plant woke me from my slumber. It was hard to argue with the horsemen's theory that you could hide anything near a chicken processing plant and get away with it. Most people who had working noses would avoid the area at all costs, and even if they didn't, the smells permeating from the chicken processing would make it impossible to detect anything other than that. Bob pulled Killer up to a small shack that, according to the GPS, was our final destination.

It was hard to believe that I missed Pestilence's plants. The location for her entrance bypassed the smelly area, but not Famine's. Nope, we had to go right into the heart of the smell to gain access.

We had no idea what to expect at the underground lab. Famine's CEOs were in full coup d'état mode, which meant we could be walking into anything. Bob hated showing up anywhere without doing his recon, but due to lack of time and because of Famine's madness, we were going in with tons of weapons and a few prayers. Hopefully, that would do the trick.

"What do you want to take?" I asked Bob.

"Everything," he replied.

"When you say 'everything,' what exactly does that mean?" I asked, wondering how we would be able to carry all the weapons we brought. Plus, that had been one of the most open-ended answers I'd ever heard. Between the three of us, we had six semi-automatic rifles, five handguns, three machetes, my scythe, about fifteen grenades, and dozens of throwing stars and daggers. We were a well-outfitted platoon of pure destruction. Luckily, most of our bullets were custom made to knock people out, the biggest impact coming from broken bones and major bruises.

"Anything we can put in our pockets." Bob had stuffed four grenades in his cargo pockets, plus two handguns, and who knew how many daggers?

"We are not playing games today." I looked over at Bartholomew, who had every pocket full of grenades and bullets.

"These people left their leader in the basement of their house for two weeks with one sippy cup and never went back to check on them," Bob reminded us.

When he put it that way, I had very little sympathy left.

"In that case, let's go full crazy on them." I slid two handguns inside my holsters, plus attached a machete on the side of my legs. And I'd been worried about being able to carry all the weapons we'd brought ...

Sometimes, the visual of being fully armed was as intimidating as actually using the weapons. If we needed to make an impression, we were going to do it today. I wasn't exactly sure what our look projected other than insane mercenaries, but either way, that should do the trick.

"Famine gave me the code to the door and said an elevator should be waiting. We have three minutes once we hit the ground before security picks us up," Bartholomew told us as he reviewed his notes one last time.

"Ready?" Bob asked.

"As ready as we are going to be," I replied.

We emerged from the vehicle hoping to avoid any wandering eyes from the chicken plant. If anyone asked, we were supposed to tell them we were inspecting the electrical panels in the boxes. I doubt anyone would ever believe us, though. No city worker showed up driving a Land Rover to a work site. I decided pointing out the obvious would not help at that time, so I focused on the task at hand. Bob and I followed Bartholomew to the entrance of the shack. The security and control panels were very similar to Pestilence's. It took Bartholomew less than twenty seconds to get us in the elevator.

The elevator was much smaller than Pestilence's but at least it provided a refuge from the smell. The descent was a smooth one. According to Bartholomew's notes, we were going ten floors underground. I still couldn't figure out how the lab was built. The chicken plant had been here for years and the lab had only been built in the last two.

Constantine was going to be even more paranoid now that he had proof that his two nemeses just kept following him around. I should check with Katrina and see if they had a secret facility near us. Unless they were using one of the bunkers at the Army Depot, which was less than fifteen minutes from us. Constantine would scream if that was the case.

"Set your watches everyone; we have three minutes," Bartholomew reminded us as the elevator stopped at the ground floor.

The doors opened painfully slowly. Bob and I were ready to charge. However, we weren't prepared to storm into the barrel of ten M16s.

"Three," I told Bartholomew and held my hands in the air.

"Move little lady or I will spray that wall behind you with your brain matter," a very tall security guard told me.

The ten guards standing in front of us were all unrecognizable. They had all donned full-body uniforms, face masks, helmets, and a lot of weapons. If the Storm Troopers needed to do some recruitment, they should definitely come here.

"They only did minor changes to their security system," Bob teased.

"Absolutely. Tiny," I joked.

"Trespassers are to be shot on sight," the overly developed security guard told us.

"Should I be feeling lucky you haven't pulled the trigger, or are horrible lectures the first part of the torture process?" I asked, sarcasm dripping from my words. Of course, I couldn't get my mouth to shut up when it was necessary. That would be way too easy.

Lesson number one for evil doers: do the deed and then talk about it. Nobody wanted to hear you ramble about nothing for minutes on end.

"You are very lucky because our boss is requesting your presence." Storm Trooper wannabe number three pushed me with the barrel of the M16.

Normal security guards would have searched and disarmed us. Either this group truly believed they were of superior power, or they just sucked at their job. The verdict was still out on the correct answer. The truth was, the three of us versus the ten of them were still horrible odds. For them. After dealing with enough supernatural creatures, they really should have brought at least two dozen more, but who was I to judge?

We followed the Storm Trooper parade to a plain, white door down a large hallway. Two other guards opened the door and pushed us inside the dimly lit room.

"Why don't we have an overly exaggerated conference room?" I asked the boys, wondering why every horseman seemed to have one.

"We thought about it, but we wouldn't have any room for the gym, so Constantine nixed the conference room," Bartholomew told me.

"I would have taken the conference room over the gym anytime." I hated our gym with a passion.

Constantine was a master at developing punishments that he disguised as weight training. At least this conference room came with a huge, one-hundred-inch TV. All we had in our gym area were boxing bags and benching tables.

"Well, well. It took you a while to come and pay us a visit," a nasally, male voice said from somewhere in the darker parts of the conference room.

"You were expecting us?" I looked at Bartholomew and Bob to make sure they heard the same thing.

"It was only a matter time before Famine sent his kill squad to stop us, but he is too late." The horrible little speech was followed by several weird, little chuckles.

"To clarify, you guys know that you work for the horseman Famine?" I hated being Captain Obvious, but confirmation was necessary.

"Everyone knows that we work for Famine—well everyone but Famine, that is," the nasally voice replied, the words followed by more awkward laughs.

"If we didn't have all these people with guns, this situation would be pretty funny," Bartholomew pointed out.

"So, who exactly do you think we are, then?" I asked, angling my head towards him.

"Probably some sad excuses posing as assassins. The Boss underestimates us. They should have sent more of you." Nasally was a little too arrogant for my taste.

"I was thinking the same thing," I told our little host. "Boys, now."

We didn't require a huge explanation, or codes to execute our maneuvers. Team Reaper had months of training taking out large and more dangerous targets than that little group. I dropped to a full split while grabbing both of my handguns from my holsters. The two Storm

Troopers closest to me went down in less than three seconds. Bartholomew set off a series of smoke grenades that, thanks to Eugene, we were the only ones immune to. It appeared their special-tactic uniforms did not come with chemical filtration.

Bob head-butted the guard holding him by the neck, disorienting the poor fellow long enough for him to kick him into the next wall. Storm Troopers were dropping like flies. I gave the overly developed spokesperson a swift roundhouse to the chest, mixing it with a kick to the groin and an elbow to the face. Those face masks were not meant to take direct hits, something I only realized when one shattered on impact. Either way, our welcoming committee was out for the count.

"You really should have ordered at least another batch of Storm Troopers to hold us down," I informed our nasally-voiced host.

"Holy shit!" screamed another one.

"Glad we got your attention." I smiled at the darkness, giving my head a slight tilt to play up the evil grin on my face.

Bartholomew ran to the side of the door and flipped the light switch on. I was expecting another set of ten old men —kind of little like Pestilence's group of Interns—hiding in a corner. Instead, three men and two women were there, all incredibly attractive and all wearing designer clothing, their hair styled to perfection.

"That was unexpected," nasally told us from the head of the table.

"You can say that again," I replied. "I guess if you are the most gorgeous of all the horsemen, your team should match the look. You guys are really beautiful."

"Why is it that nobody ever believes a woman can be smart and beautiful?" a gorgeous redhead with a pixie haircut said from the left.

"Sounds like you have identity issues, girly," I told little ginger.

"I don't have the patience for a bunch of rambling, so let's just shoot them all and get what we came for." Bob was not amused by our hosts.

"You did not make a very good impression on my partner here," I told the group, who all managed to get the picture and shut up.

"Are you here to take us hostage? The takeover is already in motion," nasally started rambling again.

I agreed with Bob. Letting this group of egotistical CEOs talk would make the whole process very painful. Since I felt a little evil, I decided to have some fun with the little group. Very slowly, I pulled out my machete and made my way around the table, dragging the blade on the finely polished surface. Bob took a seat on top of the table on the opposite side. Bartholomew wandered the room, touching all the electronics. Maybe they were right and we did look like a band of assassins, but it was too late to change our tactic now.

"Now children, let me explain something. You are not coming anywhere with us," I told the CEOs, and they all exhaled a sigh of relief. "We also don't work for Famine."

"What do you mean?" a hot, little blonde with straight hair asked. "You used Famine's codes to enter the facility."

"Yes, Famine did send us. Unfortunately for you, our boss is ten time more dangerous than Famine, and has a lot less patience." I used the machete to play with the pretty blonde's hair.

I expected at least one of them to pee their pants. Making my way around them, I retraced my steps when I came to the end of the line.

"Who do you work for?" nasally finally asked.

"Death." I let the word hang in the air and said nothing else.

This whole crazy/deadly act was actually a lot of fun. The CEOs all turned a slight green color, and I was afraid the redhead was going to puke whatever fancy, little meal she'd recently eaten.

"What do you want?" Blondie finally managed to get her shaking under control. I was impressed.

The other two pretty boys at the table said nothing. Maybe they were the backups in case two died or something, then they would step in. That made perfect sense to me since I was starting to search for my own clone.

"Nothing major. We need Famine's notes and the formula to your last, little experiment that is making all the shifters go crazy." I laid the machete next to the blonde and sat down on the table.

"We don't have it," nasally answered a little too quickly for my taste.

"What do you mean 'you don't have it?'" Bob yelled from across the room.

"It was stolen by one of our colleagues and we have no idea what he has done with it," the blonde supplied.

"How convenient?" I told them. "Listen here, children, you are playing with forces you don't understand, and you have drawn the attention of my boss. You really won't like my boss when she is mad. So, if you are lying to me, I will come back here and drag you each by your pretty little hairs to the gates of hell. Is that clear?"

Each of the CEOs turned into bobble heads.

"We want the name of this colleague of yours and where we can find him," Bob ordered.

Nasally pulled a paper from his suit and quickly started writing. He handed me the paper and looked around the room shaking.

"Did you fools miss the fact that since you work for Famine, one of the four horsemen and all that, that there are three others you should watch out for?" I asked the

CEOs, who just looked at each other. "What did you all think was going to happen when Famine's siblings came to check on things?"

"They were going to be blown away by the intense security system," Bob answered.

"That sounds about right," I told him. "I'm not sure how you are going to fix this coup of yours, but Famine will be back by the end of the week."

I slammed the machete down on the perfect table, leaving a giant gash. By the looks of the wealth in the room, the table would be replaced by the end of the day. Before that happened, though, the gash should serve as a reminder of how stupid they were.

"Time to go, boys," I told Bartholomew and Bob as I left the conference room. "We really should get a conference room and matching suits. We could pull that look off."

"Constantine already has white suits ready whenever you want them," Bartholomew joked from behind me.

"No, thanks. I'll pass." Bob shook his head.

We made it to the elevator without any more Storm Troopers joining us. It was a little disappointing. We waited for the elevator to arrive when a young Latino guy in his early twenties stepped out of a hallway. The young man was maybe five-feet-five inches, but with beautiful black hair and black eyes. He could have been of Hispanic descent.

Bob pointed his guns at him.

"They are lying to you," the young man told us.

"We know," I replied.

"Unless you are here to help us, I recommend you go back to work," Bob told him.

"I have a copy of the manifest where the supplements were delivered, but I need a secure network to show you." The young man looked up and down the hallway, licking his lips.

"In that case, it seems you are coming with us," I told him. "Bob, let's avoid any witnesses."

"My pleasure." Bob turned around in the hallway and shot all three cameras pointing at the elevator. "Better?"

"Thank you," I told him.

"How did you know?" the young man asked, inspecting the damage.

"We have a lot of practice in situations like this," I told him.

The elevator arrived and Bob shot the camera inside as well.

"If you leave with us, you won't be able to come back." I lowered my voice to sound a little sweeter. "Are you sure you want to do this?"

"I really like the boss, and it's not fair what they are doing." The young man looked sincere as he squeezed his hands in front of him.

"In that case, let's go." I escorted our new companion into the elevator.

Bartholomew pulled a small wand from his pocket and scanned the young man. Bartholomew's device beeped several times when running over the white coat the young man wore.

"Looks like the coat stays," Bartholomew told him.

"Why?" he asked.

"We don't like being tracked," I answered for Bart. "What is your name?"

"Junior," the young man said as he watched Bartholomew set his coat aflame.

The door opened to the overpowering chicken plant smell. We rushed inside Killer and made sure all the windows were up—not that it helped.

"Junior, I recommend you get comfortable. We have a long ride," Bob told him.

My adrenaline was crashing, so I decided to follow suit. I reclined my seat again and made myself comfortable.

Killer had a top-of-the-line engine, but it was a true luxury car. The ride was smooth and peaceful. I planned to enjoy it before I had to run around like a maniac for another twenty-four hours.

Chapter Thirteen

Home sweet home.

I was ecstatic when Bob parked Killer at Reapers. Our little adventure in Mount Pleasant's idea of Shark Tank took most of the afternoon. Bob—being our designated chef—deduced that everyone would be hungry by now. We did a quick stop by Texas Roadhouse since Big Jakes was closed on Sunday. Bob ordered briskets, ribs, and steaks for the boys. I had a huge baked potato with plenty of rolls, corn, and a triple side salad. One thing was for sure: nobody was ever going to go hungry at Reapers.

Bartholomew carried the food upstairs and led the way for Junior. The poor guy looked like he wanted to faint any minute. As he entered the loft, it hit me: we never warned him about Constantine.

"Junior is going to die," I told Bob.

"You don't think Famine is that mad at him?" Bob asked me.

"No, not Famine ... I was thinking of him meeting Constantine." Both our sets of eyes lifted towards the loft before we ran up the stairs.

We were too late. Junior had pasted himself against the glass wall and was barely blinking. Constantine had done his shifting trick and was the size of a bobcat. Imagine that.

Bartholomew was too busy setting up plates to pay the poor boy any attention.

"Bart, why are you not helping him?" I asked when I reached Junior.

"He is only talking to Constantine," Bartholomew replied, busy pulling dishes from the cabinet.

"I didn't know Death was a talking cat," Junior said as he slid down the glass towards the door.

"Who is this boy and why does he smell so funny?" Constantine hissed.

"Stop showing off," I told him. "Constantine, this is Junior. Junior, this is Constantine, the Guardian to the Interns and Death's right-hand guy. Can I technically call you that?"

"It works," Constantine answered. "He gets the idea. Now, back to who is he and where you found him?"

Constantine stopped interrogating Junior as the door to the back opened and Famine entered the common area.

"Junior, what are you doing here?" Famine ran over to Junior's side.

"Boss, you are alive?" Junior looked like he was going to cry.

"I thought your CEOs said everyone knew they was a horseman?" I asked Junior. "You do know they can't kill a horseman?"

"Oh, don't pretend like you were so sure yourself," Constantine called out in front of Junior.

"Thanks, Constantine." I stuck out my tongue at him and joined Bob and Bartholomew with the food preparation.

"They told us you were dead." Junior was wiping tears off his face. "I'm so sorry. If I knew you were alive, I would have gone searching for you."

"Why are you crying?" Famine asked, lowering himself to Junior's height.

"That's called caring. Humans do that stuff all the time," I told Famine in my most matter-of-fact tone. "P.S. They know you are a horseman. You need a better secret."

"They do?" Famine asked with wide eyes. "And they still tried to get rid of me?"

"Yes, your recruitment process sucks," I added. "That group of narcissists should be fired, as well as your security team."

"They are only prepared for corporate espionage, not an assault team trained by Constantine," Famine pointed out.

Constantine puffed out his chest, overly proud of himself. "Next time, they'll know not to mess with the horsemen. How did it go?"

"Isis went all Silence of the Lambs on that bunch," Bartholomew blurted out.

"I was not that bad," I defended myself.

"All she was missing was licking her lips and calling them precious and those five would have died," Bartholomew added.

"Perfect." Constantine rubbed his paws together. "Basically, all the psychological training with Katrina paid off?"

"Absolutely," Bob told him. "Boss, Isis sounded evil, demented, and even vicious. Made the job a hell of a lot faster."

"I love it." Constantine did a slick dance move and spun around. "Now, what did you find out?"

"Nothing," I told him.

"What?" screamed Constantine. "What was the point of all that training if you got nothing?"

"They were lying from the moment we got there. It was all a show." I delivered food plates to Junior and Famine, who were at the table now. "That's why we brought Junior with us."

"Famine, I know you said I shouldn't hack your system," Bartholomew said very slowly from behind the fridge, "but I left several bugs in the conference room. Before you freak, I can explain."

"Yes, please do," Famine said through clenched teeth.

"They removed your access to the system and set up an ambush for when you send somebody over," Bartholomew mumbled.

"They did what?" Famine looked at Junior, and he confirmed it.

"I figured since they took you out of the equation, their system was fair game," Bartholomew sat at the table with his fairly-gluten-free meal and tons of meat.

"You have to admit, the boy was only looking out for your best interests," Constantine told Famine as he devoured the plate of meat Bob put in front of him.

"I guess we are at war, so all is fair," Famine conceded, although they did not look happy. "I expect when I get my lab back you will turn all access back to me."

"Of course," Bartholomew told them, chewing on a bite of brisket. "I already have way too many places I keep surveillance of. I don't need another one."

"I don't think you are making them feel better, Bart," I joked as Famine stared at Bartholomew.

"I recommend everyone eat before their meal gets cold," Bob said, his tone more order than suggestion.

Everyone, including Famine, began to eat, the room falling silent other than the sound of chewing. Bob, Bart, Junior, and Famine sat at the table, while Constantine and I shared the kitchen counter. My baked potato was delicious. Bob passed fresh-squeezed orange juice out to everyone. I had no idea where he found the time to make half of the stuff he did. The man never slept. He also had made a peanut-butter pie. That thing was single-handedly the most decadent dessert on this planet. I always licked my plate twice when I had it. For the horseman of starvation, Famine had two helpings of pie.

"This stuff will make you blow up, so it's no wonder people are always going on diets." Famine rubbed their belly as they spoke.

"But it is so good," said Constantine.

"That is the dilemma, right? It is so delicious you can't resist it." Famine licked their spoon happily. "Junior, when we get back to the campus, we are adding peanut-butter pies to our menu."

"I thought you had everyone on a Kale diet?" Junior asked his boss, swallowing his brisket sandwich like a madman.

"That explains why this poor boy is inhaling his food." Constantine pointed to Junior. "You don't feed them."

"We are part of the diet industry, so we can't have overweight people." Famine gestured to their perfectly-toned frame, trying to drive home their point.

"You technically are the entire diet industry, so it wouldn't matter if your people ate real food," Constantine corrected Famine. "Besides, you are a horseman, of course you are going to look perfect."

"Constantine has a point there," I added.

"You are just agreeing with him because he is your Guardian." Famine glared at me.

"Not really. That has never been a good enough reason to back Constantine up." I gave Constantine my most brilliant smile from across the kitchen counter.

"Traitor!" Constantine spat, throwing a steak fry at me.

"Are you planning to eat the rest of your fries?" I reached over Constantine's plate and grabbed a few more.

Constantine was a pure carnivore, so fries were not his thing. He slapped my hand when I reached the second time, but it was gentle and I knew he didn't care.

"Junior, do you know which CEO was missing from the lab today?" I asked between bites of fries.

"Melvin," Junior answered as he devoured his sandwich.

"What happened to Melvin?" Famine asked.

"According to your crew of evil CEOs, he took the formula and your notes," I replied. "They gave us a note with his address, but I have a hard time believing anything they said."

"Good for you," Famine said in a cheery tone. "All my CEOs are trained in the art of deception. It would be difficult to tell what information is true."

"Having professional liars on your staff is nothing to be proud about," I told Famine.

"I hope you don't mind, Boss, but I was able to sneak this away." Junior pulled out a flash drive from his pocket.

"What's in it?" Bob asked.

"Hopefully, a copy of all the files related to that supplement," Junior told us, but his voice lacked confidence.

"It's a start," I told him.

"Let's take a look." Bartholomew grabbed the flash drive and headed towards his computer.

"Is that safe to plug into your computer?" I didn't know much about technology, but I knew enough to understand how easily viruses could infect a system through flash drives.

"Not at all. That's why I will scan it while we eat." Bartholomew was a genius. "I'm also going to start my little bugs and see if I can break into the system. I haven't had a challenge in a while."

"Am I the only one worried that Bartholomew gets bored if he is not hacking into highly-classified files?" I asked the group.

Bob and Constantine both raised their hands and paws.

"Thank you. I feel validated now." I gave Bob and Constantine a small bow.

Ring. Ring.

"What is that noise?" Famine asked, searching the room.

"The doorbell," Bob answered.

"We have a doorbell?" I asked, searching for the sound.

"Constantine, are you expecting a delivery?" Bartholomew asked from the computer station.

"Yes!" Constantine leaped over to Bartholomew, who was staring at a couple of monitors.

"What are you expecting?" I asked, making my way around the room.

"A little of this, a bit of that. You know, decorations for the equinox," Constantine announced.

"Have you lost your mind?" I shouted. "We can't have a party with shifters attacking humans. That is a recipe for disaster. Where are we having this party?"

"It's the first equinox in haven, and we need one," Constantine told us.

"This is not a good idea." Thanks to Bart's security system, I gazed at a UPS guy as he dropped dozens of boxes at the front door.

"It's going to be amazing. We will turn Union Station into a spring paradise." Constantine stood on his hind legs, expressing his vision.

"You decided the gate of hell were the perfect location to praise the goddess of fertility and spring?" I asked him, shaking my head.

"Oh, she got you there," Famine told Constantine from the table.

"That could complicate things." Constantine dropped down and stared at the screen.

"I would like to know how you are planning to explain that decision to my Godmother." I tormented him as I went back to the kitchen counter.

"I can handle this," Constantine told me, although his pacing on the computer desk told another story.

"You have no choice because she will be here in less than three days." I pointed at my watch for greater emphasis.

"Are you planning to help or not?" Constantine stopped to focus on me.

"You know I will," I said. "I'm not leaving you alone with my Godmother. But it doesn't stop me from pointing out how bad of an idea this is."

"Point acknowledged. Now, we have work to do." Constantine hopped down and headed out the door.

"Work now?" I grabbed my plate and followed him.

"Yes. We should bring all the crates inside and organize them before Wednesday," Constantine told me as he barked orders from the door.

"That is going to take us all night," I whined.

"Well, it's a good thing we don't have a lead in Famine's case," Constantine said. "Bartholomew, start checking that drive and see what you can find. Break into that system and compare the files. The rest of you are with me. To the crates!"

"Including me?" Famine asked, raising their eyebrows at the cat.

"Yes, including you." Constantine was halfway out the kitty door when he turned back. "Some manual labor might do wonders for your whiny butt. Let's go, everyone."

Planning parties was not my specialty, but it seemed Constantine was the host with the most. He had ordered all sorts of stuff, from table decorations, to chandeliers, and even exotic crystals. I had no clue what he planned to use it all for, but I didn't ask many questions, instead choosing to follow directions. After clearing the boxes through the security system, our job was to unpack, catalog, and organize everything into specific piles. It was a blessing Famine and Junior were there to help because we had more stuff than we could handle. We needed to stop Constantine from shopping. Amazon was dangerous for that cat. Based on the number of crates, we wouldn't be going anywhere for hours.

Bartholomew, please hurry.

I sent our boy genius a silent prayer in an effort that he would get me out of Constantine's torture chamber. My prayers didn't look like they'd be answered when

Bartholomew came down to help. According to him, the system scan would take a while.

Manual labor really sucked.

Chapter Fourteen

Not having a traditional job had its perks. The Monday morning blues were very rare in my world. For that matter, Wednesday hump-day or Thank-God-It's-Friday didn't apply either. The only thing that was set on our schedule was Saturday's court day. Everything else was pretty loose. We went with the flow and tried to avoid causing major disasters in North America. That was a tricky one since Constantine owned drones he used to drop bombs on his targets. Death might need to get involved with that one. I was not telling that crazy cat he couldn't blow things up anymore.

It was six in the morning and I slept in. Somehow, I was even more tired than usual. I managed to get seven hours of sleep after Constantine's sweat shop of boxes. My arms went into muscle failure and they were sore. I struggled to put on my tank top for my run this morning. Cruel and unusual punishments were Constantine's specialty. The one benefit that came out of our late-night organizing was finding more info on Famine's CEO. According to Junior, they were all competing for power but lacked the finesse of Famine. The missing Melvin had been making deals with the employees to try to get rid of the other five. That team was an episode of Jerry Springer in the making.

The morning was warm for March, so I took full advantage of it. I did fifteen miles during my run and was feeling pumped. My head was clear and I felt energized. It was a little after seven-thirty in the morning when I walked into the loft. Bartholomew was up, pressing computer keys like a pianist.

"What could be so urgent that you got up this early?" I asked the little genius, who failed to acknowledge my arrival.

"Werewolves," spoke Bartholomew in the softest tone possible.

"Werewolves what?" I was not amused, knowing full well how much trouble some of those packs could cause.

"They sold the formula to werewolves." Bartholomew stopped typing and stared at his monitors.

"Please tell me that is a horrible joke." I marched across the room to the monitors.

"What's a joke?" Constantine asked from the couch.

I jumped three feet in the air, not prepared to find him there.

"Oh God, you scared the crap out of me," I told him, leaning against the glass wall. "What are you doing there?"

"Famine has my room and Junior took Eugene's in Bob's apartment." Constantine whirled over to stretch out. "I was too lazy to walk over to the other loft across the building. That's when I claimed the couch in the name of me, Feline Extraordinaire."

"Did you just crown yourself king of the couch?" I really liked that couch. "Not fair, move over." I pushed Constantine over and sat next to him on the couch. Normally, I would have taken a shower before making myself comfortable, but if I waited too long, Constantine would never let me sit there again.

"I'm the all-supreme being of this couch." Constantine's eyes were barely open. "You should be bowing to me. Start bringing an offering and burning incense in my name."

"Are you awake?" I poked Constantine in the stomach, and he giggled in response.

"What have you done with Constantine?" I turned to Bartholomew, pointing at the strange cat lying next to me.

"Do you think he is drunk?" Bartholomew asked, leaning around his desk for a better look at Constantine.

"Can immortal cats get drunk?" I asked instead.

"Maybe Famine poisoned him and he is trying to fight off the side effects?"

Pressing my lips together, I nodded, liking Bartholomew's theory.

"Or maybe I just want people to worship me like the good old days." Constantine crushed our theories. "Can we get back to the werewolves now?"

"Never mind. He is fine," I told Bartholomew.

"I can see that." Bartholomew smirked and went back to his screen. "After decrypting Junior's file and doing some tracking on Famine's system, it appears that's who they sold the formula to."

"Why would they sell the formula and not the bottles with the supplements?" Constantine asked, sitting up on the couch.

"They sold both," Bartholomew added. "It appears they sold over fifty cases of that stuff to a group of werewolves out of Tulsa, and with the rights to the formula. They weren't lying. The CEOs don't have it."

"Who has Famine's notes?" I hoped they didn't sell that to the werewolves, too.

"Melvin stole that." Bartholomew pointed to the screen.

"Why would werewolves want to buy a supplement that would make them savage and wild?" That part did not make any sense to me.

"It's not for them," Constantine said, now fully awake. "They are planning to wipe out their competition and every other shifter in the country. Didn't TJ say he bought his pills from a special location in town?"

"Constantine, we don't need a bunch of killer shifters running around, or any werewolves targeting them." Maybe a regular job wouldn't be that bad. I wouldn't have to worry about a national disaster that involved the genocide of every race.

"Why can we never have a boring holiday?" Constantine asked. "Isis, get ready. You are heading to Tulsa. I will get Bob and Junior. Bartholomew, call the pilots and tell them to get the jet."

"Weren't you keeping the jet in Florida?" I asked.

"Only because the crew enjoyed it there," Constantine answered, shaking his head. "It seems the cost of living in Texarkana is a lot more affordable, so my peeps moved to Pleasant Grove. Now they are just a phone call away."

"That is a new level of customer service." I shook my head.

"I'm their only client, so what else do they have going on?" Constantine stretched one last time before heading towards the door. "Let's make this quick."

"Bartholomew, I recommend you get ready as well," I told him as I stood from the couch. "You are not heading out wearing a onesie."

"You know you are just jealous you don't have one," Bartholomew told me, rubbing the sleeves of his PJs.

"Right." I headed towards my room. "I don't know how I survived without one. Just hurry."

Having incredible wealth came with major perks, like private jets and crews. Constantine could own anything he wanted, yet he still stayed in whatever residence the Interns chose. As long as security was top of the line, he adjusted to any living conditions with minimum complaints. My Godmother always told me wisdom came with age. If that was true, Constantine was the wisest being on this planet, and that was a very scary thought.

According to Bartholomew's research, our werewolves owned a Casino in Tulsa, Oklahoma. Our pilot, George, was incredible and got us to Tulsa in record time. If the werewolves were trying to take out every other shifter in the country, we needed to find them fast. If Famine's calculations were correct, the supplements had been in the underground market for at least two weeks. That gave the innocent shifters who were taking them less than two weeks before they lost all control.

George pulled the jet into a private hangar where a black Cadillac SUV waited for us. I was curious how Constantine coordinated the logistics to have a vehicle waiting at every location the moment we landed. My curiosity never rose to the point of asking, though. That would translate to a very long lecture with too many moving pieces that I didn't care about. As long as we didn't have to walk anywhere and I could keep all my weapons, I was a happy camper.

"Private jet, custom vehicles … how much money does your operation have?" Junior asked as he climbed in the back of the SUV with Bartholomew.

"We have no clue," I admitted with a shrug.

"Really?" Junior stuck his head in the space between the front seats. "How is that possible? Who does your taxes?"

"Who does our taxes, Bartholomew?" I asked, having no idea myself.

"I do." Bartholomew raised his hand.

"And you have no idea how much money you are worth?" Junior faced Bartholomew.

"I know how much money Reapers reports, how much Isis claims, and the fact that the richest one on the team doesn't have a social security number." Bartholomew buckled himself up and winked.

"That is brilliant in so many ways," Junior said, a little out of breath.

"How far from here?" Bob changed the subject.

"According to my notes, it is a little over thirty minutes." Bartholomew pulled his laptop from his bag. "I'm programming the navigation system in the SUV now."

Bob started the vehicle and headed out of the hangar. As he made his way around the airport buildings, the coordinates appeared on the little screen in the vehicle.

"You are good, Bartholomew," Bob told him.

"I'm getting better with time," Bartholomew replied with a wink.

The ride to the Casino was uneventful. I spent the time cleaning my guns and polishing the throwing stars. I was not a fan of the little things because they never ended up where I wanted them to, but they did add a level of intimidation to my look, which was the only reason I kept them. Katrina liked to give me lessons with the stupid things, but her technique was flawless. She never missed and the stars always caused maximum damage. My throws ended up two feet away from my intended target and barely stuck, at least in the dummy we used for practice. I hoped I never had to use one of them in case of an emergency.

By the time we made it the casino, it was late morning. The place was deserted. It didn't look like anyone had been there in months. We walked around the building, searching for a way to get in.

"Bart, are you sure this is the address?" I asked after the fifth time around the building.

"This is the place," Bartholomew answered, peering inside through a dirty door.

"Do you want to go in and check inside?" Bob asked, pulling out a little carrying case for his tools.

Bob had taken a few lessons with some of the new members of the underground on how to break into houses. I wasn't sure if that was a good idea or not, but the skills came in handy. He was notorious for kicking down doors. Now he could open them with minimum damage.

"Not this time. This place does look dead." I ran my fingers down the window covered in a spider web.

"What do you want to do?" Junior stepped closer to us. "We can't stay here all day and look suspicious."

Junior had a point, and we were not finding anything out, anyway.

"I saw a gas station on the way here. Let's stop by and see if they know what happened to this place." Standing around waiting for a cop to show would get us arrested.

"Bartholomew, your records don't show what happened to this place?" Bob asked.

Bartholomew was busy taking photos and inputting things into his computer. I walked over to him and peeked at his computer.

"What are you doing?" I asked since he hadn't responded to Bob.

"According to my records and everything I pulled up, this place is supposed to be open." Bartholomew faced the building, then glanced at his laptop. "I even found tax records for this month, so how is that possible?"

"Aren't you always the one telling me you can create a paper trail for anything," I said softly.

"True, but this trail is absolutely odd." Bartholomew paced a few more times, comparing his screen with the location.

"Let's go check that gas station," Bob told him, dragging him away.

The only thing the parking lot was missing was a large tumbleweed to whirl across it and this place would have been the most depressing ghost town anywhere.

Bob drove cautiously, following all the traffic signs.

"There is nobody here. What are you doing?" I asked after several long minutes of watching the traffic lights change again.

"We are being followed." Bob looked out this rear window.

"For how long?" I asked, pulling out one of my handguns.

"Since we left the casino." Bob drove thirty miles an hour down the road.

"How is that possible? That place was deserted." Peering over his shoulder, Junior shook with nerves.

"They were either hiding or waiting for someone to show up, but either way, they are behind us now." Bob made a quick right turn onto an empty street. "What would you like to do?"

The last question was directed at me. As the intern on the team, most of the crucial decisions were up to me.

"It would only be fair if we had a nice little talk with our dear friends, don't you think?" I asked Bob, who grinned wickedly at me.

"I was thinking the same thing." Bob pushed his foot on the accelerator and the SUV picked up speed.

"You two, get as low as you can in that seat," I ordered. With Bartholomew's last growth spurt, getting low to the ground was becoming difficult for him.

Bob continued to speed up. I still couldn't see our pursuers, but Bob put some distance between us and them. After two long, excruciating minutes, a black truck pulled out. They were picking up speed and Bob was slowing down.

"Are you ready?" Bob asked, adjusting his gun on his lap.

"Let's do it," I answered.

Before I could change my mind, Bob did a U-Turn in the middle of the road and charged straight at the incoming truck. I lowered my window and opened fire. For incoming vehicles, I used real bullets. My goal was to stop it from hitting us, so my aim was always the hood and tires. The driver was not prepared for the assault and swerved to avoid it, but the turn was a little too much for the poor truck and the thing flipped on its side.

"Wow, that was wild!" Junior screamed.

I quickly switched guns, grabbing the one for living creatures. I doubted the people in that truck were simple civilians.

Bob was out of the truck before I was ready.

"You two stay in here, got it?" I told Junior and Bartholomew, not waiting for their answer before I rushed after Bob.

Three men were climbing out of the truck from the passenger's side. Groans from the opposite side pulled my attention and I found four more men on the ground. Two of the males were conscious, and as soon as they saw me, they made the horrible mistake of charging me. I shot both twice to make sure they stayed down. The tranquilizer took effect immediately. I wouldn't use that weird werewolf-one again, at least not until Eugene could ensure me that the target would be able to keep their fur and hair intact.

After I made sure there were no more surprises at the back of the truck, I made my way to the front where Bob was. "Back is all clear. How are you doing up here?"

Two of the men were face down on the ground, and one had a busted lip. Maybe he got it from the crash, but after glancing at Bob's posture, I had a feeling that one had come from him.

"Listen here. Unless you want to end up like your friends, you'd better talk. Now, why were you following us?" Bob pointed the gun at the man's head.

"You have two options: tell us what we want to know, or we take you back with us to haven." Kneeling down put me at eye-level with the guy, so I gave him a hard stare. "I'm sure a couple of hours locked in a room with Constantine would get you talking."

"You wouldn't." His gaze widened.

"Oh good. You know who we are, then," I said, angling my head.

"We were warned you would probably come this way." They guy's eyes traveled from Bob to me. "We were paid good money to get rid of you."

"Let me take a guess and say it was the same people you bought the supplements from who warned you, right?" I asked, a soft smile stretching my lips. According to Katrina, being ultra-sweet had a way of disorienting your target.

"You have no jurisdiction here," the man said to me.

"That's where you are wrong. I'm the North American Intern and I can go anywhere." I brushed a few pieces of dirt from the man's shirt and then pressed the tip of the barrel into his shoulder where it was already bleeding. The man screamed, then pressed his lips together. "Does that hurt?" I asked in a mocking tone, pressing harder. I kept it up until he finally had enough.

"You are too late. Everything is already gone. It's time for us to be rich," he hissed through his closed lips.

"That is a shame. I guess we came all this way for nothing." Standing, I held my gun out. "Pity, really." He held his hands out, palms toward me, and waved them around in a stopping motion, but I shot him right in the chest.

"Now what?" Bob asked as he looked around.

"Remind me to beat up Famine's CEOs next time we see them," I told Bob as I reached into the comatose man's pocket. "Let's take their phones. Maybe Bartholomew can find something that can help us."

Bob searched the pockets of the men in the back and I did the same for the three in the front. We took phones, wallets, and even a pager. Who still had a pager? We strolled back to the SUV when we finished and handed Bartholomew all the confiscated items.

"See what you can find from those. We got nothing other than that." I buckled myself in and waited for Bob.

"They said nothing?" Junior asked, his tone unbelieving.

"Besides that we were too late, and everything was gone when we arrived, so that's all we found." I tapped my fingernails on the arm rest. "They did say somebody called and warned them about us."

"This might be harder than it looks," Junior told us.

"It is always harder than it should be, trust me on that." And it was true what I'd said. It was just the nature of our jobs.

"Home?" Bob asked.

"Yes," I answered. "Constantine is not going to be happy."

We drove in silence other than the sound of Bartholomew taking phones apart. He carried minimum supplies with him on this kind of trip, so I didn't think he'd be able to get much, but he surprised me when he cracked the passcodes, meaning he would be ready to start searching the devices. I sat there hoping this madness would end soon, but it sure didn't look like that would be the case.

Chapter Fifteen

We should be happy that it was only midafternoon when we arrived, but we had accomplished nothing. All we had to show from our little trip were a few phones and IDs, which Bartholomew discovered were fake. As soon as we arrived, Bartholomew ran to his computer, surely hoping to crack the phones before dinner.

When I walked into the loft, Constantine was pacing on top of the kitchen counter. "They are driving me nuts."

"Who?" I asked, scanning the empty loft.

"Famine, who else?" Constantine growled from deep in his chest.

"Where is the infamous Famine?" I was afraid they would pop up from laying on the couch when I least expected it and scare the living daylights out of me.

"In the lab playing with elements." Constantine glared at the ground like he was able to see all the way to the first floor.

"Oh, okay. Well, I must help." Junior spun around and left the room.

"Does he know where the lab is located?" I asked.

"Not even close," Constantine shook his head.

"Let me go show him," Bob volunteered.

"Do you think he is hiding something?" Constantine asked.

"Bob?" I watched Bob's back as he headed down the stairs.

"Not him. Junior," Constantine clarified.

"Oh, sorry." I walked around the counter and grabbed a juice from the fridge. "I don't think so, but all those CEOs were a bit too strange for my taste. Why?"

"That's my problem. All of Famine's people have been conditioned to be ruthless and only care about themselves. How can this one be so nice?" Constantine was back to pacing.

"Ask him," I told him. "He is still terrified of you, so I'm sure he will confess if you push him."

"That's a great idea." Constantine rubbed his face with his paw. "What do you have going on today?"

"I was hoping to get some time to practice," I answered. "I have a few songs to compose and wanted to test how their effects work. Why?"

"I need you to head to Abuelita," Constantine said.

"Oh, that's too easy." I loved Abuelita, so having to deal with her was never a hardship. "What do you want?"

"First, everyone should eat." Constantine stared out the glass window. "I put in the order for the party."

"We are feeding people at this event?" Constantine had not told me that part of his master plan. "How many people are you expecting?"

"Oh, just a small number ... maybe three to four—" Constantine cut off.

"We require food for less than five people?" I crossed my arms and narrowed my eyes at him.

"Three to four hundred people. You know, the usual." Constantine went back to pacing. "Lots of finger foods: Taquitos, Empanadas, fried plantains."

"I don't think Mexican Restaurants are known for fried plantain, but I get it." I raised my hands to calm him down before he went all nutty on me. "I just don't get why we have to invite so many people here."

"It's a principle thing," Constantine replied.

"I thought you said principles would lead you into trouble," I reminded him.

"I was right, and now we have to plan a huge party because of principles." Constantine took a seat on the counter.

"This is madness," I told him.

"Please hurry back. Introducing Famine to food was a bad idea." Constantine looked at the fridge. "They are going to eat us out of a house if we are not careful."

"On my way," I told Constantine and headed out.

Hopefully, Bartholomew would find something while I was gone. Bad news was following us around and we were running out of time.

Abuelita's Mexican Restaurant was not that far from Reapers, just East on Highway Eighty-Two. It was a small hole-in-the-wall type of place but with the best Tex-Mex you could ever have. Abuelita was amazing—tall, full figured, and a witch. The last part I didn't know until I started working for Death. The restaurant was the social hub for most of the supernatural community in town. With the increase of those residents, business was booming every day.

For a Monday at midday, the restaurant was semi-empty. It was a little too early for the dinner crowd and the lunch one was already gone. I parked near the back and entered through the employee door. Abuelita still considered me part of the staff, and on occasion when things were hectic, I did help out. The good news was I didn't need the money anymore, so waitressing had become fairly fun.

"Isis, dear, what are you doing here at this hour?" Abuelita stood behind a large pot, mixing away.

"Constantine sent me with orders." I maneuvered around the pots and gave Abuelita a tight hug.

"How are you?" Abuelita scanned both sides of my face.

"I'm fine. What are you doing?" I pulled away before she spun me around to inspect my back.

"I heard about TJ." I looked down at the pot she was mixing. Tortilla soup.

"Oh no," I replied. "Does everyone know about it?"

"Constantine put out the warning of the tampered-with supplements, so I connected the dots when I saw that poor boy all depleted." Abuelita shook her head and moved to stir another pot. "You shouldn't be so hard on him."

"I didn't do anything to him," I explained. "Well, minus knocking all his hair out, but that was an accident."

"That's not what I mean," Abuelita told me, trying to hide her face behind the steam of the beans. "He is such a great kid; he just didn't know how to tell you."

"Wow. You had a full conversation with him?" How did she do that? In less than ten minutes, she was able to interrogate any person without them knowing it.

"I just don't want you to make any rash decisions." Abuelita refused to look away until I nodded. "Good. Now, what does your feline Fabuloso want?"

"Oh, the usual: dinner for tonight for six and enough finger food to feed four hundred people on Thursday." I managed to deliver that message without stuttering.

"You are kidding me." I was proud of Abuelita when she didn't crack up.

"I wish." I grabbed a clean spoon and mixed the large pot of white rice Abuelita had on the stove. "That crazy cat is hosting an equinox party and my Godmother is doing the ceremony."

"Ms. Virginia is coming?" Abuelita straightened to her full height and looked around the kitchen. "Ana!"

Ana rushed in the kitchen from the dining area, holding up her apron. At five-feet-four inches Ana was still a force to be reckoned with. The only true human that worked at Abuelita's, she was not afraid or intimidated by the supernatural world. She had seen enough scary stuff already to be over it.

"Abuelita, what's wrong?" Ana was a little out of breath. "Hi, Isis." She gave me a bear hug which was pretty impressive for a girl her size. I returned the hug and had to hold back the urge to play with the curls she was styling. "I didn't hear you come in," Ana told me.

"Are you that busy?" My eyes went to the bar area that connected the kitchen to the dining area.

"Not yet, but I was chit-chatting with Gabriel," Ana told me in a sweeter tone.

Gabriel was the resident Angel in haven and a patron at Abuelita's. Yes, he was The Archangel Gabriel. Too bad he was breathtakingly beautiful and beyond sweet.

"I need to say hi," I told Ana with a wink.

"Yes, you do." Ana pinched my cheeks and headed over to Abuelita. "Would you mind taking him a bowl of soup while you are heading that way?"

"That makes it even better." I poured an extra-large bowl of chicken tortilla soup and walked towards the dining area.

Gabriel was sitting at a corner table reading a book. The only other customers in the place were two men by the door. I had never seen them before, but that was no surprise. I wasn't around as much to keep up with the regulars. The two men were deep in conversation and didn't notice when I brought the soup out and took a seat in front of Gabriel.

"Here you go sir," I told him, making myself comfortable.

Gabriel glanced over his book before giving me his famous smile, the one that could set a tree on fire.

"Well, well. Look who we have here." Gabriel put the book to the side and grabbed my hand. "How are you, Isis? I don't get to see you much anymore."

"Busy, but good," I answered.

"Are you sure?" Gabriel leaned closer to me.

"Why does everyone keep asking me that?" I really hoped he didn't know about TJ.

"Because you have dark circles under your eyes." Gabriel pointed at my face.

"I might be a little tired." That wasn't a lie, just not the whole truth.

"I can see that." Gabriel gave my hand one last squeeze before grabbing his soup. "I hope you are not here to work today.

"No, just delivering messages for Constantine." I grabbed one of Gabriel's chips from the basket in front of him. "Did you know he is planning an equinox celebration?"

"For a being that has met Jesus, he likes pushing the boundaries." Gabriel laughed, a rumbling one that sounded like thunder in the distance.

"With everything going on, Constantine enjoys keeping things complicated," I told him.

"That sounds like Constantine." Gabriel dropped a few more chips in his soup before taking another spoonful. "What other madness is going on in haven now?"

"You haven't heard about the supplements fiasco?" It would be impossible for Gabriel not to know. He knew everything going on in the planet.

"That situation." Gabriel put his spoon down. "Isis, sometimes, I wish the horsemen just decided to take a nice vacation and wait for the apocalypse quietly like the rest of us."

"Do you think that will ever happen?" I knew it wouldn't, and he knew it, too, but it made a great mental picture.

"Only if you find a way to stop birds from flying and fish from swimming," said Gabriel. "Are you getting close to finding the cure?"

"No, we had a lead but it went dead as quickly as we found it." I dropped my head back and let it rest on the chair. "You know it would be so much easier if you could just tell me what was going on."

"I'm sure it would be, and that would be called interfering." Gabriel only grinned at me. "You are doing great, Isis. Just be careful. If one of the shifters bites you while they are in that uncontrollable stage, you could be infected."

"Infected?" My head popped straight up. "You mean I could turn into a shifter?"

"I have heard of some cases, yes, so you'd better hurry," Gabriel whispered the last part.

"You are full of cheerful motivation," I replied, getting up and waving at him.

"Nice to you see. Don't be a stranger." Gabriel waved back.

I found Abuelita and Ana hovering over a piece of paper at the back of the kitchen. They were both writing notes on the same page.

"Why are angels not helpful?" I asked the ladies.

"Because they are meant to watch over you, not solve your problems," Ana answered.

"Are you defending them?" I wanted Ana to be on my side.

"Only showing you the big picture." Ana was no help. "By the way, did you pick your bridesmaid's dress?"

"I thought the wedding was in April?" I pulled my phone out to confirm the date.

"It is in April, but the dress must be ordered in time to get alterations before the wedding." Ana tapped her pen on the counter. "There is a process to the madness, and you know all about that."

"I had no clue about that particular madness," I admitted. "I will make an appointment and order a dress."

"Thank you." Ana beamed brightly and went back to the paper.

"What are you two doing?" I walked around to look over their shoulders at the paper.

"Planning the most incredible menu to blow Ms. Virginia away," Abuelita said, focusing on the paper.

"You are going to do it?" I was speechless.

"Are you kidding?" Abuelita stood up to look at me. "This is the opportunity of a lifetime. It would be an honor."

"I didn't realize my Godmother commanded so much respect." I scratched my head and stepped back.

"Isis, one day you will understand how powerful your Godmother is," Abuelita told me.

"As long as we are not planning to do it today, I'm good." I made my way towards the backdoor.

"Don't forget the food," Ana yelled, pointing at several plastic bags on the counter.

"Thank you so much," I told her as I ran to grab them. "I would be stoned if I walked in without any food."

I gave each lady a kiss on the cheek and jogged out the door. After dinner, I was planning to lock myself in my room. I had several cases to review before court on Saturday. Bartholomew was busy searching for clues, which meant I had a few free hours to focus on haven stuff. As much as I didn't enjoy court, I had to be prepared. Hopefully, I would find some time this evening to practice my instruments. Running around the country had a way of draining me and putting my practices very far behind.

Chapter Sixteen

Sleep was amazing. Two nights in a row I had at least seven hours of sleep. Normally I never slept this long, and I wasn't sure why I was so drained at the end of the day. Instead of concentrating on the negative part, I celebrated the rush of energy by doing a short run mixed with intervals of squats and push-ups. Constantine's decoration episode made me very aware that I was not working my upper body as hard as I should. Weights were not my thing, but I didn't mind doing push-ups. The morning was cool, but the sun still wasn't out by the time I entered the industrial park. The park was great for sprints due to the lack of traffic in that area.

The area was a little dark, but the streetlights were still on and that helped with visibility. In another ten minutes, the sun would start peeking through the clouds. I was on lap number eight of my sprints when I heard a sound from the empty lot. I couldn't see anything from my position, though. The sounds increased, and a man crawled towards me from under some tall weeds.

"Hey, are you okay?" I moved cautiously, worry gnawing at my stomach.

The fellow was half naked with blood covering most of his upper body and face. As I ran toward him, the man shifted to attention and sprinted at me. He was faster than anyone I had ever seen. When he lifted his head and I got a good look at his entire face, I realized he was mid-transition, both legs and half his face a coyote.

When he lunged at me, I pirouetted us both to the ground where the coyote man flipped over me and landed with a thud. It appeared only fully-transformed felines landed on their feet.

Flat on his back, I thought I was safe from my new best friend, but he shifted to his side and hopped up, charging at me again. This time I was ready. I spun around and jumped on his back. With the full weight of my body, I drove him to the ground. Before he could try to twist over and bite me, I grabbed my gun from the holster in my leg. Two quick shots to the back had him out cold, and excitement bubbled inside me when I saw his hair still in place. They might need more shots but at least they would wake up with hair and not resembling raw chicken meat.

I couldn't leave him there. If he woke up in this stage, he might attack someone else. Reapers was less than a quarter mile away, but this boy looked heavy. When I lugged him over my shoulder, I knew how right my initial thoughts had been. Carrying dead weight was a new level of training, and I hadn't prepared myself for it. My little walk home had me sweating as I dragged the partial coyote around.

Getting him through the security system was another struggle. The main door almost closed on his foot since it took me so long to get inside. Once in, the lights did some weird color combination I had never seen before. They went from blue to red, and it took the door a solid three minutes to open. I banged on the door, hoping someone would hear me. When they finally opened, two rifles and a machine gun pointed at my face.

"Well, good morning to you guys as well," I told the boys. "Am I fired?"

"Your little friend set off the alarms," Constantine told me, walking inside.

I could hear the faint sirens coming from the second floor. The emergency lights inside Reapers were flashing, and even Famine and Junior were on the first floor holding guns.

"Oh, I'm sorry, everyone. I didn't realize that was going to happen." Sneaking a supernatural being inside without prior approval was not going to happen here.

"Why are you collecting strays now?" Constantine asked from inside the chamber.

"I found him in the industrial park," I told him.

"Was he knocked out?" Constantine stepped forward and faced me.

"Who is knocked out?" Bob lowered his gun and ran inside.

"No, he attacked me, and I knocked him out," I clarified.

"That's a good call," Constantine said. "But why did you bring him here?"

"Because I didn't want him to attack anyone else before he finished turning," I pointed at the half-mutated man Bob was carrying.

"It's almost sunrise. He would have finished shifting with the sun," Constantine assured me.

"Can you guarantee that?" I placed my hands on my hips and tapped my foot. I was not backing down from this.

"No, he cannot," Famine jumped in. "We have no idea at what stage he is in the process. It was a good thing you brought him. It gives me an opportunity to examine a fresh subject. Junior, please help Bob carry this man to the lab."

Famine walked away, leaving Bob and Junior to drag my new coyote away.

"For the record, I'm glad you are okay," Bob told me.

"That makes two of us," I replied.

"We are becoming the center for unfortunate souls now," Constantine muttered. "And these souls are not even dead."

"Isis, we have a problem," Bartholomew told me as he started walking up the stairs.

"You look exhausted," I told him, fixing his tousled hair. "I'm so sorry that I woke you."

"Why are you only sorry for waking Bartholomew? What about the rest of us?" Constantine complained.

"Were you asleep?" I asked him.

"No, but I could have been." Constantine flipped his tail in the air and sauntered towards the lab.

"That cat is out of control," I said out aloud, for me more than Bartholomew.

"He enjoys being confrontational," Bartholomew said in between yawns.

"Tell me what is going on and then you are off to bed," I ordered Bartholomew.

"I discovered a bidding war on the dark web," Bartholomew said.

"What does that mean?" I stopped in the middle of the stairwell.

"Our werewolves have put the formula and half of their cases of the supplement up for sale to the highest bidder." Bartholomew rubbed his face. "The deal is going on tonight and you won't believe where."

"I would believe anything after living in haven," I corrected Bartholomew.

"You do have a point," he conceded. "The deal is happening at the Cave and winner takes all."

"Bart, we need to be there." I climbed the steps two at a time.

"What do you suggest we do?" Bartholomew asked.

"Win the bid," I announced.

"Are you serious?" Bartholomew stopped mid-way down the stairs.

"Do you have a better idea?" I looked down at him.

After a few minutes, he shook his head.

"Thank you," I told him. "I'm sure Reapers has enough funds to cover any high-stakes bid. Get us the winning bid and I will recover the goods. Let's make this as simple as possible."

"Isis, there is never anything simple in our job," Bartholomew said, jogging up the stairs. "Not to mention you are playing in the Devil's playground. This gets messier by the minute."

"We don't have a lot of options," I reminded Bartholomew as I entered the loft.

"That is true, but how are you going to recognize if the stuff they are selling you is legit or not?" Bartholomew crossed his arms over his chest.

"You got me there. I really have no clue." I walked over to the fridge and grabbed another of Eric's shake.

"You have no clue about what?" Constantine asked as he entered the room.

"I thought you were checking on Famine?" Bartholomew asked him.

"I did, and it was all sorts of boring stuff, so I came back to Isis." Constantine leaped on the counter and looked at Bartholomew and me.

"I want Bartholomew to bid on the formula, but I have no way to verify if it's the real one once I get it," I explained.

"That's easy," Constantine said. "Just take Junior."

"Is that safe?" I hadn't thought of taking Junior to any other dangerous situations.

"The boy is trying to impress his boss and Famine should start trusting people, so this would be great for both of them." Constantine made himself comfortable on the counter.

"What happens if things get messy?" I placed the shake down and waited.

"You just make sure to bring him back in one piece. Got it?" Constantine had the nerve to snicker at me.

"No pressure at all," I said, my words dripping with sarcasm.

"Isis, you are a pro. You can do this," Constantine said. "It is a good plan considering we have no clues or idea where to start."

"That settles it, then." I rubbed my temples, trying to erase the small headache building behind my eyes. "Bartholomew, find a way to win that bid before heading to bed. Do either one of you know what the theme is at the Cave?"

"The roaring twenties and straight into the Prohibition Era," Constantine told me.

"You have to admit Jake does have a sense of humor." The devil couldn't make things easy for us at all. "Where are we supposed to find clothes for tonight?"

"New York City," Constantine stated. "They have a great retro shop that carries authentic pieces. Take Junior with you, too. He will need clothes, I'm sure."

"Let me take a shower and we will be on our way." I didn't wait for a reply before I exited the loft.

My head was spinning when I finally entered my room. I wasn't sure which one was crazier: the guy trying to eat my face or my shopping trip to New York on a Tuesday morning.

"This is wild," I told myself.

"Are you still talking to yourself?" Death asked from a dark corner in my room.

I screamed, and nobody could really blame me for that. I'd been expecting an empty room, not Death waiting in the corner for me.

"I'm sorry, Isis. I should have warned you I was here," Death said softly.

"How were you going to do that without scaring me anyway?" There was no easy solution in this situation.

"You do have a point." Death took a seat on my new recliner and pointed to the bed.

"Are you here to give me a lecture?" I asked as I sat across from her.

"Why would you say that?" Death tilted her head at me.

"Because any time someone tells you to sit, it's either bad news or a lecture," I explained. "Considering Constantine is the king of bad news, you must be here to deliver a lecture."

"That is a great analysis and very accurate of Constantine, but no on both counts." Death reached for my temples and pressed her thumbs softly on them. "How are you feeling?"

"I know I look awful and everyone says I should go on a vacation," I blurted out, the words rushing from me.

"They are right, and you do need a vacation but that's not what I meant." Death examined my face and head. "Mentally, how are you feeling? Are you getting any headaches?"

"That's creepy...how did you know?" I tried to wiggle out of her hands.

"I should have done this Sunday, but Famine frustrates me at times." Death took a deep breath. "This won't hurt but you need hold still. It will help if you close your eyes as well."

I did as I was told and took slow breaths, the kind you take when you visit the doctor. Death's fingertips grew warm, the heat spreading from her fingers to my temples and over my entire body. Chills ran down my spine. I focused on breathing and letting the heat move through me.

After a few minutes, Death released her hold on me. "You can open your eyes."

My eyes were watery, and it took a minute for my vision to clear. I felt lightheaded and everything looked brighter.

"Easy." Death grabbed me by the shoulder before I could face-plant the ground. "Can you still feel your headache?"

I wasn't sure if I could feel anything at all. It took me a minute to concentrate and search for any sort of pain anywhere. My mouth was dry, and my voice wouldn't work, so I shook my head instead.

"Perfect," Death said, smiling.

After swallowing three times, I found my voice again. "What did you do?"

"What do you know about Famine?" Death asked.

"Honestly, not much," I said.

"Most people know Famine as the extreme shortage of food that caused starvation and death," Death explained. "But Famine in its true essence means any shortage or insufficiency. Famine has the power to literary suck the life out of a person. Unfortunately, because you are my intern, their presence will cause havoc on your body."

"Why?" I asked, biting my lips.

"We have a unique connection and their essence feeds off mine," Death said in a low tone. "Because you are directly connected to me, Famine has been subconsciously sucking your energy. Headaches are the first symptoms."

"Would it kill me to have too much exposure to Famine?" I held my head, checking to make sure it hadn't shrunk.

"Not anymore." Death crossed her legs on the chair, but I was not relieved. "I have to place a shield around you to avoid any more accidental drains."

"Is that the reason I kept falling asleep so early?" I asked, thinking it would explain a lot of things going on lately. "I have been very jumpy lately."

"Yes, your body is trying to compensate for the loss." Death brushed a hair from my face.

"How is this affecting Bob, Bartholomew, and Constantine?" I asked, hoping Death would block them, too, if they were having any issues.

"Relax, dear. They are not having any problems, and neither will you from now on." Death stood from the recliner. "I recommend you rest for a few hours. I need the block to settle before you burn any more energy."

"Do I have a choice?" I asked, peering up at Death.

"No." With that single word, Death kissed my forehead and laid me on the pillow.

It took less than thirty seconds for my eyelids to get heavy. I felt my legs being lifted and my sneakers being removed. As my eyes closed, a blanket was draped over me.

Chapter Seventeen

The idea of crossing the country for a shopping spree was supposed to be a girl's daydream. Not for me, though. It was a giant nightmare. I hated clothes shopping, but I hated being on a short deadline even more. Death's little nap consisted of almost five hours of comatose time. By the time I was semi-conscious, I had less than six hours to head to New York and back with clothes. I also had to be ready to party. Junior and I dressed in the jet to ensure we had enough time to get back by seven p.m. when the deal was going down.

Bartholomew did his magic, and we had the winning bid. The problem was we only had five minutes to collect and transfer the funds. If we failed to do that, the next highest bid took the goods. Basically, everyone was showing up and worked on delaying the winner for a chance at the goods. This was chaos in the making. Constantine barked last minute orders through the video conference system. Struggling with my hat, I didn't pay him any attention.

"Isis, what are you doing?" Constantine asked, his tone filled with irritation.

"This is not as easy as it looks." I pushed another pin between my hair and the hat.

"Let me help," Junior stepped around his seat, took the shimmering gold hat from my hands—the color matched my dress perfectly, with more sequins and sparkles than a Christmas ornament—and fastened it on my head.

"There you go," Junior told me as he handed me a mirror.

I gaped at myself. Not only did my hat sit on my head exactly as it should, but I looked elegant. "How did you do that?" The nineteen-twenties were full of glamor, but they didn't do comfort well. Shifting, I hoped I made it through the night wearing the corset, which I had to put on to make the dress flare in all the right places.

"I have three sisters. Trust me, I'm a pro with hair accessories." Junior took his seat across from me.

"Better." Constantine nodded, then his eyes narrowed at me. "Now maybe you can focus?"

"Yes, sorry about that," I replied.

"You look gorgeous," Bartholomew added from behind Constantine. "Nice job picking that outfit."

"Thank you, Bart. At least someone appreciates our hard work." I winked at my little brother, ignoring Constantine.

"Whatever," Constantine told us. "Remember, you will not transfer the funds until Junior confirms the formula is legit. I'm not handing anyone seven million dollars without proper confirmation."

"Seven ..." I started coughing and couldn't finish the sentence. "Are you freaking serious? Junior, you better get this right."

"I'm glad you finally see the urgency in this mission," Constantine chastised me.

I didn't blame him. We had seven million dollars on the line for a piece of paper that might not even be the right one. I did not like the odds we were playing with.

"Make it quick and tell that bag of feathers this battle is not over, that I will crush him." Constantine's evil howl rang out again, so I disconnected the video call.

"Do I want to know what the last part of that call was all about?" Junior asked, his eyes frozen on the blank screen.

"Constantine has a feud with Jake," I explained, trying to tie one of my holsters to my leg without making it too obvious.

"I thought Jake was the devil," Junior said, his cheeks puffing out as if he was holding his breath.

"He is, but do you really think Constantine cares?" A sigh fell from my lips as I realized my holster experiment had failed miserably. There was just no way to hide a gun in this shimmery little number.

Switching to Plan B, I used the matching garter belt, tucking my daggers inside. Throwing knives might not be my specialty, but at least I'd have some kind of weapon with me. Sometimes, I got lucky and could sneak a gun into the Cave, so hopefully, they wouldn't notice the daggers.

We landed at the Texarkana Airport and George taxied us to our private hangar, which I didn't know we even had until this week. We were moving up in the world. I had left Ladybug parked outside for easy access. Junior had to help me down from the plane since I kept tripping over my fancy little shoes. I was not instilling confidence in that poor boy. We loaded Ladybug, and I programmed the GPS with the address for the entrance of the Cave. The Cave had many entrances across the world, and they moved depending on Jake's mood.

"Chuck E. Cheese?" Junior shouted. "You are telling me the magical entrance to the Devil's underground club is located at Chuck E. Cheese?"

"Jake likes to keep things interesting," I told him.

"Isis, we look like mobsters heading to a place where kids have parties." Based on Junior's tone, I had no clue if he was asking me a question or just stating the facts.

"Maybe they will think we are going to a costume party," I told him, trying to lighten the mood.

"Dressed like this on Saint Patty's day?" Junior was even worse than Constantine at building my confidence.

"Relax, okay? We will make the most of it," I told him, shaking my head. "Just buckle up and let's get a move on. We don't want to be late."

It took us less than ten minutes to reach the mall from the airport. Chuck E. Cheese was located at the Central Mall in the middle of town. The only saving grace of this madness was that the door to the Chuck E. Cheese was on the outside. We didn't have to wander the mall dressed like Al Capone's accomplices.

When we walked into the building, the place was empty. I paid the young girl who was at the door. She had the common sense not to ask questions. She didn't even blink when she saw our outfits. I feared that meant we were not the first people she had seen dressed this way. I dragged Junior away, and we walked the perimeter of the place. We needed to find the spot where the stupid door to the Cave was located.

We had walked half of the establishment when a shadow moved by the Skee-Ball machines. Pulling Junior with me, we stepped towards that area. Luckily, we didn't have children with us because it was darker over there and kind of reminded me of the opening scene of a scary movie.

"Aren't you Sheba tonight?" Adam stepped around the machine wearing his own version of a mobster suit, which of course he made look amazing. His muscular body was highlighted in all the right places, and with his dark blond hair slicked back, it gave his perfect face a dangerous flare.

"I have no idea what that means, and I don't want to know," I told Adam quickly before he gave me any details. "Like usual, you look stunning."

The entire staff that worked for Jake, along with Adam, probably modeled professionally on the side. Jake took the meaning of temptation made of flesh to a whole new level. I had the unfortunate experience of seeing what hid underneath those gorgeous faces last October, though, and I decided the devil can keep his demons. There was nothing warm or cozy about them.

"Oh, flattery will get you anything, doll," Adam purred in my ear. "Keep those daggers close by. You have a rough crowd downstairs."

My eyes widened. I had no idea how he saw them because his eyes never left my face. "Uh, thanks."

Adam pulled aside the velvety curtain covering the secret door to the Cave. Junior gaped at Adam, so I grabbed him by the arm and dragged him with me so I didn't lose him. The stairs to the club had a rustic feel, like we were descending to a building back in the time of Prohibition.

"This is creepy and amazing all at once," Junior told me, close enough now that I could feel his breath on my neck.

"Stay close and please don't drink or touch anything," I told him. "Dancing or singing is normally required, but it all depends on how generous Jake is feeling."

The door to the Cave opened and we were greeted by Jake himself. I almost tripped over him when I saw him.

"What are you doing here?" I asked.

"I own the place," Jake replied, running his hands over his glimmering blond hair.

"I know that," I tried to correct myself. "Why are you not standing across the room making people suffer just to see you?"

Normally, that was my experience every time I had to see him. Today, however, he was lounging by the bar at the entrance in an elegant suit with suspenders. The club was roaring with people dancing, gambling tables everywhere, and people who were dressed to impress.

"I'm not hosting the main event tonight, so I don't have to be the center of attention." Jake took a sip from his martini glass. "I'm assuming you came for the formula."

Jake looked over to the left and I followed his gaze. A VIP area had been created in a corner of the club, and it appeared as if it rested on a platform. The entrance had four large, muscled men guarding it, and I had a feeling they were probably werewolves. I angled my head at their matching hats, which all added to the elegance of their suits. The one thing about the twenties I could learn to appreciate was the fact that the men looked amazing in the outfits.

"Be very careful, Isis. This group is not one to mess with," Jake told me as he turned around to face his bartender.

"If I didn't know better, I might actually think you care," I told the devil, knowing perfectly well that the only person Jake truly cared about was Katrina.

"You know I do. You are one of my favorite Interns." Jake saluted me with his glass. "By the way, who is this lovely fellow with you?"

"Junior, and he works with Famine." I pointed at Junior, who waved in greeting.

"This is an interesting surprise." Jake put his glass down and walked over to Junior. "How is cranky pants doing?"

Somehow, I managed to hold in my giggle, while Junior let out a sharp gasp. After a minute he recovered enough to speak. "The boss is doing great, thank you for asking." He stood straighter and made his voice deeper, trying to sound more confident.

"We might as well get going," I told Junior. "By the way Jake, Constantine sends his regards."

"Tell that over-sized furball that he is going down." Jake adjusted a strand of hair that fell loose from my hat. "Nice move with the Blanco video, but this is only the beginning."

"Good to know. I will make it a point not to deliver messages between you two again." I waved at Jake and headed towards the VIP section.

I hoped Junior was following me because I did not turn around to check. The closer we got to the VIP section the less dancers and people loitering. The first set of bouncers blocked my way until I handed one of them the piece of paper with the code. I waited to see if the bouncer would give me a counter sign like we did in the military. Instead, he lifted the rope and let us through.

"This is a wonder," a huge man with one brown and one green eye told me. "I was expecting some nerdy dude with missing teeth to come in and claim his prize. You, on the other hand, are a beautiful surprise."

"I should be flattered, but I don't have all night," I told the leader, assuming that was the role he was supposed to be playing. "I will transfer you the money as soon as we validate the formula."

The leader looked me over several times, like a lion spying a sheep. Refusing to let him see the nerves spiraling through me, I shifted my weight to one side, crossed my arms over my chest, and angled my head towards him. After several moments passed, the leader smirked, then pointed to one of his assistants on the side who brought forth a briefcase. The leader opened the case and took out a manila folder. I motioned to Junior and he stepped forward. Two of the security guards blocked his way.

"You better let my associate examine the formula. I won't be paying you seven million for a blank piece of paper," I told the leader, arching an eyebrow.

"As long as he doesn't touch the paper," he told me.

"Fine," I conceded.

Junior stood by the table and waited patiently until one of the security guards opened the folder and spread out three pieces of paper on the table. It took Junior longer than I hoped to review each one. I wasn't complaining too much since one small mistake would cost us millions. Junior looked over each page at least three times before nodding at me. The security guard took the pages back and loaded them in the folder, which he stuck back inside the briefcase.

"Happy now?" the leader asked.

"Very," I replied. "I hope this is the only copy of the formula."

"It is, otherwise nobody would bother paying for it." The leader pointed to another one of his guards and the guy carried in what looked like a credit card machine. "Now the cash and we can all be on our way."

"Let's do this." I took two steps towards the guard when shots were fired.

The first one hit the guard in front of me, knocking him down and spraying me with blood. Instincts took over, and I dove back to protect Junior, pushing him underneath the table as screams filled the entire room. Once Junior was secured, I raced for the briefcase, but just before my hand grabbed it two figures that were more agile than ninjas assaulted me, one kicking me in the head while the other took the case. I pulled myself up and had enough time to fling a dagger at the duo, which sailed awkwardly through the air and stuck in the back of the one that knocked me on my butt. Good, at least he would hurt for a while.

"Lock the Cave!" Jake's voice boomed in the hall.

People were on the floor and my former dealer laid dead on the chair, a single bullet hole to the head. Jake's supermodel army emerged in the hall and started searching each of the patrons.

"At least we didn't lose the seven million," Junior told me, scrambling from under the table.

"You are not making me feel better," I told him.

"I want answers now!" Jake screamed as he marched up the stairs.

"That makes two of us," I replied.

"Who dares violate the rules of my kingdom?" Jake shouted at everyone and no one all at once. "I'm holding you responsible for this, Isis."

"Me? Why?" I backed away from the devil.

"This was your meeting. I want answers or people will pay." Flames extended from his fingers, his eyes so dark they were almost blacker than the pits of hell.

"Not my meeting...I was here to recover Famine's formula." Waving my hands in front of me, I tried to explain. "I didn't pick the place, and I definitely didn't invite those ninjas to steal the formula. Totally not my fault."

"You have until the equinox to find the culprits and deliver them to me, or all these people die." Jake pointed at the crowd. "If that's not enough incentive, I will release my demons on haven until they are found."

"The equinox? Are you mad? That is less than two days away!" I looked at Junior, but he was staring at his shoes. "I'm not responsible for this."

"I recommend you hurry," Jake whispered.

Before I could complain, Jake blew smoke in my face. I coughed, the room turning into a smoky mess. I couldn't see anything at all, and by the time the air cleared again, Junior and I stood in the parking lot of the mall next to Ladybug.

"This is not good," Junior said.

"Not good? This is a nightmare," I corrected him. "Why do I get blamed for everything?"

"You are the sheriff of haven and Death's Intern," Junior answered.

"Neither one of those answers makes me feel better right now. Let's go." I opened the door to Ladybug.

We didn't have any time to waste. I had no idea how we were going to find those ninjas or how we were going to stop the devil from unleashing hell on haven. To make things worse, how was I going to explain this mess to my Godmother? I needed prayers now.

Chapter Eighteen

Pink, cotton-candy pillows and yellow, marshmallow clouds surround me. Why am I being chased by giant Sour Patches?

I rotated over to find myself tangled in my sheets. Jazz played from my speaker system as I stared at the ceiling.

"Should I get up or go back to bed?" I asked the glowing stars that adorned my ceiling, courtesy of Bartholomew.

"Do you normally debate those things out loud?" Death asked from the corner.

"Oh my God." My hand went to my chest because I thought I might be having a heart attack.

I flipped the light on and found Death leaning against the wall wearing a dress suit. Death's hair was pulled back in a tight bun and she looked like a college librarian.

"Two days in a row, huh? This cannot be good," I told her after getting my heart rate under control.

"I came to check how my block was holding up." Death sat on the bed next to me.

"Okay, I guess," I replied, still half asleep.

"Do you still have a headache?" Death touched my forehead.

"Nope, headache is gone," I said. "Now that I think of it, I feel more rested than I have in days. Weird since I only got five hours of sleep."

It was seven in the morning and we had a late night after returning to Reapers. Constantine wanted every single detail of what went down at the Cave. I had to explain things five times before he was satisfied.

"I gave you a little extra energy yesterday," Death told me. "You looked pretty rough. It won't last long but at least it should help you get through the rest of this week."

"Did you know it was going to be this bad?" I didn't know Death could predict the future.

"Just an educated guess, dear, since we didn't exactly start the week on a high note." Death's expression softened.

"Did Constantine fill you in?" I looked at my hands to avoid making eye contact with Death. I knew what happened at the club wasn't my fault, but I still felt bad.

"He did." Death stood from the bed.

"You don't look upset," I said in a hesitant tone.

"There is nothing to be upset about," Death replied. "Having the werewolves die at the Cave did save me a trip to deliver them. Jake took care of that part for me. Besides, I can't blame Jake for being upset, not when he has a reputation to maintain. People dying at his club is horrible for business. How else is he going to convince humans to give up their souls if they get killed first?"

Massaging my temples, I tried to clear my head. "I'm not sure if I'm traumatized or just nauseous."

"Maybe a little of both, but human's life choices are not our business," Death reminded me. "Your mission remains the same: find the formula and get an antidote developed quickly. I also recommend getting dressed because you have visitors."

"At seven in the morning on Wednesday? Why?" This was not a good sign.

I rubbed my eyes with both hands. By the time I lowered them, Death had disappeared. The least thing she could have done was tell me who was outside before she left, but that would have been too simple. I rolled out of bed and made my way to the bathroom. Visitors meant I had to look presentable before stepping outside to the kitchen. My hair was matted to one side of my head due to all the hairspray I used the day before for my nineteen-twenty's hairdo. That meant a shower was required before leaving the room. Hopefully, nothing crazy happened while I got ready.

Screams echoed down the hall as soon as I opened my sound-proof door. My hair still wet, I made my way towards the kitchen while finishing my braid, knowing that would keep it out of my face. Constantine was on the kitchen counter having a very intense conversation with none other than my Godmother. Her hair floated around her like some invisible wind blew for her and her alone, and her finger pointed at Constantine as her lips moved. I had a hard time imaging my Godmother as the leader of the witches. She was always a free, loving Gypsy that had a hard time following rules and regulations.

"Sweetie." Then again, she might have supernatural powers because she somehow always knew when I was near.

"Hi, Godmother," I said walking over to her.

Godmother wrapped me in her arms and held me tight, her warm cinnamon-and-spice scent wrapping around me. Pulling back, she squinted her eyes at my face.

"What have you been doing to my child, you little dictator?" Godmother shouted at Constantine.

"Why are you blaming me?" Constantine whined.

"Look at the bags under her eyes. Of course, this is your fault." Godmother waved her fingers at him. "Where is that lazy excuse for a horseman? He promised to take good care of my child."

"Death just left. Maybe next time you can crucify her," I joked, but nobody responded.

"I needed to talk to him. Why is he avoiding me?" Constantine asked.

"I thought you just talked to Death." Peering over Godmother's shoulder, I got a nice image of Constantine's paws flailing through the air.

"Don't think for a second I don't know what you are doing. Changing the subject will not silence me." Godmother spun on her heels to face him. "Death will answer for the reason my little girl is so beat down."

I sighed. "I don't look that bad, I'm just a little tired," I told her. "And before you go all Mama Bear on me, it is my choice to work this hard. No more threatening people."

"I have not threatened any people ... well, other than a few supernatural beings with over-inflated egos." Godmother squared her shoulder and stretched her head from side-to-side like she was ready to fight.

"Stop threatening those people as well," I told her and headed to the fridge. "Are you ready for the equinox?"

"Why would you bring that up?" Constantine rumbled, covering his eyes with his paws.

"Has this demented pussy cat told you where he is planning to have the big event?" Godmother planted her hands on her hips, puckered her lips, and rolled her eyes.

"He might have mentioned something in passing." I was not going to say it out loud. "Should I assume you don't like it?"

"Don't like it?" Godmother exploded, her hands flapping all over the place as she paced circles into the floor.

"That explains all the screams I heard from the hallway." I grabbed a piece of cheesecake and popped it in my mouth. I believed in eating desserts any time of day.

"Who in their right mind would want to honor a Goddess at the gates of hell?" Godmother glared at Constantine.

I gave him my best I told you so stare. How Constantine was going to convince my Godmother was beyond me.

"But Union Station is a gorgeous building," Constantine whined.

"I'm not disagreeing with you," Godmother told him. "And I think it's great the things you are doing with the building, but we are not having an equinox celebration there. Unless you are planning to open the gates and let the demons come over."

"Very funny," Constantine added.

"You better find a suitable location by this evening," Godmother ordered. "We need to prepare the altar and cleanse the area. Don't make me regret flying all the way over here for nothing."

"Oh, it won't be for nothing," I said. "You will have the best Tex-Mex food in Texas, right here for your event."

"You have been spending too much time with this one." Godmother walked over to me. "I'm starting to worry about you."

"Oh please, you love me." I fluttered my eyelashes, hoping to look cute and innocent.

"Yes, I do, even if you do keep horrible company." Coming from Godmother, that was a pretty low blow aimed at Constantine. "I miss you and I want you to join me for lunch today."

"Godmother, I'm super busy," I whined.

"You are not getting out of lunch," Godmother said in her stern voice. "Noon, at the convention center, and don't be late."

Godmother kissed my cheeks and walked out of the loft without turning back to look at Constantine. Constantine dropped on the counter and hung his head over the ledge.

"That crazy witch is going to be the death of me," Constantine told me.

"This is all your fault for asking her to do this crazy equinox party," I reminded him.

"Why are you being so mean to me?" Constantine twisted over on his back.

"It's called the truth, sorry if it hurts." I went back to the fridge to look for more food. "What's good to eat here?"

"Bob left you a veggie quiche in the oven," Constantine grumbled from the counter.

"Bob is a saint." I rushed to the oven, pulling out the most beautiful dish I'd ever seen. Even my stomach growled at the sight and smell.

"Sometimes, I wonder if we feed you enough," Constantine said, turning on his back.

"Whatever," I replied, cutting into the quiche. "Where is Saint Bob now?"

"At Union Station getting the troops ready," Constantine answered.

"Ready for what?" I stuffed a large spoonful of quiche into my mouth, not even worried about talking with my mouth full.

"In case the demons or their little followers cross the border." His eyes wouldn't meet mine.

"Wait!" I dropped my spoon on my plate. "Jake said we had until the equinox before he released his demons on haven."

"That is correct." Constantine turned his focus to me finally. "His demons are not technically in haven right now, but they have us surrounded. The good news is the little killer ninjas can't leave haven either."

"I thought demons were only active during the day." I grabbed my spoon and stabbed the poor quiche to pieces, trying to process all the new information.

"The demons cannot roam the streets during daylight, but they have flunkies," Constantine said in a low voice. "They can have their humans do their dirty work during the day, or they can possess the human. Either way, Jake has a lot of representatives around us right now."

"One quiet week … is that too much to ask for?" I threw my hands in the air, imitating my Godmother.

"We are running a city, so no, there are no such things as 'quiet' days." Constantine smirked as if bursting my bubble gave him more enjoyment than anything in the world.

"Fine. What do you need me to do?" I asked as I went back to my quiche, which was now in tiny pieces.

"Go introduce yourself to our guests and make sure they know there are consequences for trespassing." Constantine growled deep in his throat. "Isis, just be careful. If any of those humans are possessed, they will be very dangerous and ultra-powerful. Use your third eye if you have to."

If Constantine was asking me to use my power to see the alternate reality underneath the normal veil, we were in trouble. I avoided using the sight as much as possible, mainly because of how disturbing and unforgettable the things I saw were.

"Sounds like it is time to earn my check," I said, adding extra cheeriness to my voice. "By the way, what did you do with Famine and Junior?"

"Junior was exhausted and probably experiencing a bit of shock from last night," Constantine told me. "Bob gave him a sedative and put him right to sleep. Famine has discovered Disney+ and they are hooked on The Mandalorian and baby Yoda. I love streaming services."

"I wonder how that happened," I mused, winking at Constantine.

If nonstop movies and shows kept the horseman docile, I would take it. I grabbed another slice of quiche and headed towards my room.

"I'm going to finish getting ready and I'll be on my way," I told Constantine.

"Isis, if they attack, don't hesitate," Constantine warned me. "They won't think twice about killing you. You make sure they know who is in charge. Got it?"

"Yes, sir." I saluted Constantine, and he glared back.

I shouldn't joke with Constantine when he was worried, but it was easier than facing the ugly truth. A shifter was killed in front of me last night, over some tainted supplement. I spent an hour scrubbing the blood off my skin and dress. The dead didn't bother me. Seeing the action that got them dead was a totally different story. Thinking about it made my hands shake, and I had to be steady for this little visit. If we were going to stop more killing, it was necessary that I put on a really good show today.

Chapter Nineteen

When Constantine said, "pay a visit to our little friends," I didn't grasp the meaning of the assignment. According to Constantine, the demons and their little sidekicks had set up locations at the edge of each road leading out of haven. Haven covered a large terrain, expanding across two states. This was going to be a pain in the neck. There was no sense in dragging it out, so I drove west on Highway Eighty-Two to meet the first invaders.

It took me less than five minutes to hit the edge of haven from this side. Two black SUVs were parked on both sides of the highway with dark, tinted windows. It had to be our mysterious visitors considering nothing else looked suspicious. I parked behind the one on the right-hand side. I had a pair of fabulous, black cargo pants on, a long sleeve shirt, and a light jacket specially designed to repel curses, spells, and even bullets. A girl couldn't be too careful. I loaded my pants with a water gun filled with holy water, too, just in case things got heated.

I felt like a cop getting out of my vehicle, adjusting my sunglasses and walking towards the driver side of the SUV. I didn't want to be within grabbing distance of the SUV, so I decided it was time to show off my scythe. If these were Jake's people, they knew exactly who I was and should not be surprised by my weapon. With one smooth motion, my scythe extended to its full size, the blade glowing in the sunlight. Hopefully, nobody was on the road at that time of day. If any humans saw me walking around like that they'd be scared out of their minds.

I was six feet away when I tapped on the SUV's window with the tip of my scythe. The SUV across the street had its windows up and I waved at them since I was sure the passengers were monitoring every movement I made. The vehicle in front of me was completely still, so I tapped several more times on the glass and waited.

"Oh, come out and play; I know you are in there," I told the passengers.

Two minutes later, the driver's side door opened and a gorgeous girl with silver-streaked hair stepped out. And because she worked for Jake, of course she was drop-dead gorgeous.

Could humans sue the devil for beauty discrimination? Or maybe he made them beautiful after they joined ... that could be part of the deal.

I would ponder those questions later because another gorgeous girl stepped out from the front passenger's side, moving around the vehicle. This one had spiky blue hair that looked perfect on her.

"Let me guess ... he recruited you two from a Victoria's Secret runway?" I asked the pair of model lookalikes.

"Adam warned us about you," Blue told me.

"Oh, Adam. Well, he shouldn't go around telling stories about people," I replied, using the scythe as a cane.

"Adam is actually very fond of you. He even went as far to tell us to avoid messing up your face," Silver mentioned to me.

These two were a little too cocky to be gorgeous humans, so I braced myself with the scythe and willed my third eye to open.

"HOLY. JESUS. CHRIST," I screamed, ready to launch into battle.

They were definitely not human. The demons possessing the girls were huge, at least ten feet tall in the supernatural world. Scales covered their bodies, while large horns protruded from their heads. Their eyes were empty sockets filled with a darkness so thick it made my skin crawl.

"Well, that is not fair," Blue joked, walking in my direction. "You checked under the hood without our permission."

I blinked quickly, forcing my third eye to close. At least it was easier to control the sight with demons than it was with vampires. That was truly a horrible experience I wouldn't wish upon my worst enemy.

"Did you like what you saw?" Silver purred.

I spun the scythe quickly in front of me, creating sparks every time the blade hit the pavement. The demons stopped but their smirks never faded.

"You have your orders and I have mine," I told the girls, aware of the evil underneath their beaming faces. "You cross that line and I will send you to hell in tiny little pieces. Is that clear?"

"You are really brave in the daylight," Silver mocked me. "If I remember correctly, you needed a whole army last October to take out a few of our weakest siblings."

Lord, protect me.

If what she said was true, this could quickly turn into a blood bath, and it would be mostly my blood pooling on the ground. Too bad for her I was stubborn to the core and refused to back down.

"Luckily for your siblings, I was busy with a princess." I smirked back. "Catch."

Pulling a small wooden cross from my pocket, I threw it at the demon. Silver had amazing reflexes and caught the cross in her hands. Too bad the little thing was blessed by Father Francis, our resident exorcist. The cross went up in flames as soon as it made contact with the demon. Silver screamed in agony, dropping the cross. Blue jumped to her side to put out the flames. I dared a quick peek with my sight, and the demon was gone. Silver was all alone and did not appear as tough or confident.

"Oh, I'm sorry, did that hurt?" I asked the little girl.

"You bitch," Silver screamed.

"You can call me whatever your heart desires—if you still have one, that is," I said, sounding more like Shirley Temple than myself. "Just remember if you traverse the boundaries of haven before equinox, I will burn you. We have tons more of those around town. In case you are curious, the official time for the solstice is Thursday night at ten-fifty. Stay on your side."

Feeling reckless, I turned my back to the demons. If they were searching for a fight, I was ready to have one. Too bad I had to put on that little show at least ten more times around haven. I hopped in Ladybug and made a U-turn on the road.

My Godmother was going to be furious, but I was late for our meeting. Sending threatening messages to demons took time. It didn't help that they all seemed to be ready for me by the time I arrived. The last few avoided the whole talking part and just charged at me. Shouldn't they know better than to mess with a girl who was hungry and mad? I should check with Father Francis if holy water to the eyeballs could cause blindness to possessed humans. Two of those kids looked like I had burned their retinas off. I should write a note so I don't forget.

I had called my Godmother, but one of her minions picked up instead. The man gave me strict instructions to head to the restaurant area of the hotel and meet my Godmother there. It seemed her impatience was contagious because her peeps were just as bad as her.

Godmother wanted me to drop everything as soon as she called. That worked when I was a small child, but now some things took priority over her stuff. Either way, I hated being bossed around. I had enough with Constantine, and I had to tolerate him since he paid me.

The hotel was empty except for my Godmother and two members of her security team. Godmother motioned for me to take a chair even before I reached the table. She already had a plate ready for me. I wanted to boycott the meal, but she had mac and cheese with steamed veggies and sweet rolls. Rebellion was futile when I was so hungry.

"You are late," Godmother reminded me.

"I'm sorry. My errands took longer than I expected," I confessed.

"You work too hard, dear," Godmother told me, taking a large bite of steak.

"I thought you gave up meat?" I asked her.

"On normal occasions I won't eat meat, but the ritual is draining, and I must have as much of my energy as possible," Godmother explained.

"Hence the extra layers of protein," I finished for her.

"Exactly," Godmother agreed.

"What did you want to tell me that you couldn't tell me at Reapers?" I asked my Godmother, who stopped chewing to look at me. "Oh, please don't give me that look. You didn't ask me to come just to feed me."

"When did you become so observant?" Godmother asked, cutting her steak.

"When people started trying to kill me," I replied, and when she winced, it made me a little sad. "Godmother, I'm fine. I promise."

"You work for two demented super beings who are immortal, so tell me how that is fine?" Using her utensils, Godmother pointed at me.

"They pay really well," I countered.

"Isis, this is not the time for jokes." Godmother lowered her voice.

"Why are you so excited about this? You are in charge of the order. Isn't that dangerous?" I motioned to her bodyguards in the corner.

"Exactly. I have help." Godmother focused on me.

"We are never going to agree on my career, so how about you tell me what you wanted to meet me for?" I took a bite of my mac and cheese and ignored her glare.

"I want you to be a part of the ceremony," Godmother told me, the words rushing from her.

"You are kidding?" I almost dropped the fork. "Godmother, you do remember that I'm Christian."

"Please don't use that excuse with me. You work for Death," Godmother replied. "Of all people, you should know by now that there are different levels of faith, and each have different meanings."

I internally groaned. Not another theological conversation with my Godmother. They were always so long and painful.

"Let me think about it," I told her, hoping to stop her from going on about it.

My phone chose that moment to ring, interrupting my Godmother.

Thank you, Jesus, for saving me here.

"It's Bob. I have to get this," I told Godmother. "Hi, Bob, what's going on?"

"We captured one of the werewolves from the club," Bob told me, skipping the greeting.

"Are you certain?" I asked, not sure how they did it, but if they really had, I didn't care about the how of it.

"Yes. One of your ninjas," Bob replied.

"That's great," I said, an image of the attackers cutting across my mind. "Don't shoot him, okay? I'm on my way."

"Where are you going?" Godmother asked as I disconnected the call.

"Bob found one of my potential attackers," I told her, stuffing as much food as I could in my cheeks.

"Do you have to leave right now?" Godmother looked at my empty plate.

"I have... a really... tight deadline," I struggled to speak with my mouth full. "Yes, but I love you." Jumping from my chair, I rushed across the table towards Godmother.

"I love you, too, even if you never listen," Godmother told me.

I gave her a quick kiss on the cheek and said goodbye to her and her team.

Oh, thank you, Bob, for getting me out of here.

I was going to need to get Bob a present for this. I ran out of the convention center before one of Godmother's peeps could stop me, but I was so distracted that I ran into a person right outside the doors of the building.

"I'm so sorry, sir," I apologized to the man.

"Isis?" TJ spoke.

I did a double take. Because he wore a hat, I hadn't recognized him, and I felt terrible because he had to wear that hat because he was bald and it was all my fault. He didn't even have eyebrows for crying out loud.

"TJ, I'm sorry," I told him, staring at the ground.

"Are you okay?" he asked, and guilt hit me for not checking on him.

"I'm fine, but how are you?" I folded my hands across my stomach.

"Besides not being able to sleep due to lack of eyelashes, I'm good." TJ winked at me.

"TJ, I had no idea that was going to happen, I swear," I told him.

"Relax, Isis. I know you didn't." TJ reached for my hands, but I pulled away. "Are you still mad at me?"

"I'm not mad, just processing." I had a hard time with people lying to me, but I had forgiven my Godmother.

"Just be careful," TJ said, walking slowly away.

"You, too, and don't worry. We will find a cure." I wanted to run after him but couldn't.

"I know you will." TJ never slowed down.

I took a deep breath and walked away. That was too awkward for my taste. I would worry about dating issues after this mess was fixed. Right then, I only had enough energy for one major problem at a time.

Chapter Twenty

There were never enough hours in the day to deal with family drama, boy trouble, and sociopaths trying to take over the world. Somehow, out of those three scenarios I preferred the last one. At least with the sociopaths it wasn't personal. I was just one stumbling block they needed to eliminate. The other two were all personal, and I never had the right answer.

Was I running away? You're damn right! Saving haven seemed like the safer choice of all the things going on in my life.

Union Station was buzzing with excitement. The holding cells were filled with drunken beings from too many Saint Patty's Day parties. Eugene missed one hell of a pub crawl by the looks of the crowd. I marched straight down to the lower levels to find Bob. He and Shorty had moved the werewolf to an interrogation room in the far corner of the station. Our interrogation rooms scared the crap out of me. They were completely white with a table and two chairs. It looked like a mix of a torture chamber and an insane asylum dormitory—at least the ones you saw in the movies.

"What is he doing?" I asked Bob and Shorty as I joined them at the double-glass window.

"Pacing," Shorty replied. "He has been pacing nonstop for at least ten minutes."

"Is he ready to talk?" Wasting my time with an angry shifter was not my idea of fun.

"That's the thing ... he has been rambling nonstop and every time we ask something, he just spews out the answer," Bob said, tapping the glass.

"In that case, let's go," I told the boys.

I followed Bob out of the viewing room and into the interrogation cell. The interrogation room was freezing but our new friend was sweating profusely. He was still wearing his ninja outfit, tight black pants with a snug tank top showing off too many muscles for my taste. I stayed close to the door as Bob walked over to the werewolf, who spun around at an incredible speed and charged at Bob. His velocity was out of this world, but his balance was sloppy. Bob grabbed him by the neck and dropped him in the far chair, then used a pair of handcuffs to secure him to the table.

"You are getting really good at that," I told Bob as I made my way toward the table.

"Too much practice," Bob whispered back.

"I see that." I took my seat in front of the prisoner.

The werewolf pulled on the chains holding him in place, but nothing budged. The table was steel and bolted to the floor. It would take three of him to move that piece of furniture around. I snapped my fingers in front of the werewolf to get his attention. His eyes were dilated and changing to a dark yellow.

"Let me go," he growled at me when he finally saw me.

"Soon," I said very sweetly. "What's your name?"

"Luke," he growled, pulling the chains even harder.

"Luke, I recommend you sit down and stay still." I gestured to the chair.

"Or what? You are going to teach me a lesson?" Luke licked his tongue and moved closer to me, more like a slithery snake than a wolf.

"Is he high?" I looked over at Bob.

"I was wondering the same thing. Let me check." Bob left the room.

"My body is a temple; I don't do those things," Luke answered.

"That's great. So, how about you sit your temple down before you bleed all over my table." I pointed at his hands with my chin where the cuffs were starting to dig into his skin. "The more you struggle, the tighter they will become."

Luke looked down, finally noticing the marks on his wrist.

"Something about magic cuffs." I shrugged. "Present from the Order, but if you keep struggling those little things will amputate your hands."

That did the trick and Luke sat down on the chair.

"You can't keep me here," Luke said in a hoarse tone, sweat dripping down his face.

"I can do whatever I want." I leaned closer to him. "This is haven."

"This is supposed to be a refuge for the world." Luke started shaking again.

"It is, as long as you follow the rules." I played with my braid while glancing around the room. "You and your little friend assassinated a man last night at the Cave, and that made the Devil very angry. The Devil wants vengeance and now he is threatening all of haven. You know what they say...crap rolls downhill. Guess what? You are at the bottom of the hill."

"Are you planning to turn me over to the Devil?" Luke twitched back and forth on his chair.

"I'm definitely considering the possibility. It will save me a hell of a lot of trouble, after all. But, if you cooperate with me, maybe I'll have a change of heart." I gave him a wicked, condescending smile that never reached my eyes. "Why did you kill the seller?"

"It was all a scam. He was never going to give up the formula," Luke answered.

"Even after I paid?" I asked, getting comfortable in my chair.

"Nope. He had his pack stationed outside to take it back." Luke licked his lips again. "We had a deal and he betrayed us. The lion pack is not one to be messed with."

"Lion? I thought you were a werewolf?" I glanced over my shoulder at the double-glass window hoping one of the boys would explain.

"That is the problem with you humans. You can't tell the difference between us." Luke glared at me.

"That is true. I can bring Constantine here," I told him, glaring back. "I'm sure he knows the difference, but do you really want to face his style of interrogation? Don't get smart with me."

"Constantine is in haven?" Luke looked around the room like he expected Constantine to pop out from the walls. "I thought that was just a rumor."

"Sorry, not a rumor at all." I flipped my braid to one side. "The myth, the terror ... he lives in haven and he is in a cranky mood. Should I call him?"

"No!" Luke tried to push away from the table, but his cuffs held him back.

"Fine," I said. "But if you change your mind, just let me know."

Luke shook his head, and his left eye twitched.

"Where is the formula now?" I asked softly.

"In haven," Luke replied.

"I got that, but where?" I asked, tapping my foot against the ground. I was running out of patience.

"I'm not sure," Luke replied. "We were supposed to meet outside of haven—outside of Hooks, actually—but the Demons blocked the exit before we could leave. My partner and I separated to lose their trail."

"Great." My day was filled with fantastic news. "What were you planning to do with the formula?"

"We are going to kill all the werewolves." Luke lost it and started roaring hysterically. "We have a man who can tweak it to make it airborne and target only the wolves. We just needed the original formula."

Luke was drooling and shaking uncontrollably, so I left the room. Bob was in the hallway waiting for me, and Shorty stood beside him.

"Was he like that when you brought him in?" I asked.

"No," Shorty answered. "He wouldn't even give us his name."

"What happened? He is too helpful and erratic all at the same time." I paced the hallway, not sure if I could believe Luke.

"He was sharing a cell with the resident drug dealer," Shorty said, puckering his lips.

"Bring him to me," I told Shorty. "Bob, call Constantine. Have him question Famine and find out if making the formula airborne is even an option. I'll meet you in my office. And someone please give that man some water."

I headed upstairs to my office while Shorty ran to the holding cells. Bob found one of the guards and gave him instructions regarding Luke. Shorty had everyone working today. Unlike most human police stations where everyone seemed angry and had to maintain a sense of order, Union Station was filled with laughter and jokes. The staff found everything funny and everyone was overly friendly most of the time. Most of them waved at me as I passed them on my way to the second floor.

My office was located in the far corner of the building and faced the train tracks. Shorty had Big Band music playing for me today. Somehow, everyone knew music calmed me and they played it for me everywhere. My windows were covered with wind chimes. Bartholomew gave me a few for Christmas to ward off evil spirits and the rest of the staff followed. The colors reflected beautifully off the sunlight.

My door opened and Shorty walked in with a bird cage. He deposited the cage on top of my desk. Inside he had a six-inch male pixie with the most exquisite wings I had ever seen. He wore khaki pants, a blue sweater, and a little hat. Either they shop at the Barbie section or someone is an extremely talented seamstress.

"This is the drug dealer? And you had a pixie in the same cell as a shifter?" I asked Shorty.

"Do not be fooled by his appearance, Boss Lady." Shorty pointed at the pixie. "This is one tricky SOB and a regular here. Besides, we ran out of cells." He shrugged. "It was a wild night. Do you know how often he is in and out of holding? I figured if he shared a cell with a shifter, it might teach him a lesson."

Shorty looked ready to strangle the little fellow. The pixie took his hat off, revealing a head of curly, brown hair.

"This is abuse, do you hear me?" the pixie shouted in his cage.

"Yeah, yeah, yeah," Shorty mocked. "You are going to sue us, right? Not like I haven't heard that before."

I walked over to the cage and opened the door.

"Boss Lady, what are you doing?" Shorty rushed at me. "We are going to lose him."

"He is not going anywhere, right?" I asked the pixie, holding the door open for him.

"Is this a trick?" the pixie asked, pinning himself to the corner of his cage.

"No trick. I just have a few questions for you." I sat down on my chair. "I figured you would be more comfortable talking to me outside of the cage."

"Who are you?" The pixie flew out of the cage.

"I'm sure you know who I am," I replied, propping my feet on the desk.

"Isis Black, Death's Intern and Sheriff of Haven," the pixie confirmed, landing on the desk. "What do you want from me?"

I reached over and moved the cage to the floor. Shorty stood by the wall, staring at the pixie.

"Nothing major, I promise," I told the pixie. "What's your name?"

"Why?" The Pixie put his hands on his hips, and I had to force myself not to snicker. Definitely not the most intimidating look for him.

"Do you want me to keep calling you pixie or drug dealer?" I tilted my head.

"Pete ... the name is Pete," he answered in between long breaths.

"Hi, Pete, nice to meet you," I said sweetly. "Now, Pete, you were in a cell with our little shifter. What happened?"

"What happened?" Pete walked in circles on my desk, spraying dust all over the place. "The same thing that always happens. They start talking smack and think they can intimidate us because we are small. I taught that cocky bastard a lesson."

"What did you do to him?" Pete had my undivided attention.

"He was bragging how they would never break him." A snort came out of Pete. "I sprayed his ass with enough dust that he would be singing like a canary. Did it work?" He floated above my desk, a huge grin spreading over his face as he focused on me.

"You can make people tell the truth?" I covered my mouth and looked between Pete and Shorty. "Wow!"

Shorty moved away from the wall and stood by me. The two of us were scrutinizing Pete with a new level of appreciation.

"We can make people do many things with the right combination of dust," Pete bragged, adjusting his sweater to fit his puffed-out chest.

"That is an amazing," I told him. "Why are you using it to get people high?"

"Do you know how hard it is to find work these days?" Pete dropped his head. I could relate. Before working for Death, the only person that would hire me was Abuelita.

"Well, Pete, you are hired," I told the little pixie.

"What?" I wasn't sure who was louder, Pete or Shorty.

"For what?" Shorty asked quickly.

"That was the fastest interrogation I have ever done, and I didn't even have to touch the man," I explained.

"I can be a great asset," Pete added.

"He is dangerous, out of control, and sells pixie drugs," Shorty argued.

"Sounds like seventy percent of the rest of our staff," I reminded Shorty, who stopped fidgeting.

"Okay, you do have a point." Shorty frowned.

"Pete, if you do come work for us, we have some rules you will have to follow," I said. "Rule number one is Shorty is in charge. Can you handle that?"

"Yes, Boss Lady," Pete gave me a great imitation of Shorty.

"I don't like this," Shorty mumbled.

"That settles it. You can move in as soon as you can," I told Pete.

"Wait, are you serious?" Pete stopped smiling and stared at me.

"Why wouldn't I be serious?" I asked.

"Nobody hires pixies and they certainly don't offer us a place to live." It looked like Pete had tears filling his eyes.

"I guess it's a good thing I'm not just anyone." I lowered my voice. "Haven is very young, Pete. Things change here very quickly. We could use a guy with your skills here to help. It will also free up some of our time since we won't be chasing you around to stop you from selling drugs to kids."

"But I have twenty kids," Pete confessed, kicking the desk.

"Holy cow!" Shorty shouted. "No wonder you have to sell drugs."

"That's a lot of mouths to feed," I confessed. "Shorty, is the attic still abandoned?"

"Besides that crazy ghost that refuses to leave," Shorty said, reminding me that we had our very own gangster in the building.

"Do you mind living with a ghost?" I asked Pete. "Nobody else dares to go up to the attic because of him. He is pretty harmless, just loud."

"You are giving me the whole attic?" I nodded at Pete who started doing a variation of a rain dance. "I'll take it. Can I bring friends?"

"Dude, you already have twenty kids. How many more people you want in that place?" Shorty jumped in and I had to agree with him.

"It's really hard to find housing in this area. I was thinking I could run a motel," Pete explained.

"You are truly a hustler," I told him in a mocking tone. "You will have to run all that through Shorty. We do have special codes you would have to follow if you are planning to rent space to other beings."

"Not to mention you will need to give us a cut," Shorty said. "You are not using our space and making money out of it without paying the piper."

"Okay, now that sounds like a bunch of stuff I don't want to hear," I told them both. "Pete, I just want to confirm that I can trust the info the shifter told us."

"Absolutely, Boss Lady. That fool couldn't lie even if he wanted to," Pete announced, flying up to my face.

"Nice work, and welcome to the family," I told him. "I'll let you two figure things out from here.

"Follow me, Tricky Pete. We got paperwork for you to fill out." Shorty led Pete, who was asking a million questions, out the door.

Bob walked past them as Shorty ignored the pixie flying around his head.

"You do know you can't hire every soul you meet," Bob told me, taking a seat in front of me.

"Why not?" I asked. "We have the money, they have a skill set, and we get them off the streets. It's a win-win for everyone."

"You are a bleeding heart, Isis," Bob said kindly, scratching his head.

"Thanks, but you are not happy. What did Famine say?" I dropped my feet back on the ground and waited for Bob.

"Humans couldn't possibly pull that off," said Bob.

"But." There had to be a "but" in that sentence.

"Their people can," Bob finished.

I slammed my fist on the desk and cursed under my breath. "I'm going to choke those fools."

"Constantine said something similar, only with a lot of more colorful words," Bob said. "What do you want to do?"

"Call Constantine and tell me him to get Bartholomew and Junior ready. We are taking another trip to Mount Pleasant." And I was not happy about it.

"Will do." Bob pulled his phone from his pocket and headed out the door.

That bunch of lying, greedy bastards were going to get us all killed. I took a long, deep breath to calm myself. I didn't want to lose control and hurt someone in the process. Working smarter was more desirable than working harder, especially with how drained I'd been feeling lately.

Chapter Twenty-One

Bartholomew and Junior were outside of Reapers waiting for us. I had asked Bartholomew to bring me a couple of my MP3 players. We had pre-recorded versions of my knock-out music. After our last visit, I didn't want to even know how insane the security measures were going to be at the lab. Famine was busy analyzing the last shifter and couldn't be bothered to talk to us. Constantine was going to contact Eric to give him an update on all the excitement.

The drive to Mount Pleasant was going to cost us at least two hours—time we didn't have. It was a risk I was willing to take if we got to the bottom of what Famine's team of evil CEOs were up to. The layers of this madness just got more and more complicated. Sometimes, dealing with the horsemen and their group of assistants was a notorious cycle. Did the other interns feel the same way about us? I wondered, although I had no plans to ask them.

We rode in silence all the way to the chicken plant. Bartholomew and Junior were both busy surveying the blueprints of the lab on the laptop. Bob constantly peeked over his shoulder or through the rear-view mirror. I was expecting Jake's little patrol to follow us out of town, but they just waved when we passed. That was one creepy group of people.

The chicken plant's parking lot was full of cars. Bob parked in the same location as last time. I grabbed a pair of earplugs from the backpack Bartholomew had given me and handed them to Junior.

"Put these on," I told him.

"Why?" Junior asked as he watched Bartholomew and Bob put theirs on.

"It's going to prevent you from falling asleep once the recording starts playing," I answered.

"You can do that?" Junior hurried to insert his earplugs.

"Among other things, yes." I fixed my hair one last time and opened the door. "Time to party."

"Okay!" Junior shouted.

That was the bad thing about everyone wearing earplugs besides me: they were always shouting back. I headed towards the elevator entrance. Junior pressed his codes in and the doors opened. The ride was as smooth as the last time. The cameras in the ceiling were still dangling broken, but that didn't mean they hadn't added more.

"Everyone against the walls, now," I ordered the boys and they obeyed.

The elevator reached the ground level, and I pressed play on the MP3 player as the door opened. The Storm Trooper Welcome committee had tripled.

"Freeze," one yelled but it was too late.

The vibration of my music hit them, and they all collapsed to the ground. I placed the MP3 player by the door of the elevator facing the sleepy soldiers.

"Wow," Junior shouted, ogling all the soldiers on the ground. "That is one impressive trick."

"I can do that all day," I said, flipping my hair to the side. "Where are the main offices? We don't have a lot of time."

Junior led us down a series of corridors and offices. As we walked deeper into the facility, the sterile feeling disappeared, and a sense of wealth took over. The floors were hard wood, and mosaic walls added such elegance and beauty. Soft lighting flooded the hallway, while easy radio played in the background. Junior took one last turn that led to a large door at the end of the hallway.

"That way," Junior told us. "If any of the CEOs are here, they will be in that office."

"Do they all share one office?" Bartholomew asked.

"We rarely have them all in the facility at the same time," Junior explained. "Each CEO has their own area that they monitor, and John runs this one. In his absence, one of the girls acts as his second."

Rank structure for the other interns was always confusing to me. Death separated us by region, and nobody crossed into each other's area unless it was an emergency. If something happened to one of us, a new intern would be recruited. Nobody covered our back if we required help.

"I can override the codes to let us in," Bartholomew said, rushing to a control panel next to the door.

"I'm sure you can sweetie, but that just takes time," I told him. Without waiting for a response, I took my gun and shot the lock several times. That was the only reason I carried a regular gun with bullets, in case I wanted to destroy structures or furniture.

"Bob, would you do us the honor?" I moved out of the way to give Bob more room.

One swift kick and the door flew open. I switched guns and entered the room shooting at anything that moved. The large office was massive, and now littered with bodies of knocked-out Storm Troopers.

"I hope you order these guys by the dozen. It might be cheaper that way," I told our friendly, nasally CEO sitting on the extravagant desk at the end of the room. "Hi, John."

This guy did not believe in humble. Everything in the office was over the top and a bit gaudy. Even his name plate was platinum.

"What do you want?" John asked, standing up from his chair. "I told you everything I knew. I don't appreciate this treatment."

"I'm sure you told us everything." I walked around the desk and pushed John back down on his chair. "Somehow, you failed to mention that one of your little team members was working with a pack of Lions to modify the formula."

"I have nothing to do with that. It was all Melvin," John sputtered.

"Yes, the elusive Melvin that nobody has seen or heard of." I inched my face next to him, pressing the barrel of my gun to his gut. "Why am I having a hard time believing you? Where are your other friends?" Not that I was missing the group of evildoers, but it did feel a bit empty without them.

"Damage control was necessary," John told me. "If the news gets out that our supplements are responsible for major health hazards, we will have a huge liability on our hands."

"It's all about the bottom line. So proud of you guys." I patted John's shoulder. "Too bad I don't believe a word you are saying. You are coming with us."

"He is?" Bartholomew asked.

"We have a little pixie friend he has to meet," I told him.

"We have a pixie on staff?" Bartholomew stopped moving.

"And a dwarf," Bob added.

"I should spend a lot more time at the station. I'm missing out on everything." Bartholomew shook his head.

"We can definitely work on your schedule later, Bart, but right now, do your magic." I escorted Bartholomew towards the computer area as Bob moved John out of the way. "How long do you need?"

I never knew how long it would take Bartholomew to break into anything. Bartholomew sat on the chair and connected a few cables from his laptop to the desktop.

"No time at all," Bartholomew answered, pressing a lot of keys. "Mr. John saved me the time of figuring out his password, so give me seven minutes."

"Too easy," I told him and walked towards Bob.

"Duct tape?" Bob asked, holding John down.

"That would be poetic," I replied, grabbing a roll of duct tape from Bob's backpack.

"You don't have to do this. I will tell you anything," John said, trying to squirm away.

"Yes, you will," I agreed with him. "The difference is, now you will tell us the truth instead a bunch of corporate lies."

"Got it," Bartholomew exclaimed, unhooking all his cables.

"That was faster than seven minutes," Bob said.

"They might be ruthless corporate geniuses, but they are not very creative in their electronic filing system." Bartholomew walked around and headed out the door. "I'm pretty sure Famine will be thrilled to have all their notes back."

"No, you can't do that—" John started, but Bob put a large piece of duct tape over his mouth.

"It was going to be impossible driving back with him talking the whole way," Bob explained.

"I completely agree with you." I dragged John by the shirt as Bob cleared the way.

Having John get killed by his own security team as we kidnapped him would defeat the purpose of the mission. Only a few more Storm Troopers appeared between the office and the elevator. Our welcoming committee was still sound asleep by the door. I picked up my MP3 player and turned it off as John hit the floor face first.

"That is going to leave a mark," Bartholomew said.

"I totally forgot about this part," I admitted.

"It couldn't have happened to a nicer guy." Bob smirked.

We dragged John into the elevator and left the ground floor. Junior kept poking his old boss in the chest to make him wake up.

"He is going to be out for at least another thirty minutes," I told him. "Poking him is not going to help."

"He just looks so normal like that." Junior walked to the other side of John.

"He looks normal tied up with duct tape?" Bartholomew inquired, kicking John in the shins.

"John is always screaming and giving orders." Junior kneeled down next to the guy. "I have never seen him not yelling, and I've never seen his veins not popping out from his neck."

"This guy is the ideal candidate for a stroke or heart attack." Bob dragged John out when the doors opened at the surface level. "Where do you want him?"

"In the trunk. He doesn't deserve to have a seat," I answered.

Ring. Ring. Ring.

I pulled my phone from my pocket to find it was Constantine who was blowing me up.

"Where are you?" he barked.

"Loading Famine's fearless leader in the truck, why?" I watched Bob close the back of Killer before we climbed in.

"I need you now. Hurry." Constantine sounded out of breath.

"Okay, we are on our way," I told Constantine, who hung up.

"Bob, hurry. Constantine is in trouble." I buckled up and Bob slammed his door.

Constantine was alone with Famine. If that crazy horseman did something to him, I was going to beat the crap out of them. Right now, I couldn't handle any more drama in my life, and a worried Constantine was too much for me. Bob ignored every traffic law on the road and drove like Shorty back to Reapers.

Chapter Twenty-Two

If we had a contest to see who could drive the fastest, it would be a close one between Bob and Shorty. The only difference between their driving styles was the fact that Bob was not trying to take out every pedestrian he saw. Shorty found people on the road fair game to aim for. Texarkana was becoming a very dangerous city for the few people who enjoyed walking and running on the streets.

We arrived at Reapers faster than was legally possible. Bob had barely stopped when I dove out of the SUV and ran for the stairs. My mind was racing with horrible pictures of Constantine being tortured by Famine. I questioned Death's assessment that Constantine could handle himself, at least until I crashed through the door. Constantine was sitting on the table covered in papers while Famine played games on the big-screen TV.

"You are alive?" I asked Constantine.

"Why wouldn't I be alive?" Constantine replied, slapping my hands away from him. "What is wrong with you?"

"You sounded worried, and I thought something was happening to you." I sat on the kitchen table to stare at Constantine.

"Boss, are you okay?" Bob shouted as he, Bartholomew, and Junior ran in the room.

"Relax, everyone. Grouchy Pants is fine," Famine told us. "He has been whining all afternoon, but he is fine."

"Whining about what?" I asked Famine.

"No idea," Famine replied, slamming the controller on their leg.

"I need a place for this party!" Constantine screamed.

"That's it," I said, not sure if I should smack him. "You rushed us over here because of this stupid party?"

"Your Godmother is driving me nuts." Constantine shredded the papers he had. "She keeps vetoing every place I suggest. Something to do with nature and Ostara demanding proper respect. Do you think we have enough time to get a permit for Spring Lake?"

"No!" I shouted. "We are not doing anything in that park."

"I agree with Isis," Bob told Constantine. "That place is cursed. Unless you guys need me, I will be heading back to the station. I still have to deliver our prisoner to Pete."

"Thanks, Bob," I told him, watching Constantine make little circles on the table.

"What are we going to do?" Constantine finally dropped.

"Why can't you just cancel the party?" I asked, missing the big deal here.

"Have you lost your mind?" Constantine snapped his head up. "First of all, your Godmother would try to kill me. If that isn't enough of a reason, I already announced it to the world. We can't cancel now."

"Constantine, with everything going on, you really want to do this?" Was I the only person who thought this was nuts?

"Why don't you do it outside?" Bartholomew suggested.

"Outside where?" Constantine rolled over to look at him.

"Outside of here." Bartholomew pointed to the left side. "We own all that land. If we could get it cleaned up, get some tents, and decorate the space, it would probably be really nice."

"Bartholomew, you are a genius." Constantine tossed the papers around until he found one with a list.

"I can kill the vegetation if you would like," Famine offered.

"That is a nice gesture, but we cannot have a dead crop field for the Goddess of Spring," Constantine clarified.

I had to agree with him on that one. That would create a very strange vibe that not even my Godmother would be able to cleanse.

"Do you want us to call Shorty and see how many troops he can spare?" It was going to be a struggle to get enough people here to clear that field in time.

"No time. We require some serious muscle here." Constantine was still focusing on his lists when he spoke. "The trolls owe me a favor. I have to make some calls."

"I really don't want to know," I told the boys.

"Boss, I think we found your notes," Junior told Famine as he made his way towards the very-excited Famine playing Call of Duty.

"Really?" Famine asked, dropping the controller. "I need them."

Famine looked like they were going to charge Junior but stopped at the last moment.

"I have to download them," Bartholomew said. "Do you mind if I take over?"

"Please, go for it." Famine moved out of Bartholomew's way.

"Does anyone need me here for this?" I asked the boys, not sure what to make of the whole situation.

"I think we got this," Bartholomew replied from the computer station.

"In that case, I'm heading back to the station." I pulled my phone out and dialed Bob.

"Is everything okay?" Bob asked after only one ring.

"Nothing major, but I'm not necessary here." I searched my pockets, checking for my keys. I'd left Ladybug outside

Reapers when we picked up Bartholomew and Junior. "Get John ready for interrogation. We must get answers now."

"Does that mean you are heading our way?" Bob asked with a chuckle. "Are you running away from event decorating?"

"Look who is talking. You left me here first," I joked back.

"That situation was turning scary incredibly fast," Bob admitted.

"You don't know the half of it," I told him.

I left the building through the security doors. It was incredible that it took the same amount of time to leave as it did to enter. Bartholomew was paranoid someone would walk out of Reapers with a top secret. I had no idea what kind of secret we had that someone would want to steal, but I didn't argue with him.

Once outside, I stopped to stare at the space next to Reapers. I had no idea how Constantine was going to transform that run-down area into a spring paradise. I got in Ladybug and took off before I was volunteered to help with the process.

The sun was starting to set by the time I got to the Station. I had been doing lots of driving around today and still had very little to show for it. After all the people in the station this morning, it was strange to see the place so quiet. The night crew would be coming soon to watch the phones and take over. Shorty had a twenty-four-hour operation that rarely stopped.

"Good evening, Ms. Isis," a man said from the side.

"Good evening, Mr. Mark," I replied.

Mr. Mark was the chief of the cleaning crew and he was in his late seventies. He believed in leading from the front and he even scheduled himself for mopping duties. Everyone in the underground was gainfully employed.

When Shorty hired Mr. Mark, he was too old to serve on the street crew and computers intimidated him, so he volunteered to take over the cleaning of the building. When the dorms were added to the station, he agreed to clean those as well. He was a one-man show that transformed a dirty-looking building into a respectful establishment.

Now, anyone who was too old or not physically able to work the street came to Mr. Mark. The place was immaculate, and the crew took pride in their work. It was not unheard of for someone to get hit in the head with a dustpan for dropping food on the ground. We all required purpose in our lives, and Mr. Mark gave them that. At times, he was even tougher than Shorty and Bob—if that was possible.

"You are going to be late if you just stand there, Boss Lady," Mr. Mark reminded me.

"Have I told you how grateful I am for your work?" I asked Mr. Mark.

"Every day, Boss Lady, every day." He saluted me and went on mopping the floors.

Nope, I didn't regret giving work to people.

I ran down the stairs to find Bob and Shorty in the viewing room.

"What are you two doing?" I asked them. "I thought you were going to prep John."

"No need," Bob said. "Pete said he could make him talk."

"That pixie and his army of little pixies should earn their check," Shorty told me. "I'm all about him doing as much work as possible."

"You are bad, Shorty," I told him, sliding between the two men. "How is he doing?"

"Look for yourself." Bob moved to the side to give me more room.

John was sitting on the same chair Luke had been sitting earlier, giving us a clear view of his face. Pete paced on the table and slapped a stick on his hand.

"What is that supposed to be?" I asked the boys.

"We have no idea," replied Bob.

Peter stopped in the center of the table to face John, who was trembling from head to toe. His face was covered in sweat and he looked like he was going to pass out any minute.

"Now listen here, John. My boss is a very angry man and he wants some answers," Pete told John, walking closer to his face.

"He got that right," Shorty said, straightening his shirt.

"You two are going to be really good friends." I shook my head. This was a friendship made in hell.

"What were you going to do with those supplements?" Pete screamed at John, which was really impressive, considering his size.

John flinched, trying to pull away from the diabolical pixie. "I don't know what you are talking about!" he cried.

"You don't know what I'm talking about? Really?" Pete flew over John's head, sprinkling him with dust.

Tears ran down John's eyes and loud sobs escaped his mouth. Pete flew closer and closer to John's face, tapping the bridge of John's nose with the stick.

"I don't know about you, but that would definitely scare the crap out of me," I told Bob and Shorty.

"Oh, trust me. A six-inch man with a stick to my eyeball would make me confess to anything," Bob said, agreeing with me.

"I think I like him," Shorty admitted.

"We are in trouble," I told Bob.

"Speak!" Pete yelled, making the walls vibrate.

"Go, Pete! Break him!" Shorty cheered for the pixie as I slowly moved away from him.

"We were supposed to be rich," John said, holding back the sobs.

"You are rich, you bastard." Pete smacked John in the ear with his stick. "Continue before I lose my patience."

"We were supposed to sell the supplements during the Equinox before Greg got greedy and betrayed us," John said, the information pouring from him because of the dust. "Warnings were sent to all the pack leaders that if they wanted to remain in control, they would either pay the money or watch their litters kill each other."

"How did Greg betray you?" Pete asked, sitting on John's shoulder.

"He stole the formula and the supplements, then he set up his own auction at the Cave two days ahead of us," John answered out of breath.

"Why would he do that?" Pete rocked back and forth, playing with John's earlobe and making the poor man jump every time.

"He found out we were planning to blame the whole thing on his pack." John swallowed hard. "We sent the lion boys to retrieve it and make it look like a rival gang stole it."

"Nasty." Pete gave John another smack. "You betrayed the guy, then you had him killed and blamed him for the mess. You are one evil little human."

"He is not going to last long," I told the boys.

I walked to the interrogation room and cracked open the door. I signaled for Pete to come out and he flew off John's shoulder, spraying him with more dust on his way.

"Pete, stop playing with him," I said. "We need to know where the formula is located before he passes out."

"I'm doing good here," Pete argued.

"You are doing great," I agreed. "But he is not going to last long, and I really would like to get that formula tonight."

"You know you can't rush art," Pete said, flying in front of my face and waving his arms.

"I'm sure we can't, but your artwork is drooling." I turned Pete to face John who was turning bluish.

"Oh shit." Pete flew back in John's direction and slapped John around a few times.

I went back to the viewing room to find Shorty cracking up.

"What did I miss?" I asked Bob.

"You don't want to know," Bob told me.

If Bob said I didn't want to know, I never asked. There was no reason to torture myself with unneeded information.

"John, where is the formula?" Pete was back to shouting at John.

"With Melvin," John mumbled.

"Great," Pete said getting closer to John's face. "Where is Melvin?"

"At … Oak … at …" John couldn't finish his sentence.

"Dude, this is going to hurt you more than me," Pete told him as he poked him in the neck with his stick.

John screamed but woke up.

"Better," Pete said. "Once again, where is Melvin?"

"At the Wild Oak Circle," John said, breathing deeply.

"You have unlimited funds and you picked a house there, why?" Pete was back in John's face.

"Nobody looks at discrete locations," John answered, unable to keep his head up.

"Shorty, get Pete out of there," I ordered. "Nobody cares why the evil CEOs pick their locations."

Shorty ran out of the viewing room towards the interrogation room. Pete was busy asking John ten other questions regarding choices of hideout and proper planning procedures. Shorty had to pull Pete away to stop the interrogation.

"Tell me I'm the greatest," Pete said when Shorty brought him in the room.

"You are good, but not the greatest yet," I said. "Next time, stay focused on pertinent information."

"Motives are the key to everything," Pete said.

"These motives are all about money, so nothing new there," I told the group.

"True, but now what?" In his excitement, dust sprinkled from Pete, coating parts of the room.

"First, calm down before you get us all high," I told Pete, pushing him back with my hands.

"Sorry about that, Boss Lady," Pete said as he looked at the pile of pixie dust everywhere.

"I recommend you clean that up or Mark is going to beat you tonight," Shorty whispered to Pete.

"I heard about him," Pete said in a soft tone.

"Don't mess with Mr. Mark and his building," Bob told Pete, observing the hall.

"Mr. Mark is downstairs and not what we should be focused on right now." I told them, but none of them looked very convinced. "Shorty, send a team over to Wild Oak Circle to find us the exact house. The rest of us get ready to storm the place."

"On it," Shorty announced, leaving the room.

"I want to head home to grab some weapons," I told Bob.

"No problem, I will meet you there," Bob replied. "I'm going to take John to the infirmary to get his stomach pumped before I leave."

"Great idea." Thank God Bob thought of that. "Thanks Pete."

"I like this job," Pete said, puffing up his chest. "Do you need me for anything else?"

"I think we are good for tonight," I answered.

"Good, I have a family to settle in now." Pete flew over my head. "Good night, Boss Lady."

"Good night, Pete." I watched the little pixie leave the area singing to himself.

I took the stairs two at a time while making a mental list of everything I should pack.

Ring.

I was starting to hate my phone.

"Hello," I said, not bothering to look at the caller ID.

"Isis, what is going on?" Eric asked, almost yelling at me.

"You should be more specific," I told the angry witch.

"I have strangers all around Texarkana in SUVs," said Eric.

"Those are Jake's demons and their entourage of weird humans," I told Eric as I made it outside to my private parking space. "Recommend you stay away; they are a bit angry."

"It seems Constantine forgot to mention that part." Eric's voice had dropped a few decibels.

"That sounds like him," I replied

Eric cursed, and I had to laugh. I didn't realize Eric knew such a colorful vocabulary.

"Eric, I got to go. Please stay clear of the demons." I disconnected before Eric could give me a lecture.

With everything going on today, nobody had time for lectures. I barely had time for meals and sleep. I put Ladybug in gear and headed to Reapers. This was going to be another long night in haven.

Chapter Twenty-Three

Wild Oak Circle was literally a semi-circle in the middle of Pleasant Grove, a quiet residential area with modern houses. There was nothing out of the ordinary in the neighborhood, especially no flashing lights indicating evildoers lived in the area. Shorty had sent the Triplets and two others to scout the block. They had narrowed the search to a house at the center of the loop.

Father, please don't let us blow up another house.

If blowing up houses and trucks weren't such a common part of our everyday life, I would never need that prayer. Obviously, we were those kinds of people.

Bob and I joined the team across the street from the house behind one of our SUVs. Shorty climbed down a tree and walked across the yard towards us.

"What in God's name were you doing in that tree?" I asked Shorty, trying to keep my voice down.

"Better point of view," Shorty explained. "I had a clear view of the entire area."

"Shorty, are you trying to kill yourself?" I had no idea how old Shorty was, but he was definitely too old be to climbing trees. "If you fall from that tree, the last person you will see is me when I deliver you to Death. Knock that crap out."

"Boss Lady, you cannot deny the advantage of the location," Shorty argued.

"What did you learn up there?" I looked up at the huge tree.

"Nothing yet, but if I stay there long enough, I'm sure I will learn everything about this area." Shorty looked around like he had x-ray vision.

"Shorty, it's dark and the only thing you are going to learn up there is you can't see a thing." I pulled Shorty back before he tried to climb up again.

"Isis is right, and I'm pretty sure our insurance does not cover self-inflicted wounds," Bob told him.

"You two are just jealous because you didn't think about it yourself and are afraid I will make you look bad." In order to sound even more like a three-year-old, all Shorty had to do was end that sentence with nah, nah, nah.

"Whatever you say, Shorty. Just keep your happy, little butt on the ground." I pulled him down next to me. "Here, see if your night vision can spot anything in that house."

Shorty took the binoculars and aimed towards the house. Bob reviewed the map the Triplets brought, examining it for a good entry point.

"Has anyone entered or left that house?" I asked the team.

"Nobody in the last thirty minutes," one of Triplets told me. "To be honest, we haven't seen a single soul in this entire block."

For a school night, that was strange. Bob and I did the same thing and turned around to look at all the houses. They were all dark. Like the entire area had vacated for the night.

"I don't like this," said Bob.

"Let's just get in and get out," I replied.

"I like that plan," Shorty added. "Hey, I see something by the window."

We all peered over the SUV and waited. The house was the only one with lights on, but still, I couldn't see any movement from where I stood. Hopefully, the binoculars were what helped Shorty see better and he wasn't just making things appear in his head.

"We might as well go," I told them after waiting three more minutes. "If someone is in there, we're not going to see them from here."

"We don't have a lot of options," Bob agreed.

"Follow me, and everyone keep your eyes open." I gave the hand signal, and everyone moved in on my mark.

Bob took point with me in the middle and Shorty brought up the rear. We reached the door and still couldn't hear anything from inside the house. Everyone was in position and I gave Bob the thumbs up to proceed. He took aim and kicked the door open. I busted in, running to the right while Shorty followed behind me and went left, all of us staying low to the ground. One minute, the living room was desolate, and the next minute, three lions were charging at us from different directions.

"Holy cow!" Shorty screamed at the top of his lungs as a lion pounced in his direction.

I pulled Shorty by the back of the shirt before the lion could land on top of him. Bob was right behind us and used the butt of his rifle to whack one of the lions, which made him fall flat on his back. It was probably more the shock of being hit that knocked him down, though, because the lion was back on his paws in no time. I placed Shorty behind me and switched from my gun to my scythe. I knew it had been a good idea going back to get it.

I extended the scythe in time to block lion number three from biting my head off. The beast was huge and strong enough to push me down. I landed several kicks to the lion's side, but he didn't even flinch. His jaws descended on me, and from that position I could count each one of his teeth. It sure seemed like there were way more than there should be. They also looked much too sharp for my liking.

"Take this!" Shorty's battle cry made the lion turn.

Shorty opened fire on the room. I had no idea how he managed to fire all seventy rounds before taking the three lions out. The lion pinning me crushed me when his shot hit it. I was having an incredibly hard time breathing. Then, I realized Shorty must have had Eugene's special rounds because all the hair fell from the beast, landing on me and making me sneeze. My stomach turned.

"Help," I squealed, unable to move.

"Isis, where are you?" Bob shouted.

"Underneath the mountain of hair and the huge lion." I wiggled underneath but didn't budge an inch.

"Got you," Bob told me, pushing the hairless lion off. "Oh wow, you look like a hot mess."

"Thanks," I said. "I'm going to be pulling fur out of my hair for a week. Shorty, I thought we weren't using those rounds." I narrowed my eyes at him.

"Nope. You said you weren't using those rounds," Shorty clarified. "I never agreed to that deal. Not to mention, Boss Lady, there is no way a regular tranquilizer bullet would take out one of those beasts."

"That shouldn't be a problem because you fired all your rounds, anyway." I walked over to the wall where half of his bullets landed. "Shorty, when was the last time you went to the range? Your aim is atrocious."

"It's not his aim. Shorty needs glasses," Bob informed me.

"You need glasses?" I yelled at him. "What were you doing on top of that tree you blind bat? Are you trying to get yourself killed?"

Shorty pressed his lips together, refusing to answer as he pretended to clean his gun. It took everything in me not to reach over and choke some sense into him.

"Isis, we got blood here!" Bob shouted from across the room.

"Nobody was bitten, right?" I looked around the room to make sure our team was okay.

"This is too much blood for a simple bite," Bob said, following the trail.

"Are you sure it's safe?" Shorty asked Bob, hiding behind me. "I am all out of bullets here."

"I got you covered," I told Bob, moving right behind him.

The trail led to the back of the house to what looked like the bedrooms. I made sure everyone was silent before nodding to Bob to open the door. This time, we didn't rush in but slowly peeked into the room. The scene was out of a nightmare. Blood was spread all over the walls and weird lumps were scattered around. My mind had a hard time processing all the pieces until I saw Death standing by a window with a man—or what used to be a man and was now his soul.

"Isis, keep everyone outside," Death told me.

"Back up, everyone," I ordered, holding my breath.

"I'm going to be sick." One of the Triplets left the room covering his mouth.

"What happened here?" I asked Death, trying to avoid gaping at all the scattered body parts.

"Treason," Death said softly, holding the man by the shoulder. "It seems Melvin had no intentions of keeping his part of the bargain with the lions and they were not happy about it."

"How many groups are Famine's CEOs planning to betray this week?" I asked Death.

"If you are willing to betray your boss knowing the power they hold, you will do anything imaginable," Death told me. "Melvin, it's time to go."

Death escorted Melvin to the living room where Jake stood in the middle of the pile of fur examining the hairless lion.

"This one is not it, either. Where is my shooter?" Jake asked, his voice so loud it bounced off the walls.

"Why are you here?" I asked Jake as soon as I was close enough to him.

"To make sure you do your job and I get my trespasser." Jake stopped and looked at Death. "Who is that?"

"One of the people who planned the attack on your club. I was planning on delivering him, but since you are here ..." Death handed Melvin over to Jake who sniffed the man.

"This one had a horrible, painful death. That's what I'm talking about." Jake licked his lips and handed the man to Adam, who was standing in the doorway cleaning his nails.

Melvin didn't even flinch when Adam grabbed him. His gaze was distant and not even a sound escaped his lips when they transported him back to hell.

"Just because you handed me one dead human does not mean I'm satisfied," Jake told me.

"Why are you yelling at me? Death is right there." I pointed at my boss.

"I'm sure Isis will secure your trespasser by the appointed time," Death told Jake.

"Huh?" I mouthed to Death.

Did she know something I didn't? I had no clues, no witnesses, and no idea where to go next.

"With you securing the exits of haven, it's only a matter of time until they are found." Death tapped Jake on the shoulder, and he flinched.

That was interesting news. Even the Devil feared Death.

"We really appreciate your support on this, Jake," Death told him.

"No, we don't," yelled Shorty from the door.

"My team has some cleaning up to do here. Unless you want to help?" Death walked Jake to the door where he left without saying another word.

"That was smooth, Boss," Bob told Death.

"Sometimes, it's easier to kill them with kindness than weapons, but that won't last long." Death crossed the room to inspect the lions. "These three have not been infected."

"Did Melvin say anything to you?" I asked Death.

"He mumbled something about his guy not making it to the location and his pack was blaming him," said Death. "Does that mean anything to you?"

"The two ninjas that attacked the Cave were part of this pack," I explained. "They separated when Jake locked haven down. We have one in custody but the other is missing."

"The question is who is betraying whom?" I asked the group. "Did Famine's CEOs set their colleague up to die, or did the other lion betray their pack?"

"My head hurts," Shorty exclaimed. "We have too many traitors and still one missing formula. Famine should get better friends."

"Shorty, you are so right about that," Death told him. "I recommend you get this place cleaned and keep searching. Jake is not going to give up until he gets his shooter."

Death snapped her fingers and disappeared. I sighed. The place was a disaster from one side of the house to the other.

"Shorty, call the sanitation crew," Bob told him.

"Already done, Big Bob." Shorty waved his phone in the air. "They are going to have a field day with this house."

"Isis, are you okay?" Bob asked.

"Yeah, I'm heading home, though. I'm craving a nap," I told Bob. I also wanted a hot shower, but I wasn't sharing that with the group. "Nice job, everyone."

"Nice job?" Shorty spun around.

"We breached the perimeter, took on three lions, and nobody died. That is a huge victory in my book." Lately, we needed to celebrate all the small victories.

"Looking at it that way, go team!" Shorty shouted.

"Good night," I told the boys and headed out the door.

I walked slowly towards Ladybug in the dark street. The lights in the other houses were still off, which was another huge blessing. We really didn't have much to go on, but at least our team was not hurt. With all the crazy going on, that was something to be grateful for.

Chapter Twenty-Four

The business park was glowing with strange lights that could be seen from Texarkana. I shouldn't have been surprised to find out the party responsible for the mysterious lights was Constantine. If anything, Constantine should be my first guess for everything out of the ordinary that happened around here. That crazy cat had outdone himself this time. A major construction project was taking place next to Reapers.

I had the urge to ignore the whole thing and pretend I didn't see it, but Bartholomew and Famine were outside and they saw me. I parked Ladybug next to Reapers and walked over to them. Famine and Bartholomew were sitting on the edge of the construction field on some stone benches by a fire pit. The air smelled like cinnamon.

"What are you two doing out here?" I asked them as I took a seat next to Bartholomew.

"I'm making s'mores," Bartholomew told me.

"And you?" I asked Famine.

"Waiting and spying on Constantine as he bosses people around," Famine told me, studying the construction site.

There were at least five trolls all over ten feet tall carrying rocks, moving trees out of the ground and setting up poles in a rectangular shape. Dwarves were running in between the trolls carrying tree trunks to each of them, while others moved the rocks the trolls delivered. In the center of the chaos stood Constantine, directing people like a maestro in an orchestra.

"What exactly is he trying to do?" I asked.

"It looks like a rock garden met a natural canopy," Famine explained. "If he can pull that off in the short amount of time he has, the look is going to be breathtaking under the stars."

"That is a big if," I told him.

We watched in silence as Constantine moved people from one side to the other as quickly as possible. At some point, Bartholomew handed both Famine and me s'mores. Bartholomew had toasted the marshmallows to perfection, and the chocolate was melted to hold the cracker together into a sandwich of amazing goodness.

"Is this gluten-free?" I asked him after shoving the last piece in my mouth.

"You bet." Bartholomew didn't even bother to look at me. "Bob got me all the ingredients last week. And you know he thinks of everything. Where is Bob?"

"Cleaning up a crime scene," I said softly.

"Who died?" Famine asked over their shoulder.

"Um ..." I trailed off, not sure how to tell them.

"What happened?" Famine faced me.

"Well, the victim was Melvin," I whispered.

Famine stared at the fire pit before talking. "How did he die?"

"Torn apart by the pack of lions he betrayed," I finally told them.

"Ouch, that sounds painful," Famine said and went back to watching Constantine and his project.

"That's it? You don't have any other questions or anything else to say?" Famine didn't even look sad for the loss.

"Melvin was never one of my favorites," Famine answered. "He was always too arrogant and thought he knew everything. I'm not really surprised about his ending. People should not be meddling in things they don't understand."

"You do know we still haven't found your formula?" I told them.

"I figured that much." Famine observed me. "If you had the formula, you would have told me the moment you pulled up and dragged me to the lab to get working."

"You do have a point there." I licked my fingers where the chocolate had dripped on them.

"Here you go." Bartholomew handed me another s'more. "I hate eating alone and Famine said they were only having one."

"You are missing out, Famine." I took a big bite from my second s'more and indulged in myself.

"Am I interrupting?" TJ asked from behind me.

"Good. You are my last one." Famine handed TJ an envelope they were sitting on and cleaned their hands on their pants.

"What is that?" I asked.

"Constantine's invitation to the packs for the Equinox," Famine explained. "Something about bringing everyone in as a sign of peace or something like that. I wasn't listening, honestly. My job was to hand out the invitations when the packs arrive. Mission accomplished, so I'm heading inside." Famine stood up and brushed their pants carefully, waving at TJ and skipping to the entrance of Reapers. Bartholomew and I watched them enter the building humming.

"Famine is wild," Bartholomew told me. "I'll be right back; I'm going to give Constantine a s'more."

"Bart, please be careful in the middle of that mess." The trolls were flinging rocks and not paying attention to the people moving around the area.

"You don't look very happy," TJ told me.

"Constantine is still having his equinox party tomorrow, Jake has the city surrounded by demons, and we have no clue how to find Famine's formula. 'Not happy' might be one of the many understatements of the week." I covered my face with my hands.

"If anyone can pull this off, it's you," TJ told me. "Good news, at least you didn't say you were mad at me."

I looked up and TJ was kneeling by my side. "I wasn't mad at you."

"Right. You just refused to look me in the eyes." TJ kissed my cheek. "Get some rest, Isis. Tomorrow is going to be a long day." He left before I could reply, but my hand went to the spot TJ had kissed me and a smile spread across my face.

"Aren't you precious?" a man said from behind me.

I spun around to find Iason standing there. Iason was an elf prince, six-feet-four inches with strawberry-blond hair, a chiseled jaw line, aqua eyes, and a body to make every action hero envious. His twin sister Genevieve was in love with a vampire and expecting his child.

"How long have you been standing there?" I stood as quickly as possible. The last thing I needed was to be looking up at Iason.

"Long enough to see the sweet, little shifter displaying his love for you," Iason mocked me.

"Did you know he was a shifter?" I asked.

"You didn't know he was?" Iason inched closer to me. "I thought Death had given you her sixth sense."

"If you mean the third sight, yes I have that." I tried to back away, but the fire pit was in the way. "But I don't go analyzing everyone with my third eye because that's kind of rude and creepy."

"Have you ever considered that it could save your life?" Iason glanced down at me and I felt a strong pull towards him.

"If you are doing that glamor thing, I suggest you stop it before I stab you," I told the pretentious elf.

"I'm not doing a thing; you are just changing the subject." He moved a loose strand of hair from my forehead and the touch gave me goosebumps all over my body.

I blinked several times to concentrate. "Do you know how terrifying it is to see a demon in its true form with your third sight?"

"I have seen plenty, trust me. But seeing the truth is the easiest way to stay alive." Iason angled his head towards me, somehow even closer than before.

"Iason, you made it," Constantine shouted from behind us.

"I wouldn't miss it for the world," Iason told Constantine, not moving away from me.

"Please tell me you didn't invite him," I asked Constantine, squirming to get away from Iason.

"Don't be rude, Isis. Iason and his family are our partners now, remember?" Constantine knew there was no way I would have forgotten that since I was going to be the godmother to Genevieve's unborn child.

"Are you inviting all of our partners to this party?" How many partners did we have that I didn't know about?

"It's a unity party, so I'm inviting everyone." Constantine's tone sounded very festive.

"Are you inviting Pestilence?" I looked down at my fearless guardian, knowing how much he despised that horseman.

"Sorry. We have a two horsemen limit per party, so we are maxed out," Constantine replied in that fake but cheerful voice.

"Nice comeback," I told him.

"It is my pleasure to be here to represent my family during the festivities." Iason gave Constantine a bow.

"How is Ginny?" I asked, changing the topic.

"On bed rest and hating every minute." Iason tittered. "Elf pregnancies are complicated during normal cases, but with Ginny, the risks even are higher. The midwives have her under constant observation."

Ginny was a walking miracle, or maybe a magical phenomenon. She was expecting a child from a vampire, and that made the supernatural world go wild. Unfortunately, Ginny was also one of her Father's top Generals, so staying still was not her natural state.

"I feel bad for that midwife," I told Iason.

"Why do you think I'm glad to be here?" Iason winked at me.

"You are running away from your sister, huh?" I smirked.

"I don't see you volunteering to spend some time with the little, pregnant lady." Iason was right. A pregnant elf with mood swings was too much for me.

"Fine, I will keep your secret if you keep mine." I extended my hand, and he took it.

"This is such a weird human ritual," Iason told me, holding my hand.

"You can let go any minute now." I tugged at my hand, but he held tighter.

"Do I make you nervous, Isis?" Iason grinned, coming closer again.

"No, I just have a hard time deciding when you are trying to bewitch me with your power." I wiggled my hand again, but he still wouldn't let go.

"Once. Only once and never again." Iason raised my hand to his lips and kissed it.

"Well, that is different," I said, trying to catch my breath.

"Are you two done flirting?" Constantine told us.

My cheeks warmed. I'd totally forgot he was still standing next to us.

"I was not flirting," I mumbled.

"I was," Iason confessed.

"Time for me to go." I marched to Ladybug as quickly as I could.

That was one strange situation I had no way of clarifying in my head. I really did not need an elven prince flirting with me, especially an extremely handsome one. Nope, I had enough issues with everything going on in haven so far. I drove around the building. At least Constantine had left the vehicle entrance clear from his construction. Inside Reapers, I parked Ladybug in my usual spot and headed for the loft. I still wanted a shower, or maybe a long bath would be better. Either way, I wanted some quiet time away from confusing boys.

Chapter Twenty-Five

The Equinox was in less than eighteen hours and we still hadn't caught a break. Normally, I felt energized after my run, but today was completely the opposite. I had the strangest sensation that I was being watched, even though the streets were empty. That was the nerve-racking part. There were no cars driving around anywhere. It was a Thursday and I should have seen people heading to work at the Depot. I saw nobody, and it was almost like everyone had taken the day off.

The lights were off for Constantine's construction project, so I wasn't able to see the progress on my way to my run. Now that the sun was out, I should be able to see what that crazy cat had been up to all night. It was a good thing we were the only residents in the area because people would have complained with all the noise and lights. Eric must have pulled some strings to have the cops avoid the area as well.

"Wow!" I had no other words to describe Constantine's masterpiece.

"Good morning, Ms. Isis." I followed the sound of the voice.

"Good morning, Trish." Trish was my favorite gnome in town.

She was less than ten inches tall, but she looked like a walking flower with petals and branches everywhere. Trish lived with her husband in the Sacred Heart Cemetery on Texas Boulevard.

"Please tell me Constantine didn't drag you into this?" The cat had a way of getting his way regardless what it cost.

"I'm thrilled to do it." Trish twirled around, sprinkling flowers everywhere. "I'm in charge of the flower decorations. Do you like them?"

I followed Trish inside the living pavilion they had built. The entire thing was made of trees, limbs, and natural materials. The ceiling looked like the trees had merged together to form a cover. The ground was shrouded in river rocks that created a pattern almost like waves. Rock and wood benches were scattered all around the area in a casual arrangement. He even had a small fountain in the center. The crazy chandeliers we ordered hung around the ceiling like falling stars.

"This is incredible," I told Trish. "Don't tell Constantine I said that."

Trish giggled. "He already knows."

"He is going to brag about this for months." I couldn't blame him if he did because he had outdone himself. "Are you almost done?"

"Oh, no." Trish planted a small seed next to the fountain. "I have trails to create and must make sure none of the trees die before their roots settle in."

"Are they alive?" I spun in a circle, eyeing the space with an even greater appreciation.

"Isn't it glorious?" Trish was dancing and I couldn't blame her.

"I can't imagine a better place to welcome spring than here." This was truly beautiful.

Which meant Constantine would have tons of high school kids from now on doing prom pictures here. He would lose his mind with all the trespassers. That thought made me giggle.

"Trish, I will leave you to finish your work." I waved at the little gnome.

"See you tonight, Ms. Isis." Trish went back to singing to her trees and sprinkling seeds everywhere.

"With everything going on, he is going to have a party?" Eric asked as he walked across the field in my direction.

"Good morning to you, too, Eric," I replied.

Eric was wearing his cop uniform and looked fabulous in it. I really had a thing for a man in a uniform.

"Sorry. Good morning, Isis." Eric stopped to look at the Garden of Eden. "It is beautiful."

"It is hard to deny the genius of Constantine, but on the other hand, his timing could use some improvement." I stretched my thighs while Eric spoke.

"Do you have any news?" Eric asked, watching Trish work.

"Besides the fact that we are running out of time, no. Nothing." Shifting, I stretched my calves.

"We have more demons surrounding the area and you can feel the tension in the air." Eric started pacing around me. The man was a professional pacer.

"Don't you have any good news for me? I already know about all the bad stuff." Eric's mood was making me nervous, so I switched to a tree pose to calm myself down.

"My chief wants to meet with you and the team." That news took me off guard and I lost my balance. Eric caught me before I landed on the ground.

"Chief? What chief?" I tried to recover from my near fall, but I was not very smooth.

"The police chief," Eric clarified.

"The civilian police chief?" I asked.

"Isis, why are you making this so difficult?" Eric's breath came heavier than before.

"Because you are a witch, so how am I supposed to know you don't have a witch chief somewhere that you report to?" Nobody explained hierarchies in the witch world to me.

"Your Godmother is the high priestess of the Order. How do you know so little about things?" Eric shook his head at me.

"First of all, I just found out about that, and second, I have too many issues learning about horsemen to pick up an entire Order." I was not apologizing to Eric for my ignorance, at least not today.

"The police chief of Texarkana. The same one who is terrified we are going to have another episode like Halloween." Eric planted his hands on his hips and looked like an action Ken doll.

"Got it. Calm down," I told him. "I don't think this is a good idea, but I don't have much choice, do I?

"No, you don't," Eric confirmed.

"Fine. When does your boss want to meet?" This was going to be an interesting conversation between a human and a talking cat.

"Today at eleven," said Eric.

"Okay, we are not wasting any time." I looked down at my watch and it was close to seven now. "Fine. See you at eleven."

"Great," Eric replied, breathing a little slower. "And Isis, you need to add some burpees to your regiment. Your arms are getting a little soft."

"I hate you," I told Eric as he left for his car.

Just because he enjoyed torturing himself with insane exercises did not give him the right to judge the rest of us. My arms were not soft.

"You do have a lot of suitors. And by the way, your arms look fine," Iason whispered in my ear, making me jump.

"Where did you come from?" I spun around to ask him.

"Here and there," he replied.

"That is not an answer," I told him. "Why are you here so early? Shouldn't you be sunbathing somewhere?"

"I came to ask you to breakfast. You do eat breakfast, yes?" Iason looked me up and down.

"Of course, I eat." I avoided making eye contact with him. "But I'm a little busy, so this is really bad timing."

"There will never be a good time with you, dear. Chaos follows you all the time," said Iason, getting close to me. "But as godparents to the first royal child in over five-hundred years, we have duties to fulfill."

"Duties?" Ginny had not mentioned anything about duties in her proposal.

"We have notices to send out, welcoming parties to set-up," Iason said, counting with his fingers.

"Is that like a revealing party or a baby shower?" I was not properly trained for this kind of stuff.

"A little of both, just a lot fancier and complicated." Iason was exasperated.

"Is it possible that the prince does not enjoy parties?" I teased him.

"I'm a warrior and so is Ginny, so these kinds of events are exhausting to us." Iason adjusted his jacket. "Unfortunately, some traditions have to be honored, which means we have work to do."

"Why can't we just hire Constantine?" I asked softly. "Obviously, he is a master at last-minute planning and over the top events."

"I wish, but we are it." Iason looked back at Constantine's creation. "He does have talent. I saw this quaint little restaurant with a wagon on top, so let's meet there."

"The Chuckwagon?" I asked.

"Is that what it's called?" he asked, nodding in approval.

"Yes," I replied, not nearly as excited as he was.

"Perfect. See you at seven-thirty and don't be late." Iason tapped my nose with his finger before walking away.

"What is it with men and unrealistic deadlines?" I ran to Reapers to get ready.

It never failed that every time I was running late, things took longer than I hoped for. I waited for the security system, tapping my foot. It felt like the doors were playing with my emotions and refused to open. When the last one finally did, I darted inside.

"Isis!" Junior shouted, standing by the door of the lab holding a pile of papers.

"Hi, Junior. I'm a little late," I told him, but he kept marching towards me.

"They can't do it," Junior told me in a rush.

"Who can't do what? What are you talking about?" I stopped to listen to him.

"Nobody can do it except the boss," Junior rambled.

"Junior, how long have you been up? You look awful." I normally wasn't that blunt, but he had more bags under his eyes than I did.

"I was studying the boss's notes." Junior showed me the pages that looked like a bunch of fancy scribbles. "Famine is a genius."

"It does help that Famine is a horseman and older than dirt," I reminded him.

"Yes, I know, but there are hundreds of entries here." Junior kept turning pages, and I was still not following him. "That's why it took me so long. They can't do it."

"You do know I still have no idea what you are talking about," I told him. "Start from the beginning and slowly this time."

"There is no way to change the formula without the boss. They can't mutate it to make it airborne or target any individual shifter," Junior announced excitedly.

"That is really good news," I said. "Go on."

"I was tracking his notes and there is a common ingredient that turns the products from basic to the final level." Junior looked like he was going to explode with eagerness.

"Stop with the suspense and just tell me." He was dragging this out and I was running out of time.

"Breath," Junior told me with a grin.

I just blinked. "You are kidding me." I was going to strangle him. "That does not make any sense."

"Not any breath, but Famine's breath." Junior was back to talking really fast and flipping pages like a madman. "That's what the boss calls the missing link. Famine has been adding their essence or magic to all of their most deadly supplements."

"Famine has been using magic to outperform Pestilence?" I told Junior. "Its official, Famine is moving up as one of the most cunning horsemen. I like it."

"It explains why some diets and supplements work better than others," Junior continued. "Not all are branded with the breath and only the ones designed to cause maximum damage have it."

"Are you saying this one is not as bad?" Shifters attacking humans sounded pretty bad to me.

"Oh, it's bad. But only to those who take it," said Junior. "And the people they attack. Which means we still need to get all the cases back and the formula."

"Why can't Famine develop a cure from their notes?" I asked Junior.

"The notes describe the ingredients, the intent, and findings about it." Junior showed me a paragraph. "The specific amount used for each ingredient is in the formula. It doesn't help that so many of the formulas have similar ingredients. We could be working on the wrong one."

"There is no way for you to remember the list from Tuesday night?" I was hoping Junior had a photographic memory.

"I tried, but the boss said it wasn't safe to experiment from memory. That we could make things worse." Junior looked down at his shoes.

"We definitely don't want worse," I told him, lifting his head back up. "Nice job Junior. That is really good news. But why did John and Melvin think they could do it?"

"Neither one of them were the best scientist," Junior explained. "They rose to power by taking credit for others' work and being great at delegating. At some point in time, they started believing their own hype and thought they were better than the boss."

"Pride is such a horrible counselor," I told him.

"I agree," he said.

"How long would it take to get a cure once we find the formula?" I asked Junior.

"Just a couple of hours," he answered.

"Now that is really good news," I told him. "I have an errand to run, and you need to get some rest."

"I'm tired." Junior moved like a zombie towards Bob's apartment.

I wanted to walk Junior to his bed, but I was very late now. There was no way I was planning to show up to the restaurant smelling this bad. Not that I was trying to impress Iason because that man was insufferable. I just did not want to ruin the rest of the patron's food by smelling like hell. This was going to be the fastest shower of the year.

Chapter Twenty-Six

The Chuckwagon was only open for breakfast and lunch. It had one of the most affordable prices for a sit-down breakfast out of anywhere else in town, which was probably one of the reasons the place was always busy early in the morning. It was the Triplets favorite spot, and they were the only reason I knew about it. If the Triplets planned a staff meeting, we always ended up here for breakfast. The food was hearty, and the service super friendly.

I pulled into the parking lot only five minutes late. I considered that a success, especially since my hair was still loose and wet. Iason was standing by a black Lexus LC 500 talking to the driver. I walked towards the door and he followed me.

"Is your bodyguard going to join us?" I asked, not recognizing the driver.

"Not this time." Iason held the door for me. "Do we wait to be seated?"

"Nope. We make ourselves at home and they come to us." I found a booth by the window and slid in, getting comfortable.

"Howdy," the friendly waitress said to us with a perfect Southern accent. "What can I get you to drink?"

"Coffee, please," I replied.

"The same," Iason told her.

"I'll be right back to get your order." She gave us our menus and left to get our drinks.

"Do you eat human food?" I asked Iason, not sure if that was an appropriate thing to ask.

"Every day," he answered. "Some things are better, obviously, but breakfast is fairly safe."

A group of men entered the restaurant and sat at a table near us. There was nothing special about the group, besides the fact that they all had the same boots on.

"Why are you staring at the wolves?" Iason whispered, leaning across the table.

"Are you sure they are werewolves?" I whispered back.

"You really need to start using your sixth sense," Iason lectured me.

"Probably, but right now is not the time to be busting that out," I told him. "Can you hear what they are saying?

"Is that a jab at my pointy ears?" Iason asked, his voice dripping with sarcasm as he crossed his arms over his chest.

"No. I'm talking about the fact that you are supernatural and somehow most of you have better hearing than humans." The last part was probably too loud since two of the werewolves glanced our way. "See what I mean?"

"Point taken," Iason conceded. "What are you interested in?"

"Anything dealing with our current situation." I kept my answer vague to avoid any more looks from the group.

"I'll let you know," Iason said as our waitress brought our coffee.

"Are you ready?" she asked us.

The werewolves had distracted me, and I didn't have much time to look at the menu. I ordered blueberry waffles and Iason ordered pancakes. With the werewolves so close to us, Iason kept the conversation neutral, discussing the difference in weather between Texas and

San Diego. Our breakfast was out at the same time as the werewolves. I had no idea what they were saying, but they were having a heated argument.

"I'm going to follow them," I told Iason in between bites.

"You have no idea who they are or what they are doing, but you are going to follow them?" Iason asked, lowering his fork.

"Why not?" I asked back.

"Your plan for solving your little mystery is to follow every shifter you see?" Iason made fun of me.

"Do you have a better plan?" I glared over the table and took a few more bites.

"I'm going with you," he finally told me.

"No, you are not," I said.

"You are not going by yourself to chase a group to who knows where because you have no leads. That is just asking to get hurt," Iason explained. "Besides, Constantine would kill me if I let you go alone, and especially if something happens to you."

"You are trying to avoid a lecture from Constantine," I said.

"Do you blame me?" Iason answered.

"No, I would do the same." Constantine had the power to chastise people even if they didn't work for him. "I think they are almost done. Are you ready?"

"Whenever you are." Iason cleaned his hands with the napkin. "We can take my car."

"A Lexus LC 500? Are you kidding me? We would stick out like a sore thumb." His luxury car was not one to miss in this town.

"Are you telling me your Mini Cooper is a better choice?" Iason asked, and I had to admit he had a point. Mine didn't blend in any better.

I shrugged. "True, but at least mine is smaller."

Iason raised his eyebrows. "How is smaller better?"

"Take it or leave it, but I'm heading out." I stood from the table and Iason followed.

Our ticket was less than twenty dollars, but before I could grab it, Iason took it.

"I called this meeting, so I pay," he said, heading for the cashier at the entrance of the room.

The werewolves were paying in front of us. I tried to get as close as possible to eavesdrop without acting suspicious. The werewolves left the restaurant still talking to each other. Iason handed the cashier a brand-new Benjamin and told her to split the tip with the staff. The girl was ready to kiss him.

"You are so kind," she told him in a high-pitched voice.

"Great. Now I'm going to have to leave a huge tip next time I come," I told him as we walked outside.

"Don't you leave a nice tip everywhere you go?" Iason asked, putting a pair of sunglasses on.

"Yes, but never eighty dollars." I grabbed his arm and pulled him towards Ladybug.

"Why not? You have the money." Iason walked over to the passenger's side. As he stood there, I realized it would be a really tight fit for him in my car.

"Because this is a small town and drawing attention to ourselves by flaunting money around can be dangerous in our field." I slid in the driver's seat and watched him push the passenger seat as far back as possible. "Maybe the Lexus would have been more comfortable."

"A little too late, dear," Iason said, pointing at the group of werewolves in matching trucks leaving the parking lot.

"Okay, did they say anything important?" I asked as I followed the convoy at a reasonable distance down Kings Highway.

"A lot of discussion about the ladies they spent the night with. Do you want those details?" Iason asked, and my cheeks got a little warm.

"No, I'm good without those details," I answered, keeping my eyes on the road.

"They had some discussion on how to sell the merchandise and the fastest way to make money," Iason added.

"See, I knew it." I slammed my hands on the steering wheel in victory.

"Isis, that could mean anything," Iason told me.

"True, but if you didn't think it was a good lead why are you here?" I questioned. "And don't give me the whole Constantine excuse either."

"I'm bored," Iason replied, adjusting his seatbelt in the small vehicle.

The werewolves drove down New Boston Road and parked next to the abandoned building on the corner of Texas Boulevard. The roof of the building was falling apart. I parked across the street near the Mexican store and walked over. Traffic was still pretty light even in the busy intersection.

"Are you sure you want to do this?" Iason asked as we walked around the buildings following the voices.

"I'm not turning back," I told him.

The voices were getting louder, and we found our group of werewolves fighting with another group.

"Are those werewolves?" I asked Iason.

"They are shifters, but I can't tell what breed. I'm a little too far away for that," Iason answered.

"Come on," I told him, getting closer to the action.

"You said fifty grand for a case, and now you want double?" one of the shifters yelled.

"There is a huge demand for the stuff and the supply is low," one of the werewolves answered.

"I don't give a damn about your demand and supply crap. We had a deal," the shifter replied. "Either I get my stuff now or you will pay."

Normally, when people make threats like that, it was a good idea to clear the area. My brain was not working at full speed. By the time the warning registered, it was too late. The shifters opened fire on the werewolves.

"Oh God," I screamed as Iason pulled me down to the ground.

"Was this what you were expecting?" Iason asked right next to my ear.

"Not at all," I answered. "We need to get out of here."

We stood to leave when the situation escalated. The werewolves returned fire and the noise level was worse than a war zone. I took cover behind one of their trucks.

"Isis, watch out!" Iason reached for me but it was too late.

I heard the sound of the incoming projectile as it hit the truck. After serving in the Army, I knew that sound better than anyone. The rocket hit the truck, blowing it up and sending me flying in the air. Maybe it was the explosion or the impact with the ground, but everything went dark very quickly.

Chapter Twenty-Seven

My mouth felt like it was full of cotton candy and my head was heavy. I rubbed my eyes and noticed the glow in the dark stars. How did I get to my room?

"Starting to feel like old times," Death said from the chair.

"Was I dreaming?" I asked Death, analyzing the room.

"Are you asking if the car explosion was a dream? Unfortunately, no, dear." Death put the book she was reading back on my nightstand. "Constantine has decided to triple the policies on all the vehicles due to potential Isis collision."

"How can he possibly blame me for that one?" I argued.

"He doesn't require a lot of reasoning," Death explained, sitting on the bed. "But two trucks exploding within a week and you were at both scenes has made him paranoid. How are feeling?"

"Groggy," I told her, trying to shake the feeling away.

"Iason got a little carried away with his healing magic by the looks of it." Death pushed my hair away from my face. "You are going to need a haircut. Your braid caught fire and Iason had to chop some of it off."

I pulled my hair over my shoulder and Death wasn't kidding. At least eight inches were missing, and it looked like he used a knife to cut it off.

"Lovely," I replied, tossing my hair back. "Any other great surprises that I should know about?"

"You have another full house, and most of your guests are mad." Death stood from the bed and headed to the door. "Out of all my Interns, you have the most near-death experiences. Sometimes, I wonder if you just miss me."

"I do, just not this bad," I told her, and Death left the room shaking her head.

"A room full of people? Maybe I could just stay in bed." I turned over and the alarm clock flashed eleven-ten. That meant Eric and his chief were already here. Great!

I climbed out of bed to find I was only wearing the top of my PJs. My cheeks burned.

God, I hope Iason was not the one who dressed me.

I took several deep breaths to calm down and rushed to put some clothes on. Four hours were wasted with my new incident. We still had too much going on. As tempting as it was, hiding in my room was not going to fix any of our issues.

I slowly opened my door and the shouting coming from the kitchen almost turned me around. I forced myself to walk forward and face the excitement taking place. Godmother was yelling at Constantine on the kitchen counter, Eric was following a tall man who I assumed was his chief, Bart was on the computer, and Bob was making cookies by the oven. Yeah, it was another typical day at Reapers.

"Hi. What did I miss?" I asked in the most cheerful tone I could find.

"Isis, you are up." As usual, Bob was the first one to notice me. "Let me see. The elf was right, all your bruises and scratches are gone."

"Did I have a lot of those?" I touched my face, and it was as smooth as I remember.

"I can't believe you let him use Elven magic on you," Godmother shouted at me.

"She didn't have much choice in the matter. She was knocked out," Constantine told her.

"Hi, Godmother. I miss you too." I stepped around the counter and gave her a kiss on the cheek.

"Don't you do that again!" She held me tight for a few seconds.

"I hate to agree with the screaming banshee here, but don't do that again," said Constantine.

"You are all aware that I didn't do anything." I looked around the room, but nobody seemed convinced, their eyebrows all raised in my direction.

"Gangs. We have gangs in Texarkana now." I wasn't sure if the Chief was asking me a question or making a statement.

"They were competing werewolf packs," I corrected him.

"Lord help me." The Chief leaned on the glass wall. "I think I prefer to have gangs in town."

"Isis, this is Chief Johnson." Eric jumped in with quick introductions.

"Nice to meet you," I told the chief. "You are taking this a lot better than I imagined."

"Young Lady, I have seen a lot of strange things in the last year." Chief looked at Constantine. "I'm ready for some real answers."

"How much has Eric told you?" Constantine asked, and the Chief winced but held his stare. I was impressed.

"Not much. Only that major changes are taking place in Texarkana and your group might be able to help me." Chief Johnson stood to his full height, almost six feet tall. "We need help."

"We might be the cause of all of your problems," I confessed, taking a seat at the table and signaling for the Chief to join me.

"How so?" He sat across from me.

"By me settling in town, it made this area into a haven for all supernatural beings in North America," I told him very slowly.

"You are the reason for the increase in business and people?" the Chief asked.

"Unfortunately, yes," I answered, looking straight at him.

"Unfortunately? What are you saying? Expanding the city is essential to our development," the Chief told us and the rest of us were silent.

"You understand how much trouble that brings to Texarkana?" I asked since the Chief was not getting the big picture.

"Isis ... can I call you Isis?" he asked me.

"Yes, please," I responded.

"I have been in law enforcement for over twenty years, and it is a dangerous job that doesn't pay that well." Chief cleared his throat. "Unless the city has income, our department gets cut. An increase in business, traffic, and just plain residents means more taxes to the city. I'm finally getting extra funds to hire more people."

"I like how he thinks," Constantine said, joining us at the table. "What would you like from us?"

"Most of my people can't handle all this," Chief told us, observing Constantine.

"Don't worry, most of the world can't handle all of him either," Godmother chimed in from the kitchen.

I forced myself not to laugh and answered the chief. "They don't have to. Our team can handle the supernatural community, you just have to give us a call."

"Would they listen to you?" the chief asked me.

"They have to, or they get evicted," Constantine explained. "You want to live in haven, you must follow the rules and laws of the Intern."

"You can contact our dispatcher at Union Station twenty-four hours a day." Bob handed the chief a business card. "Depending on the severity, they would notify Isis for intervention. Small petty stuff they can handle on their own."

"You have a dispatcher?" The chief looked at Eric, who nodded. "How elaborate are your operations?"

"A lot more than I care for," I replied. "If you want a tour, lets us know."

"I might take you up on the offer considering we are neighbors." Chief rubbed his temples and Bob handed him a glass of iced tea. "That explains all the activities going on down there now."

"If you have a few of your officers or detectives you trust, bring them with you," said Bob. "We are all on the same side. Our methods are the only thing that separate us."

"Yes, that is a really good idea." Chief took a gulp of his tea. "Can we stop by Monday? I need to figure out who is ready to handle all of this. Do I want to know what is going on now?"

"Short version: a crate of supplements created by one of the horsemen was stolen. The goods are being sold around town and it's causing the shifters to lose control and attack humans," I told the Chief, and by the look on his face, one might think I dropped a bomb on him. "Have you noticed an increase in animal attacks?"

"A huge spike," Chief announced. "Are those the people parked all around town?"

"No, those are demons the devil sent to find the people who attacked his club," I answered a little too quickly.

"I wasn't ready for that," Chief said, fanning himself.

"Please don't pass out. You are doing so well." I bounced off my chair and reached for the chief.

"I'm a God-fearing man, and I knew the devil existed." Chief's voice cracked and his rosy cheeks turned a slight pale color. "I just wasn't ready to hear he walks Texarkana and his demons are on the prowl."

"Let's not get carried away now," Constantine told him. "Nobody is on the prowl. The demons are not allowed to enter haven without approval from us and that is obviously not happening. They won't move from their location unless we don't deliver the perpetrator."

"How close are you to finding them?" Chief looked between Constantine, Bob, and me.

"We have the perfect trap set," Constantine announced.

"We do?" I asked before my brain could step in to shut my mouth up.

"Hello? Why do you think we are having a party outside our doors?" Constantine told me, ready to pounce on me.

"I thought it was because we liked living on the edge," Bartholomew said from the computer station.

"Now you want to join this conversation!" Constantine shouted at him.

"All the packs have been invited, so we will find our shifter." Constantine made himself comfortable like the king of Reapers.

"Do you want backup?" the chief asked.

"We are going to have representatives from the entire supernatural community here. Do you think it would be wise to bring a bunch of civilians?" I asked the chief.

"Maybe your team could provide training to my officers," Chief recommended.

"That is a great idea," Bob replied.

"For tonight, let's keep it low-key instead," I told him. "If you and Eric want to come out, that would be fine. Just no uniforms. You must blend in."

"Okay, we can handle that," Chief told Eric, who agreed with him. "What time does this start?"

"The Equinox for us is at ten-fifty. The ceremony will start at ten, and the party at nine," Constantine said, providing the itinerary for us.

"We will be here and thank you for your time." Chief Johnson stood from the chair and extended his hand to me.

"It's going to be a wild ride," I told him.

"Just don't blow up my vehicles. I don't have your budget," Chief said with a smile.

"I'm never going to live this down," I told the crowd.

"No, no you are not," Eric said as he escorted his boss out. "Thank you."

"Bye, Eric." I waved back.

"Now that you settled that, are you okay?" Godmother moved over to the table to inspect me.

"Yes. Godmother, I promise," I told her.

"You are going to be the death of me." Godmother gave me another hug. "I have preparations for tonight. I guess now that you are using the ceremony as bait, you will be too busy to help."

"I will be busy keeping you safe," I told her.

"That is my job ... to keep you safe. When did the roles reverse?" Godmother rubbed my cheeks.

"When I became an adult," I said, enjoying the touch.

"I blame this one for that." Godmother pointed a finger at Constantine and then marched out of the loft. "I love you, Isis. Constantine, you'd better keep her safe."

"Of course, Cruella!" Constantine shouted to her retreating form.

"She is going to kill you one of these days," I told Constantine.

"She can try," Constantine replied, swiveling on his back. "In the meantime, please stop trying to die. You don't get a raise for danger."

"I would be rich if I did," I exclaimed.

"Whatever," Constantine ignored me.

"Has anyone figured out why those two groups were fighting for the supplements?" I asked the boys as I headed to the fridge for food.

"We have one in custody," Bob told me. "He was badly injured, and his people left him behind. He is being treated at the infirmary. The only thing we gathered is that the supplements give the shifters extra strength and increased ability, making them even more deadly."

"Are you serious?" I asked, popping four grapes in my mouth. "They are willing to risk turning feral for more strength. This must be a guy thing because I don't get it?"

"Not a guy thing, but a shifter thing," Constantine corrected. "Pack dominance is the key to survival. Anything that can give you an extra advantage is fair game."

"Do I want to know what the going price on the streets is for those stupid things?" I grabbed a bowl of fruit and sat at the table.

"Right now, one small bottle of thirty pills is about one-hundred bucks," Bob told me.

"Did anyone tell Famine this?" I asked, scanning the room for the missing horseman.

"Nope," all three of the guys answered.

"Good, let's keep it that way," I told them.

The last thing we wanted was that crazy horseman to decide to keep making those supplements.

"What do you need me to do before the party?" I asked Constantine.

"This is going to kill you," Constantine said softly.

"Oh no," I replied.

"Nothing, just wait." Constantine spun to his side.

"I suck at waiting," I whined.

"We know that," Bob told me. "But we have everyone patrolling the streets, so if anyone moves, we will know."

"We even set up additional cameras around town to monitor traffic and pedestrians," Bartholomew added.

"You can't possibly tell me there is nothing for me to do." I popped more fruit in my mouth.

"You can always go help Abuelita with the food," Constantine said, eyeing my empty plate. "It will get you out of here and doing something productive besides munching on grapes."

"That is not a bad idea," I told him.

"You can make sure that all the food is here and ready by eight-thirty," Constantine ordered. "You know we will have early arrivals and we want to look perfect."

"I'm not sure if I should be impressed or traumatized by how your mind works," I said to Constantine as I headed for my room for shoes.

"Be impressed, child, because I'm brilliant," he said. "While you are out on the town, you should also get your hair fixed. It still smells like smoke."

I stopped short and smelled my hair. It didn't smell like smoke to me, but if Constantine said it did, I knew he was right.

"Fine," I mumbled. "I will go get my hair cut before heading to Abuelita. This is not what I meant when I said I wanted something to do."

"You need the distraction. Just make sure we have food here by eight-thirty," Constantine ordered.

With everything going on, getting my hair done did not seem like a big priority. Unfortunately, I had nothing else to do right at that moment. I would head over to Fringe on Texas Boulevard and hopefully, one of the ladies could help me. I didn't trust many people with my hair, but the ladies there did magic. This was the calm before the storm, so I might as well enjoy it.

Chapter Twenty-Eight

Why did I think getting my hair cut and styled was going to be easy? Iason probably saved me from getting burned to a crisp, but his cutting style left a lot to be desire. That man cut my hair at an angle with one side longer than the other. How was that even possible? My poor stylist had to chop at least five inches from one side to even my hair out. I never had people apologize so much over a haircut. It was a blessing I wasn't attached to my hair or I would need therapy after this little episode. After fixing my fiasco haircut, getting it washed and dried took too long. She wanted to give me highlights, but who had the time for that?

Abuelita was almost done by the time I made it to the restaurant in the afternoon. If I thought cooking food for four-hundred people was difficult, transporting the food was a nightmare. It took us over three hours to get the food prepped, loaded, and moved to Reapers. Once at Reapers, we had to set up stations all around the outside of the pavilion. Some food had to be refrigerated and others kept warm. Constantine had ordered catering equipment to get all that done. Anybody who was not decorating was arranging food. By the time we were done, I had a new appreciation for event planners and chefs. I couldn't do that work for a living.

I barely had enough time to dress for the evening. Eight thirty was upon us faster than I was prepared for. Constantine wanted everyone ready prior to any of the guests arriving. He had a safety briefing to give us before the event. That sounded a lot more terrifying than the ceremony itself.

"Glad you decided to join us, Isis," Constantine called to me when I tried to sneak in.

"Hair issues," I told him.

"This is not the time to get all girly on me," Constantine shouted. "Now, is everyone here?

There were over fifty of us in attendance with Constantine standing on top of the fountain to take a survey. Bob gave Constantine a thumbs up after doing a head count.

"Listen up, everyone. The party is about to start in less than twenty minutes." Constantine looked around the crowd. "Is everyone here fully armed?"

Without a word, each one of us pulled out our weapon of choice, from knives to semi-automatic guns. This was one scary crowd.

"Good," Constantine announced proudly. "Each one of you has a job. If you are not sure what your role is tonight, check with Bob. Make sure your headsets are on at exactly nine o'clock. I want everyone working your stations or areas but keeping your eyes open. Anyone who looks suspicious or acts up, take them out."

"Are we shooting first, asking question later?" Raising my hand, I let the question fall from my lips.

"I don't care if you ask questions, but definitely shoot first," Constantine replied, and the crowd nodded.

Thank God for Eugene and his tranquilizer bullets. Without him, this would end up being one giant massacre instead of a celebration of life.

"Any questions?" That was the end of Constantine's motivational speech.

"We are so in trouble," I said to myself.

"This is going to go down bad," Bartholomew told me.

"What are you two mumbling over there?" Constantine growled at us as he walked in our direction.

"That's all the guidance we are going to get?" I asked, watching the crowd disperse across the area.

"With this many people, the less complicated the plan, the easier to execute," Constantine said.

"I hope you are right." I did not have warm, fuzzy feelings about the evening's agenda.

"Here are our guests of honor," Constantine announced, and I turned searching for my Godmother and her group.

Instead, the Triplets were making their way to us dragging two figures with hoods. They headed to a bench at the far side of the fountain. Bartholomew and I followed Constantine towards the bench.

"Who exactly are those two and why are they in hoods?" I asked Bartholomew.

"I have no clue, but this is getting exciting." Leave it to a thirteen-year-old boy to find danger and chaos exciting.

"Perfect. Drop them in that one," Constantine told the Triplets.

The Triplets arranged the two men side-by-side on the bench. They faced them towards the crowd and then removed their hoods.

"This just hit a new level of scandalous." Bartholomew bounced with joy, unlike me.

"Why on God's green earth are Luke and John here?" The two men looked high out of their minds as they sat on the bench drooling.

"Just think, if we add Matthew and Mark, we will have the whole gospel," Constantine joked, hopping on John's leg.

"You are not funny," I chastised Constantine.

"Yes, I am, and you know it." Constantine waved a paw in front of the two men. "A little too much with the dust. We need them to recognize their partners, not die on the bench."

"Not a problem, Mr. Constantine." I recognized Pete's voice from somewhere in between the two men.

I walked over and found Pete standing on Luke's shoulder. He was wearing black cargo pants with a black top—Bob's mandatory uniform for all the underground troops. Pete looked so cute I wanted to pinch him.

"Hey, Boss Lady, I got these two secure." Pete saluted me with so much military precision that all I could do was give him a nod.

Hard to be angry when people took their jobs so seriously. Constantine was working every angle and every loophole available, but we were still fighting trained shifters a lot faster and stronger than most of our team. Oh God please don't let us die tonight.

"Constantine, what if they don't show up?" I asked.

"Are you not seeing the brilliance in my plan?" Constantine kept talking before I could reply. "They will come. All the leaders of each pack will be here. They don't have a choice if they want to stay in haven."

"You ordered them to come?" Now that was impressive, even for Constantine.

"What is the point of ruling a county if I can't boss people around?" Constantine jumped off the two prisoners and walked over toward one of the food tables. "Pete will handle the two traitors over there. The rest of us have to move fast to catch them when they point them out. Simple enough?"

"There is nothing simple about four-hundred people wandering around with potential killers in the mix." I worked at keeping my voice low.

"Nothing like adding a bit of spice to your life." Constantine continued his walk around the area. "Nine o'clock, earpieces on."

With that order, we all turned on our communication devices. I followed Constantine around as I looked for my station. Bob and I were in charge of the drink table. Bartholomew was handling the light and sound system from a small booth on the far end of the pavilion. We didn't have a lot of time to talk as our guests started arriving. Eric and Chief Johnson were not far behind and Constantine placed them both with Bartholomew to give them a better view.

My Godmother and her crew did not arrive until nine-thirty. At least two-hundred people and supernatural beings were present when the witches marched to the center of the pavilion in single file. My mouth dropped when I realized their shimmering black gowns were see through, including the one my Godmother was wearing at the back of the line. I tried to hide under the table when Bob stopped me.

"Too late for that now," Bob told me.

"It's never too late to hide in shame," I replied, measuring the distance between my table and Reapers.

The witches spread around the fountain, taking positions like marble statutes. Their skin glowed under the chandeliers and they resembled Greek gods and goddesses. A throne-like seat was brought over for my Godmother and musical instruments were placed in front of some of the other witches. The crowd watched in silence.

"I haven't seen this ritual in decades." Famine appeared next to me.

"Are you supposed to be here?" I asked.

"I couldn't miss all this fun." Famine waltzed away.

"We must work on their definition because 'fun' does not mean the same thing to the two of us," I said to Bob.

"I feel like we just gave a grenade to a three-year-old," Bob replied as he shook his head.

"You are not making me feel better." I eyed Bob one more time and turned to scan the party.

The witches started playing, and the crowd fell into a hypnotic dance, keeping step with the music. As a fellow musician and one who could control people with music, I had to give them credit. The witches were good. Between the music and the group of dancers my Godmother had, everyone was focused on the center stage, giving the rest of us enough room to do our jobs.

"Boss Lady," one of the Triplets said over the earpiece. "Drool boy, here, says the group entering the tent are all lions and part of his pack."

Bob and I faced the incoming group. Seven of them strolled towards the witches. They moved with a grace that looked like they were floating. Four of the people in the group were male and three were female, all wearing black pants and dark shirts.

"Which one is the shooter?" I asked. "We need to get the formula and that group has it?"

"Pete is checking now," the second Triplet answered.

"We have trouble," Triplet number one said.

"We've been having trouble, so be more specific," I replied.

"The new group entering is the werewolf pack Mr. Evil here sold the supplements to," Triplet one clarified.

"Do we know who the leader of that one is?" Bob asked this time.

"Not yet, but we are working on it!" Pete shouted.

"Somebody please lower Pete's mic before we all go deaf here," I ordered.

"Pete doesn't have a mic, so he is just shouting into mine," Triplet number three said.

"In that case, make him stop that," Bob commanded before scanning the crowd. "Gentlemen, more people are coming and everyone is packing heat, so you should hurry."

The music picked up speed and the dancers increased their movements to match it. The different packs placed themselves in various sections of the pavilion, which made the area look like the stage of the Wild West.

"Guys, hurry. I don't like the looks of this," I told the Triplets and Pete.

"Everyone be on high alert," Bob told the crew. "Something is about to go down."

"Keep your eyes on the lions and werewolves who just arrived," Constantine ordered from somewhere near my Godmother.

Servers moved around the crowd getting closer to the shifters. The crowd was too busy watching the dancers to notice all the extra movement around them. The music reached a crescendo and the crowd held their breath in anticipation. As the music ended, the crowd erupted into applause. The dancers bowed like professional ballerinas. My Godmother rose from her throne and the applause stopped.

"Welcome, my friends, to this celebration of the equinox." Her voice carried through the night. "We are here to celebrate as one community, as one family."

Everyone clapped with excitement. I lost track of the two packs of shifters.

"Does anyone have eyes on the lions or the werewolves?" I asked, my voice competing with the cheers.

"Isis, move in," Bartholomew told me from his booth. "They are facing each other in front of your Godmother."

Bob and I left our table and pushed our way towards the center of the pavilion.

"You killed my husband!" an angry female shouted.

"That's the leader of the werewolves!" Triplet number one shouted.

"A little too late now," I replied.

"Maybe you want to join him," a male with a deep voice replied.

"Let me guess. That's our killer?" I said to the Triplets before they could speak.

"You are good, Boss Lady," Triplet number two added.

I ignored the praises and made my way through the crowd.

"Get those two out of here," Constantine shouted at the Triplets.

"Moving the gospel members to Reapers," Triplet number one announced, and I didn't have time to confirm it with the crowd when my Godmother started frantically moving.

"What happened to the music?" Famine shouted.

Bob and I looked at each other and pushed harder through the crowd.

"Die!" the female yelled.

Bob and I reached the center of the pavilion in time to watch as the scene unraveled. It was like everything went in slow motion. The female shot across the dance floor right as the lion pushed Famine in front of him. Junior ran in front of Famine and got shot in the chest. A second shot was fired, hitting Famine and knocking them to the ground.

"Lord," I said on an exhale, but really, I could barely speak.

The crowd froze. Famine rose from the ground as blood poured from their side. Tentacles of smoke spread from Famine's fingers and they levitated off the ground.

"You. Dare. Attack. Me?" Famine's voice echoed through the night and vibrated inside my skull. "You will pay!"

Famine unleashed their power across the group. Everyone the smoke touched slowly started to shrivel up. Bob gasped for air next to me, collapsing to the ground. Bartholomew fell next, landing next to Eric and Chief Johnson. Even the ones that tried to run were dragged back by the smoke.

"Isis, charge!" Constantine screamed, snapping me out of my trance.

Constantine and I were the only ones not affected by Famine. By the time I reacted, Constantine was halfway to Famine in mid-pounce. Famine was too fast and swatted Constantine away like a fly. I pulled my scythe out and extended it as I ran towards the demented horseman.

"Famine. Stop!" I used my scythe as a javelin and threw it as hard as I could.

Famine caught it with one hand, but it gave me enough time to run across the dance floor. I landed one quick blow to their midsection that did absolutely nothing. Famine broke my scythe in half and punched me halfway across the dance floor. I didn't know if it was the fall that crushed all my bones or the force of Famine's impact, but everything hurt. I tasted blood in my mouth and couldn't even move my arms to get up.

"Constantine, Famine is killing everyone," I whined, unable to breathe, let alone drag myself across the rocks.

"I'm way ahead of you," Constantine stuttered.

"Famine. Enough." Death grabbed her sibling by the shoulders.

Famine tried to move but Death was stronger. She snapped her fingers, and they both disappeared. It took several minutes for the smoke to dissolve. People started twitching and coughing. That was the greatest sound I'd ever heard.

"If anyone can move, grab the lions and the werewolves now," Constantine ordered.

Triplet number one rushed out of Reapers. "What in the hell happened here?"

"We will explain later. For now, just get the leader!" Constantine shouted, and people began to move. "Isis, can you move?"

"I think Famine broke my ribs, and who knows what else?" I told Constantine as tears rolled down my face.

"Baby." My godmother was by my side in an instant, holding my hand.

"Virginia, we've got her." Constantine pulled my godmother away.

"What?" Godmother refused to let go of my hand.

"Take control of the situation and continue with the ceremony," Constantine told her very sternly.

"Are you crazy?" Godmother tried to push him away.

"What are you going to do for her?" Constantine asked.

"By the Goddess!" Godmother cried. "I hate you, Constantine!"

"You can hate me all you want, but you have people to lead," Constantine pointed to the disoriented crowd trying to wake up. "Death is inside, so we will take care of Isis."

Constantine slowly pulled my Godmother's hand away.

"I'll be fine," I whispered.

"Hurry, get her inside." Godmother kissed my forehead and went to her throne.

Bob picked me up as gently as he could, but I still had to bite my lips to keep from screaming. Bartholomew picked up the broken pieces of my scythe.

"Stay here and help Virginia with the rest of the ceremony," Constantine told Bartholomew softly.

"But—" Bartholomew started.

"We all can't leave, please," Constantine cut him off.

"Okay," Bartholomew replied with tears streaking down his face.

"Bob, hurry," Constantine told him as he made his way through the crowd. "Everyone else, make sure everyone eats."

I heard muffled replies, but the pain was too great. For every step Bob took, it was like shards were digging into my chest and crushing me.

"Isis, stay with me," I heard Bob say somewhere in the distance.

"Death, we need you!" Constantine shouted.

I looked up at the stars and felt like I was being pulled to them. My head pounded, and every breath was a struggle to take. I just wanted to close my eyes for one minute and make everything stop.

Chapter Twenty-Nine

The sun was shining, and I was floating on fluffy, pink-marshmallow clouds. My eyelids were heavy, so all I wanted to do was sleep, to float on my marshmallows and let the sound of the sea put me to rest. Unfortunately, lightning struck.

"Ahh." It took me a minute to recognize that I was the one screaming. "Oh my God. I was dying."

"Not yet. You just got shook by Death," Constantine whispered in my ear.

I held my chest and tried to breathe.

"Isis, can you hear me?" Death hovered over my head.

"Yes," I replied.

"That's my girl." Death patted my cheek. "This is going to hurt. Bob, Triplets, hold her still."

"Are you going to hit me with lightning again?" Tears fell from my eyes.

"Something like that," Death told me. "Now."

I screamed at the top of my lungs as the heat spread across my chest, and my body thrashed against Bob and the Triplets. Death ran a cool cloth over my face.

"The hardest part is over. Now sit still while things settle down," Death ordered. "It's been years since I had to repair that many broken bones and internal organs. My intent was to block you from Famine's power, not from a direct hit. Not many humans could take that kind of impact and live to tell about it."

"I wouldn't call this living," I countered.

"You are breathing, so that's surviving," Death reminded me. "Bob, get her a shake and something to eat. I stopped the internal bleeding, but we need fluids in her quick."

"Got it." Bob took off to the loft.

As my vision cleared, I found myself lying on a mat on the floor of the gym. One of the Triplets helped me lay on my side. A few feet from me were Junior and Famine. Death was working on Junior first, doing a similar treatment as she did on me. Famine was on their side whining.

"I'm going to die," Famine said.

"Can a horseman be killed by a gunshot?" I asked anybody who would listen.

"No," Constantine told me while marching over to Famine. "Get a hold of yourself."

Constantine slapped Famine over the head with his paw. Famine twisted over to face Constantine, who looked ready to pounce on their head.

"You hit me!" Famine shouted.

"You are lucky I didn't rip your eyes out after that stunt you just pulled," Constantine hissed.

"They attacked a horseman, so they deserved to be punished," Famine stated.

"You were not the intended target," Constantine said. "If you would have stayed by Bartholomew where I left you, this wouldn't have happened. But no, you wanted to see the show up close. You almost killed Isis and the rest of my guests."

"She tried to stab me." Famine turned again to face me.

"In my defense, you were killing everyone," I said softly. "I just wanted to break your concentration. Besides, you broke my scythe. Death, can you make them pay for it?"

"I have replaced your scythe already." Death pointed to my pocket.

I reached inside to find a new scythe, which I held tightly as I rested my head on the mat.

"Is he going to be okay?" Famine asked Death as she worked on Junior.

"His wounds are not as bad as Isis's," Death explained. "Unfortunately, because he is not my Intern, I can only do so much without overwhelming his body. If you would just claim your people, I wouldn't have to be doing this."

Famine sat up and turned away from Death. Constantine walked around to look Famine in the eyes.

"Would you please heal yourself now?" Constantine told Famine. "You are spilling blood all over my gym. Do you know how long it takes to clean up blood?"

"You only care about your floors; what about my pain and suffering?" Famine yelled at Constantine.

"You are NOT in pain!" Constantine shouted. "You are being a spoiled brat and throwing a tantrum. Knock it off."

"Famine, Constantine is right. Enough is enough." Death walked over to her sibling and kneeled in front of them. "Either you heal yourself or I will close that wound for you. If I do, you are not going to like it."

"Fine, you evil dictators." Famine closed their eyes. In a matter of three breaths, the wounds were sealed, and the blood stopped flowing. Famine snapped their fingers and they were wearing a fresh suit.

"Are you serious?" I wanted to choke Famine. "You went psycho over a flesh wound?"

"If I was human, I would be dead by now," said Famine. "A lesson needed to be taught."

"But you are not human!" I shouted this time.

"Isis, you stay still and stop stressing yourself," Death said softly.

"Here you go." Bob was back with the biggest shake I had ever seen. "Let me help."

Bob slowly picked me up, which made everything spin. I held my breath to make sure I didn't puke all over Bob. It took a few minutes for my head to stop whirling and for me to see straight again. The sharp pains in my chest had stopped, but I was aching all over.

"Big Bob, is Boss Lady...?" Shorty couldn't finish his sentence.

"I'm alive, Shorty," I answered before Bob.

"Thank you, Jesus." I couldn't see Shorty, but his voice was getting closer.

"Mr. Shorty has been praying nonstop while he kicked some butt outside," Pete told me as he flew down to my face. "We thought you died for a minute."

"I was feeling rough," I admitted.

"At least you have some color to your cheeks again." Pete pinched my cheeks and it made me squeal. "We do have a surprise. Guess who we found?"

Nobody guessed. Instead, we just waited for Pete to continue.

"You guys are no fun," he told us. "We have the murderous countess herself, and the treacherous lion."

I tried moving to see them, but Bob held me still, pushing the shake towards my mouth. He was not going to let me move until I finished it.

"Triplets, grab us a couple of chairs and some duct tape." Constantine's solutions to major dilemmas always ended with duct tape. "We need some answers and this pair is going to give them to us."

"You will have to kill me before I talk," the female told us.

"Be careful what you say around here because you might get your wish," I warned her.

"Don't worry, dear, we can arrange that," Famine told her, and they made their way towards the prisoner.

The Triplets secured both the female and male in the chairs in front of Famine, who stretched their arms over their head.

"You don't scare me," the female told Famine, and I didn't have the heart to warn her to keep her mouth shut.

"Obviously, you are not very smart then." Famine cracked their knuckles and stood over the woman.

She tried to wiggle away, but Famine held her face. "This is going to hurt. A lot." The words were a soft purr.

Famine dragged their hands into the female's scalp and tentacles of smoke wrapped around her face. The female opened her mouth to scream, but instead the tentacles crawled down her throat. Famine's powers were literarily sucking the life out of her. Her skin was being pulled tighter and tighter towards the back of her skull.

"Are you ready to talk? Because I can do this all day." Famine was only inches away from the female.

The female couldn't speak, and I wasn't sure if it was because of the smoke down her throat or if Famine's powers were destroying other things from the inside out, but she eventually nodded.

"That's more like it." Famine receded, giving Constantine room to jump on her lap.

"Where is the formula and the supplements?" Constantine asked and the female just looked at Famine.

Constantine didn't waste any time asking again, instead slapping the female hard enough to leave scratches all over her face. It seemed Constantine enjoyed slapping people.

"Don't make me ask you again, or I'll let Famine finish you off." Constantine looked at Famine over his shoulder and the female trembled.

"No, please!" the female cried. "The supplements are at the Cowboy, but we don't have the formula."

"The Electric Cowboy?" I asked. "Isn't that place condemned?"

"Not as well as I'd hoped," Constantine told me. "Next time, we will blow it up and avoid this hideout crap again."

"How many times have you been to the Cowboy?" I asked Constantine, who ignored my question.

"Who has the formula?" Constantine asked the female.

"This disgusting beast and his pack have it." The female spat at the lion.

"Don't hate because we are better than you at executing our mission," the lion told the werewolf.

"Listen, boy, I don't have time for this," Constantine told the lion. "You have two seconds to talk before I let Famine turn you into a younger version of a mummy."

"In a safe in the boss's house," the lion spilled.

"That's it? You are just going to give us all the necessary info, no questions asked." Constantine switched laps and sat on top of the lion.

"I already experienced the wrath of Famine once, so I don't want a second taste of that hell." The lion kept his gaze on Famine. "Besides, I don't get paid enough by those fools to put up with torture sessions. We were promised immunity from the side effects while we became stronger than ever. We haven't seen either one yet."

"Triplets, you three go with this one and Pete to retrieve that formula and bring it back," ordered Constantine.

"We will make it happen, Boss." Pete saluted Constantine.

The Triplets dragged the lion away still duct-taped to the chair. Are they not planning to un-tape him?

"Bob, you take Shorty and as many of the team you can find to the Cowboy. Get those supplements." Constantine walked over to us.

"You will never make it back alive," the female told us with a bitter howl.

"You don't know our team very well," Constantine replied, cuing Death.

Death tapped the female on the back of the head and she passed out.

"Do you see how simple that is, Famine?" Constantine asked. "One little tap and bang—human knocked out. Why can't we get you there?"

"Does it look like she learned her lesson? No!" I hated to agree with Famine after the last episode, but I was sure they were right.

"Bob, I'm going with you," I finally spoke, sitting up by myself.

"You are in no condition to go anywhere," Bob told me.

"I can go with you, or I'll just meet you there. You pick." I was not backing down. "You need me if the situation is as dangerous as she hinted at."

"Isis, you almost died," said Bob.

"She didn't almost die; she was almost murdered. Big difference." Constantine was not dropping this subject.

"Death, can you please talk some sense into her?" Bob begged.

Death walked around the mats and sat in front of me, placing one hand over my chest and the other over my forehead. She inclined her head to the left and then to the right. I wasn't sure what she was doing, but I waited patiently.

"You are not going to be able to keep her here," Death told Bob. "All internal wounds are healed, but you are going to be in pain for a few days."

"Can you make the pain go away?" I asked Death, who looked at me even closer. "Just for a few hours."

"I can but when you do crash, you will be out for a while," Death told me.

"Sounds great," I said. "I don't have any big plans."

Death kissed my forehead softly. "Isis, this is only going to last a couple of hours. I have done a lot of healing tonight, and your body requires rest."

"As soon as we are done, I will come straight home to sleep." I made the sign of the cross over my heart to seal my promise, enjoying the fact that I could breathe without wincing. It was such a beautiful feeling to be pain free.

"You won't have a choice because you will probably just crash," Death corrected. "You'd better hurry.

"Constantine, could you tell my godmother what is going on while we are gone?" I didn't want to worry Godmother anymore.

"I got this here, but please be careful," Constantine said.

"I don't like this," Bob told me.

"Let's just make this fast and then I can get to bed." That sounded simple enough.

Bob gave up arguing and helped me stand up. I stretched myself, making sure all my body parts were still functioning. Once Bob confirmed that I wasn't screaming in pain, he led us to Killer. If he only knew how much I wanted tonight to be over, he wouldn't be wasting time.

Chapter Thirty

Ever since I moved to Texarkana, the Electric Cowboy had been closed down. I had heard rumors of the wild nights people had at the former club. Pulling up to the old, run-down building, it was hard to imagine. There was nothing special about the place, besides the boarded-up doors. The placed looked dead, not a car in sight.

Bob parked to the right of the establishment away from the front door. I had a feeling he was planning to avoid another incident like we had with Storm. Shorty parked on the opposite side with four more trucks forming a semi-circle.

"Are you sure you want to come in? You don't have to," Bob said.

"I can handle a couple more hours. You heard Death," I replied softly. "Thank you for watching my back and keeping me alive."

"You are my family." Bob bit his lower lip and grabbed my hand. "If I had a daughter, I would love for her to be just like you."

Bob squeezed my hand and stepped out of the truck. I was stunned. Tears were threatening to come out and I couldn't afford a crying fit now. I waved my hands quickly in front of my eyes and took a deep breath. That was the sweetest thing Bob had ever said to me. If something happened to him ... I stopped myself before those thoughts took root in my soul. God, please protect my team.

The team was assembled around Bob, who was giving instructions. I walked slowly to join them, stretching my neck and upper back.

"What do you think, Isis? We can sneak in and surprise them?" Bob asked, inspecting the building with the rest of the team.

"Or we can bust the front door down and shoot everything that moves," I replied.

The entire group stopped and stared at me. Shorty moved closer to me and took my temperature.

"Are you sure you are feeling alright?" Shorty finally asked, pretending to take my pulse like they do at the doctor's office. "Our sweet Boss Lady would never suggest something so drastic and wild."

"I'm tired of sneaking around," I told the group. "We have been running around in circles because of this group. Let's go in, get the supplements, and call this a day. Any problems with that?"

Shorty raised his hand and I signaled for him to speak. "Boss Lady, I'm out of the regular tranquilizers. The only ones I have left are the hairless ones."

"Use them." I gave the team my blessing. "This group is aiming to kill us all. If they end up bald, it's not my concern. Everyone, stay with your buddy and cover each other. And in the famous words of Constantine, 'anything that moves, shoot it.'"

"Remind me not to get her mad," Shorty told Bob, and I had to laugh.

"Suit up, everyone," Bob ordered. "Team A, get the ramps ready. On my signal, I want that door down. Gas team, you are up first, so everyone put your masks on."

"You really should worry about not making Bob mad," I told Shorty. "At least I won't grenade your house after I demolish your front door."

"You don't need to tell me twice," Shorty answered. "Big Bob is one scary dude at times."

Shorty headed towards his truck to put his gear on. Bob recently ordered new body armor for the team. The jackets were ballistic-level and super lightweight, top-of-the-line models with matching headgear. Bartholomew had ordered us custom gas masks with night-vision goggles. If the apocalypse was happening this week, we were ready to battle zombies, aliens, and drug-dealing werewolves.

"Radios on everyone," Bob shouted before putting his gas mask on. "Team A, door."

Team A consisted of the three largest men in our group. They each rushed the door at full speed carrying a large battering ram. I was sure the running was not necessary but who was I to destroy their motivation? Two young men followed closely behind carrying grenade launchers. I hadn't seen one of those since I left the military. Normally, nobody needed a grenade launcher while living in the states.

Team A gave the door a few swift knocks with the rams, breaking the poor thing down. The grenade team maneuvered past Team A and into the former club releasing grenades left and right.

"You three stay here and cover us," Bob told Team A. "Anyone gets past us or sneaks away, take them out. The rest, follow me."

Bob was a true sergeant, even after being out of the military for so many years. If he was sending troops into battle, he would be right there with them. We followed Bob inside. The grenade team had created a path from the door to what looked like a dance floor. I couldn't see more than three feet in front of me, but I could hear the sound of coughing all around. Tear gas had a way of taking the toughest soldier out of the picture. With their highly developed senses, the shifters were getting a double dose of the gas.

One of our guys screamed.

"They are all around us," another one of our team told us through the earpieces.

"Don't let them bite you," I ordered the team. "Everyone, turn on your infrared lights. Our jackets are tagged with a skull that glows in that light. Anything without it, shoot it."

When Bartholomew told me what he was planning to do, it seemed over the top. Now it made perfect sense.

You are a genius, Bart.

Lights went on all around me, followed by gunfire. The dance floor become a madhouse. Werewolves jumped at us from all different directions. They had to have over thirty people in this pack and they just kept coming. My senses were heightened, and I wasn't sure if it was the adrenaline or Death's extra power moving through me. I didn't care either way because I felt like I was floating. I moved swiftly through the room and shot two werewolves in the chest. The next one that jumped at me ended up kicked in the head. Our group was small but lethal.

By the time the smoke cleared, all the shifters were down. The team walked around the room checking each body. Unlike the military where double tapping was against the Geneva Convention, our team did it automatically. We were not taking any chances that one of them would decide to walk up and eat our face off. The team was meticulous in their assessment of enemy combatants.

"Has anyone found the supplements?" I asked.

"Not yet," Bob replied.

"DJ's booth," one of our guys told us. "I have tons of crates here. What do we do with them?"

"Make sure the supplements are inside the boxes," I told him. "We don't want to carry all that stuff outside and find nothing worth our time."

"Checking now, Boss Lady," he replied.

I used my communication system to call Constantine back at Reapers. The phone barely rang once when Constantine picked it up.

"I'm hoping you are calling because you have everything under control," Constantine told me.

"Actually, we do," I replied, feeling very satisfied with our work. "What are we supposed to do with all the supplements?"

"Burn them," Constantine shouted into the phone. "Hold on a minute. Listen here, Famine, you said as soon as we returned your formula and your notes you could design us an antidote."

"The other side of your conversation sounds awful," I told him.

"It's even worse than you might think," Constantine added. "Famine is not cooperating and is still complaining that they were attacked. They want to punish people."

"How is Junior?" I asked, feeling a bit guilty I didn't check on the young man before leaving. "Could he get Famine to help?"

"That is a brilliant idea, or he could start making it himself." Constantine was a little too happy for my taste.

"Good luck with that. We will finish here before heading back," I told Constantine and disconnected the call.

"Okay, everyone, I have orders from Constantine," I said to the team. "We are setting all the supplements on fire."

"In here?" shouted Shorty over the mic.

"No!" Bob responded quicker than me.

"First, we are moving them outside. Then we'll set them on fire," I clarified for everyone.

"Too easy. Half of you drag the wolves outside and handcuff them all," Bob ordered. "The rest start taking out all the supplements. Find a way to get through the plastic or the glass, depending on what material the containers are made of."

"Leave that to us," the grenade team told us, grabbing the first case of supplements and heading out the building.

"What are you two planning on doing?" I asked.

"It is so much safer if you don't know, Boss Lady," one of the grenade boys told me.

"You are right." I was always better off not knowing the methods behind the madness. "Everyone, move with a purpose. We have an equinox ceremony to witness. Go!"

With everyone working double time, it still took us twenty minutes to move all the shifters and supplements outside. The grenade team had set up the supplement station as far away from the vehicles and people as possible. On our last trip out, flames ten feet tall were coming from the boxes of supplements.

"Oh my God!" I screamed, pulling off my night vision goggles and mask.

"You said set them on fire," Bob reminded me.

"I didn't mean the entire parking lot," I told him.

"There is nothing around here." Shorty walked over to us and watched the flame.

"That fire needs constant supervision, do you understand?" I directed my glare at Shorty.

"That should not be hard." Shorty crossed his arms over his chest. "I'm sure our little pyromaniacs will have a field day playing with that thing."

"Isis, what are we going to do with the werewolves," Bob asked me, removing his mask.

"We will take care of that for you." Shorty, Bob, and I turned to find Jake and Adam strutting towards us.

"What are you two doing here?" I asked, keeping my voice steady.

"Collecting our side of the bargain," Jake replied. "And you had twenty minutes to spare."

"What are you planning to do with them?" I watched as demons materialized in front of the wolves and carried them away one by one.

"We are just sending a message that you should never double cross the Devil." Jake clapped his hands and the few remaining wolves disappeared.

"All those people are not guilty of treason," I defended. "You shouldn't punish them all for the deeds of a few."

"You are so sweet." Jake pinched my cheeks. "Unfortunately, I don't play fair. We already collected the lions and now this group. People will learn never to place me in the middle of their greedy little wars."

"Jake, that's a lot of people," I pleaded.

"It will make a great teachable moment," Jake said, adjusting his tie. "Besides, you should be grateful."

"Grateful that you are dragging a bunch of people to hell?" Had Jake lost his mind?

"I'm doing Famine a favor," Jake answered. "Now they don't have to hunt them down and kill every soul they encounter trying to do it. Yes, I know. You're welcome."

"That is madness." I shook my head to try to wipe away the sight of Famine sucking the life out of people.

"Well, sounds like we are done here. Goodnight, Isis." Before I could protest, Jake was gone, along with all of our shifters.

"I don't know how I feel about that," Bob told me.

"I've been to hell," I said. "Trust me, I wouldn't wish that upon my worst enemy."

I yawned and started to feel very tired. I looked over at the burning crates. The flames were a little more manageable, but they were still too intense. That fire was going to burn for at least a couple of hours.

"Shorty, call Chief Johnson and post some guards to watch that fire until all the supplements are gone." I marched over to Killer. "Everyone else can return to Reapers, or you can release them for the night."

"With all that amazing food Abuelita made?" Shorty asked me. "You know we are heading back to party."

"In that case, let's go." I told them. "I'm tired."

"It's about time," Bob replied.

We all jumped in our respective vehicles and headed back home. This week had turned out to be full of excitement and just plain madness. At that moment, the only thing I was craving was my nice, comfy bed. Constantine could deal with Jake and how to bring back those people. At the same time, I was afraid Jake was right and letting Famine take their revenge could result in more dead bodies all across the US. Those were all things I could ponder later, though. I was too tired and beat down to have philosophical discussions with myself. That would be a project for a different day.

Chapter Thirty-One

The party was in full swing when we pulled up to Reapers. The Equinox had officially started, and every witch was standing outside the pavilion with wands raised. Godmother was in the middle directing the group. In a synchronized move, fireworks erupted from their wands. The most beautiful display of lights decorated the sky, ushering spring to come. I watched from the edge as I leaned on Killer. Minus the almost massacre of the guests, the party looked like a huge success.

"You're back." Bartholomew crushed me in a huge bear hug.

"Were you doubting it?" I asked him while playing with his hair.

"When Bob carried you away, you didn't look too hot." Bartholomew poked my side and I giggled.

"I'm okay. I promise." At least I was going to be after a long night's sleep.

Junior waved at me from across the pavilion. Death had done a great job healing his wounds. That was ironic... Death saving someone's life. Junior had a line of people in front of him who he was giving shots to.

"Death convinced Famine to make an antidote?" I asked Bartholomew.

"Not exactly," Bartholomew said with a smirk. "She ordered Famine and Famine refused. Junior begged and Famine agreed. Strange dynamics in that family."

"No kidding," I replied.

"Death said to get in bed as soon as you got back, so off to bed." Bartholomew gave me one last hug and pushed me towards Reapers.

"Enjoy the party, Bart," I told him, heading towards the pedestrian's entrance.

"Is almost dying part of your job description?" Iason asked as I approached Reapers.

Iason was leaning against the building looking ravishing in a midnight-blue suit. He looked like he was glowing with his hair slicked back.

"I like to make an impression," I replied.

"You do that very well." Iason walked with me to the entrance. "I'm not sure if I'm glad I was late or not."

"You should be very glad," I told him. "Famine's tantrum was spectacular and deadly."

"There is never a dull moment with you." Iason looked me up and down. "We still have to get together and start planning baby parties. I have to fly out tomorrow but will be back next week. Stop avoiding my calls."

"I don't know what you are talking about," I said with a hand over my heart.

"Go get some rest, Isis." Iason kissed my cheek and returned to the party.

I got goosebumps everywhere, but I was too tired to explore the meaning of that. Baby parties could wait because I was starting to drag. I entered Reapers and didn't care how long the security system took to inspect me.

The inside of Reapers was quiet and most of the lights were off, which allowed the glow from the fireworks to shine in through the tall windows. I took a minute to enjoy the silence of the place, especially after the celebration going on outside.

"I'm sorry," Famine told me from behind.

"Hi," I replied as I turned around.

We stood in the dark space just staring at each other. Famine's clothes were wrinkled, and their hair was messy like they'd been running their hands through it.

"Did Death ask you to apologize to me?" I finally asked.

"Death wouldn't try to influence those types of decisions." Famine walked toward the stairwell and I followed.

"Then why are you apologizing?" I really wanted to know if Famine could be sorry for something.

"For centuries, I have been feared by the humans. We coexist in this space but never truly interact." Famine stopped in the middle of the stairs to glance at the fireworks. "How does Death do this?"

Famine was not watching me, so I focused my attention on the inside of Reapers. Everything about our space was very human, but all funded by Death. The life we currently had was because Death gave it to us.

"Death never lies," I told Famine. "You created an empire based on deception and the idea that you are not a horseman. It's hard to create lasting relationships when nobody can trust your word."

"Humans are not ready to know the truth." Famine spun around to face me.

"Not all humans are ready, but some are." I grabbed Famine's arms with both hands and waited for another hit to the chest. When nothing happened, I continued, "Junior took a bullet for you. The guy admires you, and I have no idea why. But that is the stuff Interns are made of. You need an Intern, someone who knows what you are and will still follow."

"What if he dies?" Famine looked so young and vulnerable with their lips quivering and eyes shining with unshed tears.

"We are all going to die; it's the only thing we know for sure in this world." I rubbed Famine's shoulder before letting go. "Goodnight, Famine, and I forgive you."

"Thank you, Isis," Famine replied.

I was tired and everything ached by the time I entered the loft. Constantine was somewhere outside directing the madness. If anything happened, he could handle it. I didn't have the mental energy to care. I strolled through the kitchen and went directly to my room. Marshmallow clouds were all I craved.

The smell of coffee hit my nose, and I slowly opened my eyes. I turned on the light and a large mug sat on my night table with a note from my godmother.

I'm so proud of you, my precious Isis. I had to head back to Salem. Please call me when you wake up. Love you, Godmother.

I took a sip from the mug and the coffee was delicious. A strong Texarkana blend with a hint of creamer. I glanced at the clock on the night table and it read seven am.

That's not possible. Death said I would sleep for hours.

I reached for my phone and the time was right. It was seven am, but the date was Saturday, March twenty-first and not Friday. I had slept for over twenty-four hours. The responsible part of my brain said to get up and get ready for court. With all the excitement of the week, we had plenty of stuff to get done today and I'd lost a full day. The kid in me boycotted that idea. Turning the light off and going back to sleep sounded like a better idea. I contemplated both ideas for a minute, then I dialed Katrina.

"Didn't I tell you to stay away from Famine?" Katrina shouted as soon as she picked up.

"Hi back to you," I said as cheerfully as possible.

"I left you like ten texts," Katrina continued. "Are you just waking up?"

"Yes, and before you start with another lecture, is that offer still on the table?" I asked before she cut me off again.

"What offer?" Katrina asked in a more civilized tone.

"Hawaii," I answered.

"Yes!" Katrina screamed.

"Do I have to pick you up or do you want to meet me there?" I climbed out of bed and headed to the bathroom with my coffee.

"Girl, you have a jet. Pick me up," Katrina said full of joy.

"In that case, get ready. I will let you know when we land." I disconnected the call and dropped the phone on my vanity table.

I had never been to Hawaii and had no clue what to wear, but I had a credit card just for clothing allowances that I was planning to put to good use. All I was planning on taking were bathroom essentials and a change of clothes.

Twenty minutes later, I emerged from my bedroom carrying my backpack. Bob, Constantine, and Bartholomew were all up watching TV.

"Good morning, everyone," I announced from the sink area.

"Well, look who decided to join the world of the living," Constantine replied.

"How are you feeling?" Bartholomew rushed across the room to give me a hug.

"Better, much better," I told him, squeezing him back.

"You are looking better," Bob informed me.

"Thank you for the coffee," I told him.

"I figured you might enjoy a good wake-up call." Bob walked over and grabbed a plate from the table. "Made you waffles. As soon as you are ready, we can head to court."

"I won't be going to court today." The room went silent.

"I thought you said you were feeling alright," Constantine bounced to the kitchen and sniffed my face.

"Stop that," I told him trying to push him away. "I'm fine. You've all been saying that I need a vacation, so I'm taking one."

"I really think she is suffering from a concussion," Constantine told Bob. "Maybe we should call Eugene over."

"I'm fine." I grabbed the plate and started eating. "Bob, would you mind taking over court this weekend and next?"

"Are you serious?" Bob asked, leaning against the wall for support.

"Yes, people, I'm serious," I said with my mouth full.

"It would be an honor to fill in for you," Bob answered. "I have to make some calls to get things adjusted."

"Constantine, can I borrow the jet?" I asked as sweetly as possible.

"Where are you going?" Constantine asked, walking closer to me.

"I'm going to Hawaii with Katrina," I replied.

"In that case, no problem." Constantine hopped from the kitchen table and headed back toward the computer area. "Let me call George. He will get the jet ready for you in thirty minutes."

"Where did you think I was going?" I asked, putting my plate in the sink. "On second thought, it doesn't matter. Do you mind calling Will for me and letting him know I will be in his territory?"

"I'll do it," Bartholomew volunteered. "Will is my man."

"Thank you, Bart," I told him. "What should I bring you?"

"I don't know but I will think about it and give you a call." Bartholomew picked up his phone and dialed.

The television was on the news and the reporters were talking about some breaking information. According to the announcers, one of the major pharmaceutical companies was conducting a recall on several of their supplements due to harmful side effects. The announcer was getting ready to interview the spokesperson for the company. I hated the news since it was always so depressing, but I stopped to watch as Junior appeared on the screen wearing a tailored black suit.

"Junior is the spokesperson for that company?" I asked the boys.

"Junior is now Famine's first Intern and doing a major overhaul on their companies," Constantine told me. "Famine was very moved by a conversation they had with you."

I smiled at the TV and walked back to the kitchen.

"Am I good to go?" I asked Constantine, giving him an elaborate salute.

"George will be waiting for you at the hangar," Constantine answered.

"Have fun and tell Katrina we miss her," Bartholomew told me.

"I will have a blast and please don't burn down Texarkana before I get back," I said to Constantine.

"It will be hard, but we will do our best." Constantine rolled over on his side. "Have fun, Isis."

I grabbed my bag and left the loft. It had been years since I took a real vacation. For most of my adult life, I couldn't afford one. This job paid me well enough that I could afford multiple trips a year, but I was always too busy. After several near-death experiences, I'd earned this. The dead could wait a few days for me to return.

I was going on vacation!

If you enjoyed Unstoppable Famine, then you don't want to miss the final installment of the Intern Diaries Series:

Judgement Day! This time Isis is going to need all of her friends to battle the enemies heading her way.

Acknowledgments

Dear Reader,

I don't have enough words to express how I thankful I'm to each one of your for reading this book and being a part of this journey. Thank you so much for all the love and support you have given Isis and the team. A special thanks to all of Constantine's fans. The feline extraordinaire has changed my life as much as he changed Isis's. Thank you for opening your hearts to this special little family.

During this journey, I'm so blessed that my tribe continues to grow each time. A huge thanks the amazing Mr. J. Patton Tidwell for being super-beta-reader. To Cassandra Fear and Michelle Hoffman for editing this baby. Sending tons of love to my family for believing in this dream. Absolutely, it takes a village to get this done.

If you enjoy the story, please consider leaving a rating and possibly a short review. Your reviews help others find the books you love.

With love,

D. C.

About Author

D. C. Gomez was born in the Dominican Republic, but grew up in Salem, Massachusetts. She studied film and television at New York University. After college, she joined the US Army, and proudly served for four years.

Those experiences shaped her quirky, and sometimes morbid, sense of humor. D.C. has a love for those who served and the families that support them. She currently lives in the quaint city of Wake Village, Texas, with her furry roommate, Chincha.

Also By D. C. Gomez

In The Reapers' Universe- Urban Fantasy Books

The Intern Diaries Series

Death's Intern- Book 1

Plague Unleashed- Book 2

Forbidden War- Book 3

Unstoppable Famine- Book 4

Judgement Day- Book 5

The Origins of Constantine- Novella

From Eugene with Love- Novella

Rise of the Reapers- Novella

The Order's Assassin Series

The Hitman- Book 1

The Traitor (coming soon)

The Elisha & Elijah Chronicles (UF and Post-Apocalyptic)

Recruited- Book 1

Betrayed- Book 2 (coming soon)

Humorous Fiction

The Cat Lady Special

A Desperate Cat Lady (coming soon)

Young Adult

Another World

Children's Books

Charlie, What's Your Talent? – Book 1

Charlie, Dare to Dream – Book 2

Devotional Books

Dare to Believe

Dare to Forgive

Dare to Love